Keep 2011

Crime Brûlée

Crime Brûlée

Nancy Fairbanks

WHEELER
CHIVERS

This Large Print edition is published by Wheeler Publishing, Waterville, Maine USA and by BBC Audiobooks Ltd, Bath, England.

Published in 2006 in the U.S. by arrangement with the Berkley Publishing Group, a division of Penguin Group (USA) Inc.

Published in 2006 in the U.K. by arrangement with the Berkley Publishing Group, a division of Penguin Group (USA) Inc.

U.S. Hardcover ISBN   1-59722-239-9   (Cozy Mystery)
U.K. Hardcover ISBN 10 1 4056 3820 6   (Chivers Large Print)
U.K. Hardcover ISBN 13 978 1 405 63820 3
U.K. Softcover ISBN 10 1 4056 3821 4   (Paragon Large Print)
U.K. Softcover ISBN 13 978 1 405 63821 0

The text of this Large Print edition is unabridged.
Other aspects of the book may vary from the original edition.

Set in 16 pt. Plantin.

Printed in the United States on permanent paper.

═══

British Library Cataloguing-in-Publication Data available

═══

Library of Congress Cataloging-in-Publication Data

Fairbanks, Nancy, 1934–
    Crime Brûlée / by Nancy Fairbanks.
      p. cm. — (Wheeler Publishing large print mystery)
    ISBN 1-59722-239-9 (lg. print : hc : alk. paper)
    Blue, Carolyn (Fictitious character) — Fiction.   2. Women food writers — Fiction.   3. New Orleans (La.) — Fiction.
4. Large type books.   I. Title.   II. Wheeler large print cozy mystery.
PS3606.A36C75 2006
  813′.6—dc22   2006007675

For the Gourmet Group

1982 to 20–

In celebration of
good food,
good wine,
and good company

Lillian Mayberry
Jack Bristol
Becky Craver
Lionel Craver
Doris Drow
Gregg Drow
Nancy Herndon
Bill Herndon
Joyce Keller
Randy Keller

Acknowledgments

Many thanks to my editor Cindy Hwang, who suggested that I start a culinary series; to my literary agents Richard Curtis and Laura Tucker; to John Shoup of Great Chefs Publishing for granting permission to use material from *Great Chefs: The Louisiana New Garde*, a book that was as helpful to Carolyn Blue as it was to me; to good friends Mike and Carol Eastman of Northern Arizona University and Larry and Dawn Scott of Boston College with whom my husband and I roamed the French Quarter and even the swamp in search of adventure and good food; to Carol Lee Griffin and her late husband, Gary, whose hospitality gave us an early introduction to the delights of New Orleans; and to Joan Coleman for her friendship, encouragement, and time in reading this manuscript.

Grateful acknowledgment is made to John Shoup of Great Chefs Publishing for permission to reprint recipes and use material from *Great Chefs: The Louisiana*

New Garde by Nancy Ross Ryan with Chan Patterson and to the New Orleans chefs whose recipes are used. Their names are listed in the recipe index.

Visit the author's World Wide Web site at:
http://www.nancyfairbanks.com

Author's Note

Characters and events in this book are inventions of the author. Although real restaurants, meals, and New Orleans scenes are described, the action is fictitious. Any resemblance to actual people and events is purely coincidental.

Nancy Fairbanks

Prologue

Life doles out the most amazing surprises, not all of them pleasant. For instance, who could have imagined that I would find myself in New Orleans trying to solve a mystery, which no one, including the police, seemed to find mysterious at all?

To point out how incongruous the situation was, I should introduce myself: I am Carolyn Blue, a forty-something professor's wife, mother of two, and novice food writer — not a promising résumé for even the most amateur of detectives, and my adult life heretofore contains nothing to recommend me for my self-imposed assignment, the location of a missing person.

How astounded I would have been at the age of twenty had I been able to foresee myself enmeshed in a mission that ultimately proved to be quite terrifying. As an undergraduate, I believed, with my contemporaries, that thirty was the age at which adventure and commitment to ideals ended, the age when one, if still alive, became a fuddy-duddy. Which is not to say that Jason and I were rebellious types, storming administration buildings, occupying the offices of deans, and shouting unpleasant epithets at police officers. We were much too busy for that, he working on a doctorate in science, I pursuing an undergraduate degree in medieval history. We didn't even smoke pot or take hallucinogenic drugs.

I'm sure our children are profoundly appreciative of that abstinence, since they are both normal, intelligent young people with no sign of chromosomal damage. Also they are now away at college, the beneficiaries of generous scholarships that save their gratified parents from being dragged into poverty by the weight of onerous tuition payments.

Jason, my husband, is a university professor and respected scientist. I, having resisted the feminist impetus to go out and accomplish something in a high-powered job, spent my twenties, thirties, and a bit of my forties raising my children and giving charming dinner parties for my husband's colleagues, both foreign and domestic.

Although I was quite content during those years, I must admit that I no longer have much interest in elaborate gourmet projects. In fact, I have become quite addicted to OPC (other people's cooking). I'll eat just about anything that isn't prepared in my own kitchen by me.

Being a semiretired mother and hostess, I have become an Accompanying Person. Perhaps you're not familiar with the term. An Accompanying Person is the spouse or significant other of a scientist attending a conference away from home, perhaps even in another country. I find travel a delightful pastime, one of its greatest benefits being that the traveler is not expected to cook. Entertainment and even meals are provided for Accompanying Persons by the scientific group hosting the conference. I am showered with tours, lunches, and banquets in exotic places.

Even more amazing, this new freedom to accompany my husband has provided me with a career, one that is beginning to generate an income. I haven't had a paying job since I fell in love with Jason, who was the graduate assistant in a perfectly deadly science course the university forced me to take. We married after a year's courtship and were supported by my family and his fellowship while he completed his doctorate and I my bachelor's degree in a subject that was, although fascinating to me and approved by my father, not one with much appeal to prospective employers.

I had Christopher, my first child, while Jason was a postdoctoral fellow and Gwen, my independent daughter, when he became an assistant professor at another institution. After he became a full professor and the children had gone off to college, Jason decided, to the astonishment of all, including me, to take a different job in an unlikely place, but that's another story.

Not a very exciting history, you might say, until I took it into my head, after a trip to Spain, to write an article for the newspaper in El Paso, Texas, our new location. The story was entitled "Goats Are Tastier Than You'd Think," and was probably accepted for publication because people in El Paso and Mexico actually eat goat. My inspiration was a mildly amusing series of events, or mishaps, if you will.

In Madrid, Jason and I went to a charming restaurant that had a menu in many languages, English among them. I ordered lamb, of which I am very fond, and there was some confusion with the waiter, who didn't speak English or understand it and couldn't read the English menu when we pointed to my selection. Then the entrée arrived, a dainty leg of something crisscrossing my plate. Knowing what leg of lamb looks like, I was sure I hadn't gotten it. Nonetheless, I was inspired to adventure by the novelty of eating in a new country and sampled my mystery entrée. The meat was very rich, somewhat greasy, and had an ambrosial marinade on the skin.

"What can it be?" I marveled.

When I gave Jason a bite, he informed me that I was eating goat, or *cabrito* (baby goat), as it is called in Juarez, Mexico, where Jason ordered and enjoyed it while entertaining a seminar speaker from Belgium. You can imagine how taken aback I was. Jason, however, expressed envy. During the second half of our trip, when we were attending a meeting in Catalonia, a province on the eastern coast of Spain, I once again ordered lamb. This time Jason ordered goat, but when our plates came, I had received another goat's leg, and Jason had been served fish. We were both frustrated and complained, not that our protests registered with our non-English-speaking waiter or influenced his employer, who settled the dispute by pointing to the menu entries we had chosen and then to the entrées we had received. As far as the owner was concerned, I had ordered goat and my husband had ordered fish. Jason admitted that his fish was very tasty but claimed half of my goat to assuage his disappointment.

I found the whole incident much more amusing than Jason, although I never did get to sample lamb in Spain, where I had assumed it would be not only excellent but readily available. I have read that many immigrant shepherds in the western United States were Basque. Actually, I don't suppose the Basques consider themselves Spanish. For that matter, the Catalans don't, either, and they speak a different language, which may account for the fact that I missed getting lamb a second time.

But as I said, I submitted an article about eating goat in Spain to our local newspaper. For a wonder, they published my contribution, which was then picked up by other papers in the chain and evidently appeared all over the country. One day while I was loading the dishwasher, I received a telephone call from a literary agent in New York who said that she had read my goat piece and asked if I did much traveling.

"Well, yes, a bit," I said modestly. "I travel with my husband."

"I wonder if you'd be interested in writing a book of anecdotes about eating abroad?"

Needless to say, I was quite astounded and replied, "My next trip is not abroad. We're going to New Orleans."

"Even better," she said. "I know just the publisher for a book on eating in New Orleans." As it happened, she did. The publisher was duly contacted and offered me an advance to write the book, which is why, as I said, I have a sort of job and why I found myself searching a strange city (and New Orleans really is strange) for Julienne Magnussen, although none of our friends seemed to think she was actually missing. However, I knew that my childhood friend would never have missed the crawfish Etienne, much less the seafood gumbo, unless something dreadful had happened to keep her from the table.

1

The Menu at Etienne's

Any cook who aspires to duplicate Cajun or Creole cooking must be willing to master the art of making roux, that seemingly simple mixture of flour with oil, butter, or — horror of horrors! — lard. To produce a cup of roux, begin with a cup each of all-purpose flour and of the oil or fat of choice. Place the oil in a large, heavy-bottomed skillet, and whisk in the flour. (Traditionalists and those who have sufficient upper-body strength recommend a cast-iron skillet.) Then cook slowly, stirring without pause while keeping an anxious eye on the mixture. If your roux burns, it must be discarded. Otherwise, it will ruin whatever dish you add it to — unless you happen to favor food with a bitter taste. How long must you stir? That depends on the color at which you're aiming.

For tan, 10 to 12 minutes; for medium-dark roux, 15 to 18; for dark-brown roux, 20 to 25 minutes.

In these days of public consciousness regarding repetitive motion injuries, one must wonder if New Orleans doctors are keeping statistics on such ailments as *roux elbow* and *roux-induced carpal tunnel syndrome*. I'm told that a treasured gift in Louisiana is a jar of roux made by a master of the art. Perhaps you can make friends with such a person. I, for one, would be delighted to exchange an artfully arranged Christmas assortment of Mesilla Valley pecans for a jar of New Orleans roux.

Carolyn Blue,
Eating Out in the Big Easy

The opportunity was a meeting of the American Chemical Society to be held in New Orleans, the occasion a dinner, which I would arrange for three other couples, companions from our student days. I was somewhat nervous about my plan, although the eight of us were the closest of friends when we attended the university together, working on graduate and undergraduate degrees.

But I haven't seen most of them in over twenty years. Of course, Jason, my husband, runs into those who attend the same scientific meetings, but for me it's been a matter of garnering news of the others at second hand, and my husband isn't given to collecting personal details and passing them on. He's much more likely to tell me about a paper given by one of our friends and the questions asked by the audience.

There have been notes at Christmastime, to be sure, and they sometimes included pictures of children and pets, and I have kept in closer touch with Julienne Magnussen. We talk by phone several times a year, send letters and E-mails, and get together when we're both home to visit our families. Julienne and I have been best friends since childhood. Several times a week for the last two months, she has E-mailed me to add to the list of sights she plans to show me when we meet in New Orleans, the city of her birth. But the other five people, including Julienne's husband Nils, are in the nature of friends one remembers with affection from youth, friends whose lives are familiar in outline, although when one thinks of them at all, one wonders whether they might not have changed into entirely different people over the years. Several of them have.

Julienne and Nils, for instance, were passionately in love both before and after marriage. She told me that they once made love on the sofa in the office of the math chairman, who had left the campus and his graduate students to participate in deer-hunting season. However, I now get hints from her that things aren't as rosy as they once were. I've wondered whether their problem, if there is one, might not be professional jealousy. Julienne is now a full professor with many papers in prestigious journals. She's been an invited speaker at important professional meetings, chair of sessions, editor of journals, recipient of government research grants, and mentor to graduate students. Moreover, Julienne served as chair of her department (an honor about which she complained constantly during the five years of her tenure) and was even proposed as dean of the college, an appointment she firmly declined.

Nils, although he's had a perfectly respectable academic career, is still an associate professor and not nearly as well known in his own field, mathematics, as she is in hers. And Nils tends to be depressed because everybody says mathematicians do their most brilliant work in their twenties, which he is, of course, long past.

Then, I'm somewhat uneasy because the other three women all obtained graduate degrees and made their mark in their chosen fields, while I've drifted through motherhood and helpmate-hood, coming only now in my forties to start a career outside the home. It's entirely possible that I'll be viewed with some disdain by my female friends, while, ironically, the males will probably envy Jason his full-time wife.

Oh well, such are the ironies of gender competition. (I have at last given in to the use of *gender* as the indication of a person's sex rather than a grammatical term, *sex* having too many libidinous connotations these days.)

Then there is the dinner, which I suggested and planned, having established myself as the group's culinary expert. Everyone is coming a day early to attend and will, if I remember them at all, have no hesitation in telling me if they don't find the meal worth their time and trouble. That's not to say that they are rude, just outspoken. But even in the matter of the dinner, I had to work with the restaurant that Julienne insisted on. She pointed out that she has often been in New Orleans, having, in fact, moved from Louisiana to

Michigan as a child, and knows where to order the best gumbo, her favorite dish.

I like gumbo myself but rather resent having to organize a whole meal around some stranger chef's expertise in making roux, a talent that I personally never mastered, even in the days when I wasn't addicted to other people's cooking. I've always hated the idea of spending long periods of time stirring flour over a fire in the faint hope that it won't burn.

The owner and chef, Etienne something or other — his last name is French and completely unpronounceable — has been rather cavalier and even impatient about my desire to choose the menu, which he would much rather have chosen himself, quite possibly from the leftovers of the previous night's offerings. However, when he learned that I am a food writer, he became extremely charming and loquacious, at my expense. I was tempted to insist that he call me back so the long-distance charges would be billed to him. It cost me $21.25 to plan the following menu, which I hope, and Etienne assures me, is the epitome of New Orleans cuisine.

We are to start with deviled alligator puffs and drinks. The deviled alligator will be followed by gumbo, then avocado stuffed with shrimp remoulade, crawfish Etienne as the main course, and finally bread pudding, which I detest but was bullied into by Julienne, the chef, and even my husband Jason. Appropriate wines and brandies are to accompany each course.

Thank God, Jason and I don't have to foot the bill for this dinner. The cost is to be divided evenly among the couples, as long as I keep it below $60 a person, bargained up from $35 in an E-mail negotiation with Broder McAvee, who teaches Calvinist theology at a small but highly regarded liberal arts college on the West Coast. His wife Carlene is a microbiologist and department head in a bioengineering company and has been invited to the meeting to give a plenary address on computational something or other. I'm sure she makes lots of money, but Broder doesn't and says Carlene might be able to afford $200 dinners, but he personally thinks $50 is outrageous; he can eat all week for $50. Well, maybe he can, but it makes one wonder *what* he eats and whether he makes Carlene eat the same things, and especially what they served their four children when the children were at home.

Incidentally, the alligator puffs, which I

chose as a conversation piece and to satisfy my own curiosity, have generated a veritable blizzard of humorous E-mail notes among the group. Everyone is now calling our reunion "the alligator dinner."

2

Deviled Alligator Puffs

Whatever man's original motivation for eating a creature as ugly as an alligator (perhaps it was an eat-or-be-eaten situation), I can certainly recommend deviled alligator puffs. Alligator meat may well have a nasty reptilian tang; if so, it's completely disguised by the herbs, spices, breading, and frying that go into making the puffs, which are light, crispy, and very flavorful (in a nonfrightening way). The alligator meat is also low in calories and cholesterol, although the breading and frying undoubtedly negate any health benefits.

Not the least of an alligator puff's charms is that it breaks the conversational ice at a cocktail party or before a dinner when the guests haven't yet imbibed enough alcohol to be easy with one another.

However, I am not including a recipe

for alligator puffs because it is unlikely that the reader will be able to find alligator meat, ground or otherwise, in the local supermarket. I certainly couldn't, but at that time I foolishly imagined alligators being captured in the swamps by daring hunters called "alligator wrestlers."

Silly me. Alligators have evidently become domesticated. There are over one hundred alligator farms in the state of Louisiana, so I can only surmise that the delicacy is consumed in cities more sophisticated than my own. In fact, I am told that in New Orleans the much favored turtle soup is often made with alligator meat. However, I have never seen turtle soup on a menu in El Paso.

Carolyn Blue,
Eating Out in the Big Easy

Our reserved private dining room at Etienne's was gold and cream with French doors opening onto a patio we couldn't use because rain was falling steadily on the lush shrubbery, the flagstones, and the ornate, white-painted, wrought-iron furniture. Jason and I arrived early to monitor the preparations, but we were joined before eight by Lester and Miranda Abbott.

I remember Lester as a husky young graduate student; now he is the fat dean of a college of science with, to hear him tell it, a very active research group. He wore a brown, double-breasted suit that didn't particularly flatter him.

Ever so slight a smile touched my husband's mouth as Lester bragged about his fourteen graduate students and three postdoctoral fellows and the twenty-six papers his research group had placed during the last year in the very best journals. That little twinkle in Jason's eye was a reminder that Lester Abbott is garnering a reputation as the king of irreproducible results, in all probability, according to Jason, because Lester doesn't monitor the research in his labs closely enough; he's too busy wheeling and dealing at the administrative level.

Jason harbors a mild prejudice against interfering administrators, not to mention the fact that his own research group has published more papers than Lester's, and Jason has aged much more gracefully. My husband is a runner, swimmer, and racquetball player. He is still slender, his hair still dark and thick, with just a touch of distinguished gray at the temples and in his neatly clipped beard. Poor Lester, although he and Jason are both forty-seven, has become rather pompous and self-congratulatory and isn't at all attractive anymore. It's hard to believe that we once called him Les and considered him one of the jolliest persons in the group, especially when he'd been drinking, and he did a lot of that in the old days.

Miranda, his wife, who had once been slender, has grown stocky and developed a thriving practice in tax law. She let us know within two minutes of arrival that she was now billing $350 an hour. Can you imagine? She'd make almost as much in a day as I received as an advance for writing a whole book. Having come straight from taking depositions in a "very important" tax case, she was festively attired in what I took to be a power suit. The garment was so well cut that you could hardly tell she was overweight and so severe that no one could ever accuse her of attempting to make points with feminine wiles.

I felt decidedly frivolous. I was wearing one of those new, almost full-length dresses whose straight-line tailoring belied the pretty flowers on the cream background. Miranda's hair is iron gray and cut very short. Mine, still blonde with the help of a biweekly rinse, is curly but rather carelessly tied back with a scarf whose color, that evening, matched the flowers on my dress.

For all our differences, the conversation was amiable enough, the reminiscences pleasant. Then Julienne and Nils arrived, and suddenly the room hummed with the antagonism that flowed between them. Jason shook hands with Nils, who towered over him. Nils is six three, while Jason is what I consider a perfect height, five seven. He sometimes teases that I chose him because his height gave me an excuse to eschew big hair and high heels, and I'd be the first to admit that such considerations certainly increased his husband-desirability quotient during our courtship. High heels, in my opinion, were designed by males to hobble females who might desire to flee. Nils still had that Nordic blond hair, although thinner than it once was, and the Viking chin and body had softened with the years. He now seemed somewhat indecisive and sulky, while Julienne was as vivacious as ever.

She kissed Jason on the cheek and said, "How are you, you handsome thing?" to which Jason replied, "Never as gorgeous as you, Julienne." Nils scowled at them.

Then Julienne turned to me, breaking

into infectious laughter and hugging me. "You look wonderful, Caro!" she exclaimed. "I'll bet if we took a vote, everyone would agree that you're the youngest-looking person here."

"I *am* the youngest person here," I replied, "even younger than you by a month and a half."

"Oh well, rub it in," said Julienne. She was wearing a dress that I'd never have dared to buy: bright red, sheer floating fabric, with one bared shoulder, one covered with a short, flared sleeve, and a low-cut, crisscross bodice with a full, layered skirt falling in an uneven handkerchief hem that flirted with her knees.

"You look gorgeous, Julienne," I said admiringly. "What a wonderful dress."

"Just what any high-priced call girl would wear for a special customer," muttered Nils.

I couldn't believe my ears and didn't know what to say. Julienne, however, said quite clearly, "Screw you, Nils."

Then she turned back to me, as if her husband had never made that ungentlemanly remark, and said, "I hope you're ready for the grand tour of New Orleans, Caro. First, we're going to meet every single morning for chicory coffee and beignets at Café du Monde."

"Wonderful!' I agreed, imagining the taste of delicious, deep-fried donut squares dusted with powered sugar, a New Orleans delicacy about which I'd read but had never experienced.

"And we're going to the voodoo museum. You don't want to miss that."

"I don't?"

"You don't. And the swamp. We have to take a swamp tour, and don't give me that dubious look, Caro. You'll be perfectly safe. Daddy and Philippe and I went fishing in the swamp lots of times."

Philippe was Julienne's older brother, who had, as older brothers are wont to do, pretty much ignored the two of us. I couldn't imagine the oh-so-serious Philippe fishing in a swamp with his little sister. Still, I didn't want to seem a complete coward. If Julienne could brave the swamp when she was just a tyke, surely I could face it on a tourist boat in her company. "All right," I agreed. "We'll visit the swamp."

"And the French Market and Lafitte's Bar and the tacky clubs on Bourbon Street. You haven't lived until you've seen the tassel twirlers."

She was bubbling with laughter, and I

had to wonder what a tassel twirler was.

"I'm sure, my dear wife, your department chair will appreciate your skipping sessions to watch a bunch of overaged strippers," said Nils sarcastically.

"And if no one else tells him, you will? Is that your plan, Nils?" she retorted. Nils flushed with anger while Julienne turned her back on him. "And Le Bistro for crème brûlée. That's a must, Caro. You and Jason and I can go for dinner one night. It's at Maison de Ville on Toulouse, very romantic. We won't invite Nils since he's being such a shit." She sent him an angry look.

"Crème brûlée sounds good," I agreed in a weak voice. Marital discord in public places always makes me uneasy.

"Miranda! Lester!" Julienne hugged Miranda and patted the stolid Lester on the cheek. Jason, ever the diplomat and always ready to move the conversation into areas scientific, said to Nils, "If you don't mind my picking your brain, old friend, I have a couple of projects that need input from a mathematician."

"Why not," Nils replied. He picked up a flute of champagne from the tray a waiter was passing and tossed down half. "Ask away," he said. "It's common knowledge that chemists don't know dick about math."

I was about to pass him the alligator puffs, but since he'd insulted both my husband and my best friend, I passed them to Lester, who had two, probably to make up for the fact that he'd refused alcohol. When Miranda explained that he was now in AA, Lester didn't look particularly pleased to be exposed as a reformed drunk. For a moment, I was afraid that they might embark on a quarrel, too, but Carlene McAvee breezed in at that moment with Broder plodding behind, looking anxious; no change there.

What a surprise Carlene was: very California, with long, frizzy gray hair and a gauze skirt topped by a shirt that looked to have been made by Southwestern Indians who favor the colors black and turquoise. She radiated enthusiasm. Broder wore a black suit and looked like the Calvinist theologian he was: serious, responsible, and weighted down with the consciousness of a sinful world. His hair had receded, his middle thickened, and the creases deepened between his eyebrows.

Miranda was saying, "Lester Junior has his degree in law. Now he's going for a doctorate in chemistry."

"Trying to please you both?" asked Julienne.

Miranda ignored the question and continued with evident satisfaction, "Do you have any idea how much money he's going to make over a lifetime with those two degrees? Millions!"

Carlene laughed. "I'll bet Broder and I haven't produced a millionaire in the bunch."

"What *are* your brood doing, Carlene?" Miranda asked. "If anyone had told me you'd have four children, and a full-time job, well, I —"

"Nothing to it," said Carlene. "I've got energy to spare. Everyone pitches in on the boring domestic stuff, Broder keeps us all virtuous and out of jail, and I make the money and do the childbearing." She linked her arm through her husband's and squeezed affectionately. "Broder's a daddy in a million. Our oldest girl is in seminary."

Lester looked astonished. "I'm not sure I approve of women pastors."

"What are the rest of them doing, Carlene?" Julienne asked, laughing. "Any other shocking career choices?"

"The eldest boy is in a Central American jungle doing a post doc in archaeology,

35

and the two younger kids are studying microbiology. How far along are they, love?" she asked her husband. "Do I have to get them jobs yet?"

"Jason, what about your two?" Miranda asked, turning to us.

"Undergraduates," he replied. "Gwen in drama, Chris in chemistry."

"Drama!" Miranda exclaimed. "Good lord, you'd better hope she finds a wage-earning husband, or you'll be supporting her for the rest of her life."

I felt rather resentful on Gwen's behalf. "She's already supporting herself, Miranda, and she's only a freshman," I said.

Jason nodded. "Gwen never ceases to amaze us. She talked someone last summer into giving her a job computer programming. She's been a trigonometry tutor and a — what else, Caro?"

"Well, she directed a children's theater and served as an assistant to a muralist working in a downtown bank. She's very talented." I suppose, as a proud mother, I can be forgiven for bragging a bit.

"Takes after my mother in her politics," Jason added. "If she'd gone to school in the sixties, she'd have been out burning her bras."

Jason's mother is a feminist critic and professor of women's studies at the University of Chicago. She finds me a most disappointing daughter-in-law. But Jason is wrong about Gwen and bra-burning. My daughter isn't loath to trade on her beauty, and she wouldn't think of going without a bra.

"You've got a child don't you, Julienne?" said Broder.

"And only one," Nils muttered.

"Diane," Julienne replied, ignoring him. "She's in prep school in New Hampshire and doing very well."

"Since her mother can't be bothered to keep her at home," said Nils.

"Oh?" retorted Julie combatively. "You want to put a sensitive, intelligent girl into the public schools?"

"Since we took her on — and God knows where she came from." Nils turned to the group at large, ignoring his wife. "Julie simply arrived with this baby one day and said she was going to adopt it."

Julienne whirled on him in a flurry of red skirts, and I knew that trouble was imminent. "Well, you *did* want a child, Nils," she snapped.

"Of our own," he retorted.

"Of course. The child-of-my-loins syn-

37

drome. If you were so set on begetting your own —" Her voice dripped with sarcasm. "— maybe you should have gone to a doctor to find out why we weren't having any."

"The problem was that you've always been more interested in career than family, Julie. That's the problem." His eyes, usually so blue, seemed to bleach with malice.

"Nils, you wouldn't know a problem if it bit you on the ass," she sneered. "The fact is, you don't want to hear about problems unless they're your own."

"Case in point," he persisted as if she hadn't spoken, "you can't be bothered to keep Diane at home with us. You —"

"That does it, Nils." Julie slammed her champagne glass down on the dinner table, splashing golden bubbles across an unoffending white linen napkin. "I've heard just about as many of your complaints as I can stomach." With red skirts whirling again, she announced that she was going to the ladies' room and stalked out.

Conversation was somewhat stilted after her exit, and Nils said nothing. He was busy sulking over by the French doors.

3

For Lack of Seafood Gumbo

Gumbo tells, in its ingredients, the tale of the many national groups that immigrated to New Orleans and influenced the city's cuisine. With the original French settlers (from aristocrats and soldiers to prostitutes and transported felons) came the recipe for roux, the necessary first step in the making of gumbo. The soup is thickened with filé (powdered sassafras leaves introduced to the colony by the Indians) or okra, the seeds of which arrived in the New World in the hair and ears of slaves from Africa. The Spanish, who ruled for a short time and imposed their most lasting influence on the architecture of the Vieux Carre, provided the spice of peppers. Arcadians (Cajuns), who were driven from Nova Scotia by the British, make the andouille sausage found in many gumbos, and Croatians farm the oysters, while the whole, whatever its ingredients, is served over rice grown in Louisiana fields by Chinese settlers.

The gumbo at Etienne's in New Orleans is everything a good gumbo should be — with a thick, flavorful stock and enough rice and seafood to make it less a soup than a stew or dish with sauce. If you know a restaurant in your hometown that serves tasty gumbo, patronize it. Otherwise, it might go out of business and someone suggest that you make the gumbo yourself. Only a professional paid to do so should have to attempt the difficult and time-consuming task of making the roux that is the basis of a good gumbo.

Carolyn Blue,
Eating Out in the Big Easy

The alligator puffs disappeared as everyone pretended not to notice that Julienne had failed to return. Then, while waiting for the presentation of the gumbo (the gumbo that had dictated the choice of restaurant, recipe of the chef chosen by the very lady who was missing), I set off to find the rest room and retrieve my friend. If she couldn't face sitting beside her husband, I'd simply change the place cards and move him to the other end of the table. Let Jason put up with him.

But Julienne was not in the ladies' room. After calling her name several times without receiving a response, I peeked under the only closed door in case she was proving to be as sulky as her husband; Nils hadn't said a word to anyone since she left the dining room. The door under which I peeked — and I just bent down to take a look at the shoes — burst open, nearly knocking me over, and an irate lady in flowered lavender silk stalked out and demanded to know what sort of pervert I was.

"I'm looking for a friend," I stammered.

"We in N' Awlins know all about folks who want to make friends with strangahs in public toilets," she retorted disdainfully, bringing home to me how much different indignation sounded in a Southern drawl than in, say, the crisper accents of the Middle West.

"I only wanted to look at your shoes," I responded.

"Mah shoes! Well, Ah nevah! Ah'm goin' to report you to the maître d'." She had been vigorously washing her hands during the conversation and left after making that threat, which, I have to admit, kept me from searching further for Julienne. Instead, I crept back to the dinner, where seven of us sat down to seafood gumbo.

"She wasn't in the ladies'," I whispered to Jason before I took my seat at the other end of the table.

Unfortunately, Nils heard me and said, "That's typical of Julie — inconsiderate to a fault."

He sounded so self-satisfied that I switched his card with Broder's so that I wouldn't have to sit beside him and neither would Julienne when she returned, which she would. I *knew* that she'd never miss the gumbo. Maybe she was making a phone call, perhaps reserving her own room. The Magnussens were staying at the same hotel in the French Quarter where we had reservations, although we hadn't seen them during the afternoon.

As the waiter distributed our bowls, Broder told me how worried he was about his youngest children, who were away at university, no doubt being chased by drug dealers and receiving sexual overtures from lechers with communicable diseases. Poor Broder! He's a dear, but he does fret about sin. I gave him a weak smile and looked down at my gumbo. Where were the crab claws, the sausage, the shrimp, and the oysters? And what were those chopped, hard-boiled eggs doing on top? I frowned, sniffed, then tasted. "Waiter!" I called. "What is this?"

"It's the turtle soup, ma'am."

"What turtle soup?"

"Well, actually, ma'am, Ah believe the chef used alligator insteada turtle, but that's by way of bein' a N'Awlins tradition, an' Ah know you're gonna find it's the best turtle — well, alligator — soup you ever did eat. Etienne is famous fo' his —"

Jason was chuckling and leaned forward to say, "Well, we *have* been calling this the alligator dinner, Caro, but I never realized you were *this* fond of reptile meat."

"I ordered gumbo," I informed the waiter. "My friend insisted on this restaurant because of Etienne's reputation for wonderful gumbo."

"Since the friend who insisted didn't even bother to show up for the course," said Nils, "it doesn't much matter, does it?" He looked smug while he ate his soup as rapidly as possible, no doubt in order to prevent me from having it removed.

"Etienne, he's even mo' famous fo' his turtle soup," said the waiter, who was clasping a tray in a white-knuckled grasp.

"But turtle soup is not what I ordered, and this is not, by your own admission, turtle soup. I want to see the chef."

"For heaven's sake, Carolyn," said Miranda. "This is delicious. Don't make such a fuss."

I gave the waiter what I hoped was a suitably steely and commanding glance, and he was soon back with Etienne himself, a short, round man, wearing a ludicrously tall chef's hat and glaring majestically.

"Madame does not like my famous soup?" he demanded.

"Madame ordered gumbo, as you very well know."

He looked blank for a minute, then slapped his forehead with the palm of his hand. "But of course, Mme. Julienne, who loves my gumbo. How could this mistake have taken place? Discipline shall be meted out to where it is deserved. *Bien?* You will eat my ambrosial turtle soup —"

"Alligator," I reminded him.

He glared at the waiter. "Turtle, alligator. It makes no difference."

"Broder, doesn't the Bible have prohibitions against eating alligators?" asked Carlene, eyes twinkling.

Broder looked thoughtful and admitted

that there was a prohibition against eating crawling things, snakes for instance, and alligators might be included, although they did have feet. On the other hand, such dietary restrictions were practiced by Jews, not Christians, and in fact, he thought crocodiles were native to the Middle East, not alligators, so alligators wouldn't have come up, as such, in the Bible.

"Madame will accept my most profound apologies," Etienne ordered, although Broder was still talking about dietary laws, "and enjoy her turtle soup, and tomorrow I will send to her hotel a container of my excellent gumbo. And one for Mme. Julienne as well." He bowed and left before I could protest.

Well, what could I do? I ate the soup, and it was indeed delicious, flavored with sherry, chicken stock, herbs, chopped vegetables, and the meat. (I later discovered that not only could turtle meat be replaced by alligator but by ground veal, as well.) In fact, the next day when I returned from the less-than-exciting refreshments at the American Chemical Society welcome mixer, Etienne's gumbo awaited me, and it was as wonderful as Julienne had promised: spicy, rich, thick, and loaded with delectable crustaceans caught locally. I amused myself while eating it by imagining

Etienne himself, chef's hat askew, apron bespattered, scrambling down some muddy bank to harvest crabs.

As the soup bowls were being cleared away and new wine poured, I excused myself to go in search of my friend, but before I could get out of the room, Nils said, "If you're still looking for Julie, maybe you should try locating her hot-blooded Italian stereochemist."

That comment stopped the conversation cold until Lester tried to break the uncomfortable silence by saying, "Wonderful soup, whatever they put in it. Are there seconds?"

"Certainly, sir," said the waiter, who had been in the act of removing Lester's bowl and was obviously relieved that the restaurant's mistake was not causing table-wide anger and thus promising a substantial diminution of his tip.

"Lester, you don't need seconds," snapped his wife.

"Well, what's next, Caro?" Jason asked with an eagerness that was unlike him on any subject other than scientific research.

"Avocado-stuffed shrimp remoulade," I replied and escaped, wondering if Julienne could have discovered when she left for the ladies' room that gumbo was not to be

46

served, upon which discovery she left the restaurant entirely. But it wasn't my fault the wrong soup had been served, so if she left, it was because of her husband or because something dreadful had happened to her.

I checked the ladies' room again and found two women sitting on poufy, low-backed, wire-legged chairs. The ladies were renewing their makeup in front of gilded Cupid mirrors. One other woman stood at the marble sinks, but the stall doors were open, and Julienne was not there. Through a window covered with stirring rose silk drapes, I could hear the rain and studied the window as if my childhood friend might have pulled over a chair and crawled out into an alley. But that was a ridiculous idea. For one thing, anyone who tried to stand on one of those silly little seats would have been tipped onto the floor with resulting bruises.

And if Julienne had wanted to leave, she could have walked out the front door. In fact, and although our hotel was only a four-block walk through the Quarter, she would have called a cab rather than exposing her lovely dress to the rain.

Unless she called the mysterious Italian stereochemist, a little voice whispered in my head. Then the Carolyn who had grown up with Julienne and shared adolescent secrets rejected that disloyal notion, and I went out to question the restaurant staff.

But first I noticed that the hall leading to the rest rooms had a door at the end. What if someone had kidnapped her in the hall and dragged her out through that door? I hurried down to try it and found the door locked. But the abductors might have had a key. *Oh nonsense, Carolyn,* I told myself. *Don't be so melodramatic! She's probably in the bar having a drink, making a new friend, and paying Nils back for being such a pill.* I checked the bar, which was very crowded but harbored no one with curly black hair and a stunning red dress.

Next I tried the maître d'. Was it my imagination, or did he look at me peculiarly? Surely that obnoxious Southern belle in lavender hadn't reported me to him as the lesbian shoe fetishist in the ladies' room. In reply to my query, he said that he had seen Julienne come in with a tall, blond man, but he had not seen her leave, alone or accompanied.

"I'm afraid something terrible has happened to her," I cried, allowing melodrama to overcome me once more.

"Nothing terrible happens to the customers at Etienne's," he assured me in a heavy, if unconvincing, French accent. "Only the most delightful of culinary experiences. Is madam not happy with the meal thus far?"

"Aside from the fact that you served the wrong soup," I replied, "the dinner has been tasty."

Evidently he had expected more enthusiasm, for he eyed me with all the approval he might reserve for a fly discovered in the crème brûlée, a dessert I would have preferred to the bread pudding I'd been coerced into ordering. If Julienne didn't show up for the bread pudding, I'd never forgive her. Unless she had no choice in the matter. "The door at the end of the rest room hall — where does it go?" I asked urgently, once more picturing my friend being shanghaied by swarthy men in evening clothes.

"Outside, madam," he replied, "but she could not have escaped your dinner party in that manner, for the door is locked, and I have the only key."

I went on to the tuxedoed person who presided at a too-precious antique desk, dispensing haughty condescension to those who had come in off the street without a reservation, perhaps not even suitably dressed. I wondered how my friends had been treated when they arrived — Miranda in her business suit (of course, at $350 an hour, she could condescend with the best of them) and Carlene in her California hippie outfit. But then Carlene wouldn't have noticed any but the most blatant snub, say, if the gatekeeper at the desk had refused to let her in.

He, too, remembered Julienne's entrance but assured me that she had not departed past his station, nor had she ordered a cab. "No one has yet ordered a cab, madam," he asserted. "Who would eat at such an unfashionable hour as to be finished with dinner already?"

What could I say to such an incontrovertible piece of logic? I stopped a few waiters and busboys passing between the kitchens and the main dining areas, but no one had seen Julienne, and I had to return to my avocado-stuffed shrimp remoulade. Incidentally, it was superb, the avocados soft and buttery, the shrimp firm, plump, and shrimpy, and the remoulade — ah, it was perfect.

But before I sat down under the disgruntled eyes of the waiter, who wanted to clear that course and serve the crayfish Etienne, I leaned down and murmured to Nils, "I'm really terribly worried. Perhaps you should call the hotel to see if she's safely back."

"Nonsense," Nils retorted testily. "She's fine. Just willful."

Broder didn't help my state of mind when I finally sat down to my second course. Having finished his own avocado, he regaled me with stories about the white-slave trade in New Orleans, the corruption of the police, and various murder and drug-dealing statistics. I was so panic stricken by the time I had swallowed my last delicious shrimp that I nodded to the waiter to serve the main course and rushed out to call the hotel myself.

Julienne didn't answer.

Carol Lee's Avocado Stuffed Shrimp Remoulade

Combine in a small bowl $^1/_4$ *cup tarragon vinegar, 2 tbs. horseradish mustard, 1 tbs. catsup, 1$^1/_2$ tsp. paprika, $^1/_2$ tsp. salt, $^1/_4$ tsp. cayenne pepper.*

Slowly add $^1/_4$ *cup salad oil,* beating constantly.

Stir in $^1/_4$ cup ea. *minced celery and minced green onions* with tops.

Pour sauce over *2 lbs. cleaned, cooked, shelled shrimp* and marinate in refrigerator 4 to 5 hours.

Halve and peel *4 medium avocados.*

Lift shrimp from sauce and arrange 4 or 5 in each avocado half.

Serve and pass leftover remoulade sauce.

4

Crawfish Etienne

Crawfish. Not the most pleasant sounding word for something so tasty, but then natives of Louisiana object to the more inviting *crayfish.* In fact, a popular local name for the crustacean in question is *mudbug,* while I myself prefer *minilobster.* New Orleans mythology tells us that the crawfish is a lobster that walked all the way from its native Maine and arrived in Louisiana seriously diminished in size, a cautionary lesson to dieters: eat crawfish, which are low in calories, and walk a lot. However, if your cholesterol is high, eat oysters. They have fewer calories and one-third the artery cloggers.

Whatever you call its main ingredient, crawfish Etienne is not a dish you can make at home. I did try, but the recipe is the secret of Etienne, the talented New Orleans chef, and I didn't come close to imitating his culinary triumph, even though I shelled all those miserable minilobsters. Actually, they're delicious, but essentially only one bite per creature. Consequently, you have to feel sorry for the poor, no doubt underpaid, serf in the kitchen at Etienne's who cooks and then cracks open hundreds of shells in order to produce all the delicious crustacean bits. The bits are then bathed in a glorious cream and wine sauce enhanced by mystery herbs. Even the direst circumstances are mitigated by the consumption of crawfish Etienne.

Carolyn Blue,
Eating Out in the Big Easy

"Isn't crayfish a peasant food?" asked Miranda, who had moved over to talk to me, filling the seat that Julienne would have occupied had she not disappeared. "I always thought they were something that swamp dwellers, the sort who marry their cousins, fish out of the muck and eat."

"Viva la swamp!" I said, having had quite a few glasses of wine in an effort to drown my worries about my missing friend. I picked up my pen and scribbled more notes, dutifully keeping in mind that I had been paid to write a book about food in New Orleans.

I noticed that Miranda was eating her way steadily through the *peasant food* on her plate. Maybe I should have sicced Etienne on her. It was hard to believe she'd once been a rather radical protestor with waist-length hair and beads — until she'd been arrested and was so horrified by the inadequate hygiene facilities at the jail that she never joined another protest. Somehow or other, her father, a prominent Cincinnati lawyer, managed to get her out of jail without her presence becoming part of the public record. Having learned her lesson (she was always a good student), Miranda immediately changed to prelaw, went on to law school, and look at her now. She's a Republican!

"At least you're finally working," she said. "How could you stand staying home all those years?"

"I enjoyed it," I replied defensively. "I really don't see why we stay-at-home wives and mothers should have to apologize."

"You enjoyed staying home?" Miranda rolled her eyes. "I'd have felt selfish. I mean, *one* income? And a college professor's at that?"

"Nothing wrong with my income," Jason called from the other end of the table. "The kids and I are the lucky ones, having Carolyn at home." He gave me a very sexy smile, which I returned. Jason really is a love.

"Hear! Hear!" muttered Nils. "Every man should be so lucky."

"Well, I call it financially feckless," continued Miranda. "Because I make a lot of money, Lester can afford to indulge himself in all sorts of esoteric research and administrative skullduggery, and we're still very comfortable financially."

I was beginning to feel a bit beleaguered, although I couldn't see that my staying home had thrown us into poverty. Still, if the children hadn't been so smart and received scholarships . . .

"Oh, knock it off, Miranda," said Carlene. "I think women should get to stay home if they want to. I mean, kids are fun! I wouldn't have minded mothering a couple more, but I just didn't have time for more pregnancies."

Lester looked horrified. "You'd have wanted *six* children? Or eight?"

"Why not?" replied Carlene. "As long as they do their own ironing, the more the merrier."

"They are a responsibility, however," said Broder. "In this world, one thinks twice about having children. And we certainly couldn't have afforded those we have if Carlene hadn't been working. Theology professors are not well remunerated."

Carlene giggled. "Now, Broder, when did you ever *think twice?* Unless it was after conception."

Broder turned red. I had to put my hand over my mouth to hide a smile. I wouldn't embarrass him for the world, but the idea of a hot-blooded Broder begetting children with abandon was amusing.

"I suppose your move to El Paso had something to do with your sudden need to become a working woman," said Miranda, evidently miffed because others, even the very successful Carlene, had supported my right to stay home. "Why in the world would you take a job in El Paso, Jason?" She looked at my husband with a mixture of horror and pity. "Some trouble with your previous position? Goodness, you'd been there for *years.*"

"Toxicity," said Jason, looking energized at the very thought of a favorite subject. "I was offered a chaired professorship in the chemistry of environmental toxicology. With a mandate to found an institute."

"But in El *Paso?*"

"Where better?" Jason replied. "The toxins in the air, soil, and water are a researcher's dream."

"Still, old man," Lester chimed in smugly, "it is a step down from your old position."

"My research group at this point numbers over thirty," said Jason mildly.

Lester frowned; Miranda added, "But it must be a cultural wasteland. How can you stand it, Carolyn?"

"We have a very presentable symphony, a good opera company, and even a local ballet," I replied defensively. Initially, I had been quite reluctant to leave all my friends and associations when Jason announced this marvelous opportunity that had been offered to him, out of the blue as it were. And the children had been furious. Especially our daughter, who had just been accepted to college. She threatened to stay in her dormitory during all vacations if she had to come home to El Paso. Not that I intended to admit any of these problems to Miranda. "And I do have a maid," I added slyly.

"A maid?" the women breathed.

"In fact, our house has a maid's room and bath."

"A *live-in* maid?" Miranda's mouth dropped open.

"Actually, she lives in her own house," I murmured, "but she has a car. I don't have to pick her up or even pay transportation, and her wages are very reasonable." I didn't mention that Ippolita speaks Spanish and I don't, that we communicate through a Spanish phrase book, and that the book doesn't include the phrase, "The vacuum cleaner is on fire; maybe you should turn it off." Ippolita only understands the instructions I find in the book when it suits her to understand. In fact, she does pretty much as she likes, although she does get the house cleaned. Needless to say, the vacuum cleaner repairman considers me his best customer.

"Well, I still think —" Miranda began.

Broder cleared his throat and interrupted diplomatically, "The owner at our bed and breakfast recommended a gospel brunch that occurs tomorrow in the warehouse district. She says it's very colorful — a black choir and leader, ethnic food. It's rather expensive, unfortunately, but —"

"— but we can afford it," said Carlene. "We heard that the audience is dancing in the aisles by the time it's over. So why don't we all meet there at quarter to eleven? We don't have to register at the convention center until late afternoon. Then there's the reception at the aquarium afterward."

"Complete with cheap wine, American beer, and dubious canapés," said Miranda. "Unless you attend a conference abroad, you never get a decent thing to eat at a meeting of chemists, present company excluded."

"Well, whatever they serve, it will take care of dinner," said Carlene, ever practical for all her offbeat wardrobe. Maybe she only wore things like that when she was away from home, or always wore them because they were inexpensive.

"Sounds fascinating," said Jason.

I was signaling the waiter to clear and produce the dreaded bread pudding.

"Nils, be sure to tell Julienne about the gospel brunch," Carlene added. "She'll love it."

"And remind her to bring her camera," said Miranda. "She promised to send pictures to all of us, and now we have none of our reunion."

"Maybe we should try to call her again," Broder suggested, digging enthusiastically into his bread pudding. "She must be back at the hotel by now."

I hope so, I thought nervously.

"As I suggested, you might have better luck calling her favorite colleague, Linus Torelli," said Nils.

"Linus?" Lester looked interested. "Was he named after Linus Pauling?"

"He's young enough to have been," Nils snarled.

"Oh, knock it off, Magnussen," said Carlene angrily. "If you'd work a little harder yourself, maybe you wouldn't have to be jealous of your wife."

"What's that supposed to mean?" Nils demanded.

"Why, that when we were all in school together, you were the fair-haired boy," Carlene replied crisply. "Now it's Julienne who's the star."

Nils stood up, knocking his chair over, dropped his napkin on top of his bread pudding, and stalked out.

I sighed, foreseeing an acrimonious divorce in the future of my dear friend Julienne. It's so sad to see a marriage end, especially a marriage that was once marked by great love; but obviously, in this case, a fragile male ego had overridden a warm female heart. I didn't for a minute believe that Julienne had been unfaithful to her husband. Nils was simply substituting sexual jealousy for professional jealousy because the latter made him look small-minded and exposed his own inadequacies while the former placed the onus on Julienne.

One has to wonder how many modern marriages break up on the rocks of professional competition. Had I become a famous medieval scholar instead of a mom, would Jason have come to resent me? Probably not, I decided. In the first place, Jason isn't like that. In the second, he considers the study of the Middle Ages more in the nature of an indulgence, while the study of chemistry is serious business.

Feeling better, at least about my own marriage, I took a bite of the bread pudding. Oh my. This was not like any bread pudding Mother used to make. In fact, it was a sort of bananas Foster, which I love, plus bread pudding, plus whipped cream. Bathed in a delicious banana-rum sauce, even bread pudding can send a shiver of culinary delight up the spine. I ate every bite, as, I noticed, did all the others, except the bad-tempered and absent Nils. Lester confiscated and ate Nils's serving when Miranda wasn't looking. Would the rum sauce knock him off the wagon? Maybe not. He didn't drain Nils's goblet of dessert wine.

"Wonderful dinner, Carolyn," said

Lester, looking as if he'd like to mop up the sauce left on Nils's plate. He was the first to break the uncomfortable silence that followed the angry departure of a second Magnussen.

"Anyone care for a brandy?" Jason asked.

I placed my fork properly on my empty dessert plate and slipped away to call Julienne's hotel room again. Her telephone rang uselessly and ominously in my ear. I could only hope that she was in the room but refusing to answer, anticipating the caller to be her husband.

When I returned, the five remaining diners were preparing to disperse after the expected compliments to me on the menu and an exchange of directions to the gospel brunch. Then Jason exercised his preference for walking in the rain — actually, he would have preferred to jog, but I demurred — and we shared his giant, black umbrella during the four-block walk to the Hotel de la Poste. I don't think we've used that umbrella since we moved to arid El Paso, but Jason, always foresighted, thought to find and pack it.

The trip home was very pleasant as the sidewalks were neither so crowded as to be troublesome nor so deserted as to make us uneasy. My moisture-deprived skin was sucking in the precipitation as we passed under streetlights that glistened on wet pavement. Even the sounds of revelry seemed muted in the fine rain. Or perhaps the visitors were just quieter; I didn't notice as many go cups in festive hands. But then why buy a drink to go when raindrops would quickly water it down?

The hotel glowed warmth into the wet darkness as we approached on Chartres Street. Three flags, of which I recognized only that of the United States, dripped from poles that slanted out above the cream columns in front. What were the others? French and Spanish? Louisiana and New Orleans? I'd have to ask. At my insistence, we turned left into the small lobby with its antiques and its somnolent desk clerk to ask after Julienne.

"Haven't seen a lady in a red dress pass by," he answered. "Sure didn't notice one comin' in here. You all want me to buzz her room?"

I thought of Nils, with his disgruntled attitude toward Julienne. He would take such a call amiss. Therefore, I shook my head unhappily, and Jason and I went off to bed. Our lights were out within fifteen minutes. Inspired by our exotic surroundings, we had had a romantic interlude that afternoon, which sufficed for our first day in New Orleans.

I will never again speak slightingly of bread pudding after having it in New Orleans. What a treat! The following recipe is actually that of Chef Frank Brigtsen but produces results close to the marvelous dessert I had at Etienne's. Try it if you are long on time and desire for a wonderful final course to some special meal.

Banana Bread Pudding with Banana-Rum Sauce and Whipped Cream

Preheat the oven to 300° F.

Put *6 cups bite-sized pieces of day-old French bread* in a 9 x 12 x 2-in. baking pan and set aside.

In a blender or food processor, blend *3 large eggs, 3 cups milk, $^2/_3$ cup sugar, 2 large very ripe bananas, 1 tbs. ground cinnamon, $^1/_4$ tsp. ground nutmeg, $^1/_2$ tsp. vanilla extract* until smooth.

Pour mixture over French bread pieces;

fold in $\frac{1}{2}$ *cup ea. seedless raisins and roasted pecans* and let mixture set for 20 minutes.

Top with *3 tbs. unsalted butter* cut in small pieces.

Cover pudding with aluminum foil and place pan into larger pan. Add warm water to depth of 1" in larger pan. Bake 1 hour. Remove foil and bake uncovered for 15 minutes or until set.

In a deep, medium bowl, whisk $\frac{3}{4}$ *cup heavy whipping cream* just until it begins to thicken. Add *1 tbs. sugar* and $\frac{1}{4}$ *tsp. vanilla*. Continue whisking until soft peaks form. Cover and chill.

Sauce:
Heat a large sauté pan over low heat. Add $\frac{2}{3}$ *cup unsalted butter* at room temperature, $\frac{1}{2}$ *cup packed light brown sugar, 6 large ripe bananas quartered, 1 tsp. ground cinnamon,* and $\frac{1}{4}$ *tsp. ground nutmeg.*

Moving skillet back and forth, cook until butter and sugar become creamy and bananas begin to soften, about 1 minute.

Remove skillet from heat and add *3 tbs. dark rum* and *2 tbs. banana liqueur* (optional). Return pan to heat, tilt, avert face, light liquid with long match, and shake skillet until flames subside. Add $^1/_2$ tsp. vanilla, remove from heat, and keep warm.

Serve:
Place a large scoop of bread pudding in the middle of each plate or bowl.
Place 2 slices of banana on each plate and top with about 3 tbs. of sauce.

Spoon whipped cream over pudding and serve immediately. Serves 12.

Carolyn Blue,
Eating Out in the Big Easy

5

Soul Food

On Sunday morning, while Jason went to buy a newspaper, I called the Magnussens' room in search of Julienne. No answer. Surely Nils hadn't disappeared as well. This was not the reunion of old friends I had looked forward to. Worried and tired after a restless night, I began the slow process of getting dressed for the gospel-brunch excursion planned the night before. Did one dress up as for a church service or opt for casual clothing like the tourists who were already crowding the streets below my window?

Some were even carrying go cups and sipping liquor at ten a.m. This was the Big Easy indeed, and I wasn't sure I approved of street drinking, especially on Sunday morning. Had he known what I was thinking, Jason would have laughed and remarked on the vestiges of a Protestant Midwest background that clung to my psyche like crumbs of Styrofoam to a wool dress.

I chose casual and pulled on beige slacks and a brown turtleneck sweater with a bit of gold jewelry and an autumnal print scarf to tie my hair back. Before I could complete my toilette, a stocky black woman with powerful arms and a gold tooth that winked at me from an amiable smile knocked at my door and entered the room.

Black? Or African-American? I seem to have lost track of which is currently the politically correct designation. Before the Civil War, *black* was the term used to refer to slaves in New Orleans, while free Negroes were *men and women of color.* Of course, *colored* would now be considered old-fashioned, if not downright insulting. It is, no doubt, a sign of encroaching middle age that I am behind the times on modern racial terminology but knowledgeable about the relevant linguistic history.

At any rate, the maid's accent was so Southern as to make me think I might need an electronic translator. One thing I can say for El Paso: the natives do not have Southern accents, although many have Hispanic accents, but those aren't at all hard to decipher, unless, of course, said native is actually speaking Spanish. Maybe

I should get an electronic translator to aid in communication with Ippolita. Or maybe not. I have the suspicion that she can understand me perfectly in either language if she chooses to, but perhaps I do her an injustice or give myself more credit than I deserve in my use of the phrase book for communicating with my Hispanic housekeeper. And is *Hispanic* preferable to *Chicano* or *Mexican-American?* I have no idea.

"Please do stay," I said to the maid, hoping that I'd understood correctly her presumed offer to come back when we were gone if that would be more convenient. She began immediately on the bed while I brushed my hair back and tied the scarf. Was she responsible for the Magnussens' room as well? I wondered.

"Excuse me." I had finished fastening conservative gold button earrings to my ears. "Do you make up this whole floor?"

"Mostly, yes, ma'am." She finished the bed and headed for the bathroom with an armload of fresh towels.

I followed to stand in the doorway. "I have friends on this floor, the Magnussens."

"Miz Julienne you mean? An' her husband? Don' know his name. He didn' introduce hisself like dat nice Miz Julienne. Dem as had such a terrible fight yesterday afternoon. Cain't say as I blame her, not comin' home to da likes a him last night."

"She didn't sleep in her bed at all?" I asked, thoroughly alarmed. Then it occurred to me that the maid could hardly know that for certain. If the room had one king or queen-sized bed, they would have shared it, and Julienne might have fluffed her pillow up when she rose. If the room had separate beds, they were probably full or queen-sized, and they might have made up their differences and shared one. "You can't be sure of that," I pointed out anxiously.

"Oh, Ah be sure," said the maid. She stopped work and put both hands on ample hips. "One bed been slept in an' got his 'jamas layin' on de sheets. Other bed ain' even got de spread rumpled. An' dey be twin beds, only twin-bed room on da floor. Hafta ask fo' dem twin beds. Folks do dat don' wanna be sharin' a pilla. Course it ain' none a mah business." She went back to work, but I could see that the woman was beginning to regret having spoken so freely.

"Julienne's been my friend since we were little children," I hastened to explain. "I'm so worried —"

"Yo'all don' sound like you from N'Awlins," said the maid suspiciously. She had turned from cleaning the tub.

"I'm not. Julienne moved to Michigan when she was little."

"Po' chile," the woman commiserated. "Mus' be terrible cold up dere."

"Julienne shivered for three years," I agreed. "Even in the summer." How had we moved from Julienne's frightening disappearance to her childhood intolerance of Michigan weather? "I'm so terribly worried about her," I said to the maid, who was now swishing a brush around the toilet bowl. "She left the dinner party last night, and it seems that no one has seen her since."

"Well, likely she run off, or he done sumpthin' to her. He was a-yellin' so bad Ah couldn' hardly git no one to answer da door when Ah come to deliver dem extra towels Miz Julienne wanted fo' washin' her hair with."

Oh lord, I thought, more worried than ever; Nils and Julienne had been quarreling even before the dinner party. By the time the maid had finished the room and I had prepared to go out, Jason returned with a rumpled copy of the *New Orleans Times-Picayune* under his arm. He couldn't say enough about the delights of having a morning café au lait and a beignet at the Café du Monde on Jackson Square. How could I have forgotten? Julienne had said last night that we would meet every morning for breakfast at Café du Monde, and I had missed the meeting.

"Did you see Julienne?" I asked.

" 'Fraid not," said Jason absently.

"Didn't you look for her?"

"Carolyn, why would I? She's probably just getting up. We are, after all, going out to brunch shortly."

"Then why were *you* eating breakfast?" I couldn't resist teasing my husband for having eaten immediately before our eleven-to-one seating at the Praline Connection.

"New Orleans is for stuffing oneself with the local cuisine," Jason replied. "Isn't that the gist of your book?"

I could hardly argue with his logic, but then I wasn't interested in logic; I was interested in the whereabouts of my missing friend. "Julienne didn't come back to the hotel last night."

Jason looked surprised. "Really? Then it would appear that the problems between her and Nils are serious," he said thoughtfully. Then he smiled. "But she'll show up.

I imagine she's giving Nils something to worry about, and I must say, he was pretty unpleasant to her last night."

"He was beastly," I agreed furiously. "I'll never forgive him for the things he said and for driving her away. I just hope she's safe."

"Now, Caro. Of course, she's safe. She's probably staying with friends or relatives in New Orleans."

Was she? I don't remember her mentioning friends or relatives here, not since her great aunt died several years ago. Julienne and her brother Philippe had come down for the funeral of Beatrice Delacroix, a jazz funeral, which Julienne arranged, over the objections of her brother, and later described in detail to me, along with the cemetery in which her aunt was interred. She had said I'd have to see it. Did she still want to go? I'm not a devotee of cemeteries, although they can be a useful tool for historic research.

I rushed Jason out before he could suggest that we call the Magnussens' room and meet Nils in the lobby. I was so irritated with Julienne's husband that I didn't care to walk however many blocks with him.

Jason obtained a map from the front

desk showing the route from Hotel de la Poste to the Praline Connection. How glad I was that I never wear heels; it looked to be a good distance and proved to be worse than I expected. We turned left and walked several blocks on Chartres to Canal, where we turned left again and walked two and a half very long blocks to the confusing five-way intersection that led us to South Peters and the Warehouse District, where the blocks were even longer. The area gave me an eerie feeling. Once we had left the bustle of the French Quarter, we passed one featureless warehouse after another and in a neighborhood where few people were on the streets. Under gray skies, heavy with the threat of impending rain, I found myself glancing apprehensively into alleys and down cross streets, as if some threat lurked there.

Unable to secure a cab, had Julienne been snatched off the street as she walked home through the rain to the hotel? I shuddered to think of how terrified she must have been, perhaps calling for help and ignored by hurrying passersby, or unable to call out because a dirty hand was clamped over her mouth. Or had her abductors used an ether-soaked rag so that they could drag her, unconscious, into a waiting car?

As my imagination ran amok, I clutched my husband's arm in a death grip, but Jason only glanced at me, briefly puzzled, and patted my hand. He seemed immune to my low spirits. Having met, at the Café du Monde, a fellow scientist whose conversation had lured him away from the sports page of the newspaper, Jason was intent on telling me about an exciting new compound the fellow had synthesized and planned to talk about at the ACS meeting.

"It's a dilemma," Jason confessed. "His paper and Julienne's are scheduled for the same hour on Wednesday."

"Julienne's missing," I reminded him gloomily.

"Believe me, Caro, she won't skip her own paper!" Jason laughed and, having previously disengaged my clutching hand, now took my arm as we crossed the last street and approached the Praline Connection. Miranda and Lester arrived at the same time but from a different direction. They were staying, as Miranda had pointed out last night, at an expensive, high-rise hotel on the riverfront, conveniently situated near the convention center. Personally, I preferred the exotic ambiance of the French Quarter. Why, if one had a choice, would one elect to stay elsewhere? Unless it was because the walk to the meeting would be shorter. When Jason pointed out that we were only a few blocks from the Ernest N. Morial Convention Center ("Dutch" Morial was the first black mayor of New Orleans), I realized what a long walk Jason would have every morning, possibly in the rain. The one umbrella we had brought was not going to suffice when we parted company in the morning.

While giving half an ear to Broder McAvee, who was seven or eight places behind us in the line and complaining audibly about the cost of admission, we paid for our tickets, then claimed a table for eight. Ours wasn't near the stage; those tables had already been taken, mostly by black women dressed as if for church, which made me somewhat embarrassed over my choice of casual, touristy clothes. We *were* near the soul-food buffet. I am, personally, unfamiliar with soul food, but I was prepared to write about it and even like it, although I had heard that collard greens are somewhat bitter. On the other hand, they are supposed to be very healthful. As it turned out, I found that I prefer spinach to collards in the dark-green, antioxidant-rich, healthful-vegetable category.

Oh, for the days when we knew less about the benefits, beyond simple sustenance, of the food we were eating. What would a medieval European peasant make of the advice that one should choose chicken and fish over red meat or suffer the cholesterol consequences? Since medieval peasants rarely had any meat in their diets, they would, no doubt, have been quite indifferent to any diet consideration other than the benefits of having a full stomach.

There was a second buffet with more ordinary offerings — bacon, eggs, sausage — but I decided that it was my duty as a newly minted food reviewer to sample and write about the more exotic, more regional cuisine. The food was just then being set out by platoons of young African-American waiters and waitresses, all wearing black hats that made them look as if they expected to desert the service industry and join jazz bands momentarily. Some of them frowned at me, probably thinking that I wanted to fill a plate before the lines were officially open. A third, and rather well hidden, buffet offered coffee, orange juice, and desserts: cake, pralines, peach cobbler. The room itself was very large with metal rafters in the dark loft space overhead and tiny white Christmas lights twinkling everywhere. It was also very noisy and becoming more so as it filled up.

During my investigations, Carlene and Broder joined the table, Broder still complaining, and as I sat down next to Jason, Nils straggled in, looking as sulky as ever.

"Where's Julienne?" Carlene demanded, even before he could take his chair. The unoccupied seat beside him reminded me, rather terrifyingly, of Banquo's empty chair at Macbeth's banquet.

"Gone," Nils snapped. "I haven't heard from her since she walked out last night."

Before I could quiz him further, the opening of the buffet tables was announced, and the throng in the cavernous warehouse stampeded toward the food. Miranda and Lester refused to try soul food; they opted for eggs and sausage, as did Nils. Jason had some of everything; my husband has a healthy appetite and an appreciation for whatever is put in front of him. When we order something particularly memorable during our travels, Jason will even join me in trying to reconcoct the dish in our own kitchen, although I suspect that he sees the effort as akin to a lab experiment.

Broder and Carlene accompanied me to the soul-food buffet, and we helped ourselves to red beans and rice, which was a traditional Monday dish in New Orleans, slow-cooked on the fire all day while the wife and/or servants did the weekly washing. At home I make a Caribbean recipe that includes not only rice and beans but green onions, salt pork, olives, and various other delicious ingredients. Although I prefer my own recipe, the Praline Connection served a tasty and, I suspect, lard-rich version. Best of all, I didn't have to spend my time cooking it.

Their barbecued beef proved so tender that it disintegrated between the teeth in a swirl of tangy sauce. The jambalaya was packed with chicken, ham, and sausage and left the flavors of thyme, garlic, and chili powder dancing on the tongue. The peppers were so lavishly stuffed that the filling squeezed from the ends and even burst from the side veins. Then there were the bitter greens: perhaps they are so popular with soul-food lovers because they cut the taste of grease, or perhaps some instinct for survival shows itself in the popularity of collards, which the body believes will chase plaque from the arteries and dread oxidants from the cells. Grits completed the menu.

I have had grits before and have never

been a fan. I consider them even more detestable than Cream of Wheat, which my mother served on freezing mornings to protect us from frostbite of the fingers and toes by warming us in advance from the stomach outward. Does that make sense? I never thought so. At Praline Connection I was tempted to seek out their chef and suggest a more interesting recipe. My next door neighbor at home, a seventy-five-year-old Hispanic matron whose husband's company built her house, my house, and hundreds of others, introduced me to a local hominy dish that is easy to prepare and quite delicious.

Vastly amused by the conviction that, like her namesake, Lazarus, she will rise from the dead to terrify her droves of children, grandchildren, and great grandchildren, Lazara has arranged to have this dish served at her funeral dinner. It involves sautéing chopped onion and chili peppers, mixing in the hominy, then baking the whole with grated longhorn cheese on top. You will never mistake this dish for some wimpy breakfast cereal.

Of course, I didn't find the chef, although I wanted to obtain the instructions for his barbecue sauce, but I did take notes on every bite I ate. That practice earned me impatient glances from my friends, puzzled stares from strangers, and a visit from a waitress who asked if I worked for the *Times-Picayune*. She seemed disappointed to hear that I didn't.

While I tasted and took notes, Lester, Carlene, and my husband chatted about the amazing growth of research on "bucky balls," a huge, soccer ball–shaped molecule discovered in the relatively recent past. Broder told Miranda about the lamentable lack of impact made by Calvinist theology on African-American Christians. Miranda responded with the suggestion that Calvinist hymns might not be lively enough to attract converts, a theory that Broder declared frivolous. Never having considered herself a frivolous person, at least since leaving jail in the early seventies and electing a career in law, Miranda refused to talk to Broder any further and turned her attention to the heretofore silent Nils.

"Did she take her clothes with her?" Miranda asked.

Startled, Nils looked up from his peach cobbler (which tasted of fresh peaches, although March is certainly not the peach season) and barked, "No."

"Isn't that just like Julienne?" Miranda responded. "Running away without a word to her friends, causing us all sorts of worry —"

"Well, she *meant* to worry me," Nils interrupted, "but I'm not falling for that ploy."

"Julienne may be intelligent," Miranda continued as if he hadn't spoken, "but she's always been flighty, thoughtless, and self-centered."

If I hadn't been so worried by the revelation that Julienne had left her belongings behind, I'd have taken exception to Miranda's harsh assessment of my oldest friend. Flighty, thoughtless, and self-centered didn't describe Julienne at all. "Nils, if she were leaving you, she'd certainly have taken her clothes," I pointed out. "Could she be staying with relatives or friends?"

"There aren't any left alive."

"Then you've got to contact the police and report her missing."

Nils glowered at me. "I have no intention of asking the police to find my runaway wife," he muttered. "Why should I embarrass myself when she's probably staying on the riverfront with Linus Torelli?"

I almost exclaimed, "Without her clothes?" but caught myself in time. Such a remark would not have convinced Nils of anything but the presumed sexual infidelity of his wife, a suspicion I didn't entertain for a moment. However, I was considering the idea of contacting the police, even if I had to do it myself, when the lights on the stage bloomed, music drowned out conversation, and the gospel show began. It was an experience! Choruses of young people, featured performers in sequins, and a master of ceremonies/preacher wearing red boots and a gray Ghandi suit with flashing gold chains and medals. By the end of the performance, the audience was indeed clapping, swaying, and dancing in the aisles — well, not at our table. College professors and tax lawyers aren't given to dancing in the aisles, although some of us did join in the clapping, and I noticed that Carlene was tapping her foot.

6

Hurricanes

New Orleans is the birthplace of the cocktail, the first having been concocted by Antoine Peychaud, who escaped the slave rebellion on Santo Domingo in the late eighteenth century and set up a pharmacy in New Orleans. There he sold a brandy-based drink guaranteed to cure whatever ailed his customers. His cocktail, the Sazerac, was served in a *coquetier* or eggcup from which the word cocktail derived. Peychaud himself invented the bitters that, with a dash of absinthe, added flavor to the Sazerac brandy.

One can imagine the traumatized Frenchman, having barely escaped with his life from the violence in the Caribbean, dealing with post-traumatic stress disorder by sipping his new medicinal cocktail from the large half of an egg cup. Would he have approved of the changes made in his recipe over the years? Probably not. The brandy has been replaced by rye whiskey and the absinthe, now outlawed in the United States, by Herbsaint, an anise liqueur, but the bitters still carry his name.

So delighted was I with this delectable piece of culinary history that I determined to sample as many of the famous cocktails of New Orleans as I could. In moderate amounts, of course.

Carolyn Blue,
Eating Out in the Big Easy

When the performance at the Praline Connection ended, Nils took the opportunity to slip away while Jason and I were saying good-bye to the rest of the party, all of whom had different plans for the time between one and the opening of registration at the convention center. I assume that Nils's plan was to avoid going to the police station to report his wife missing. Therefore, I did it for him.

We asked directions from the young man taking tickets for the second show, and he, looking insulted, demanded to know if we thought something had been stolen from us during our visit. Given the master of ceremonies' many narrations about young people being saved from unfortunate circumstances by embracing Christ and the Praline Connection, I can see that my inquiry was ill advised. I assured the young man that we had been not only unmolested but also pleased with our experience and wanted to consult the police about a missing friend.

Miranda, who was directly behind me, muttered, "Oh, for heaven's sake, Carolyn, give it a rest. Think how embarrassed she'll be when she turns up and finds that the police are looking for her."

I replied, "If you read your guide book, you'd know that female tourists are warned against walking alone at night."

"You got that right, lady," said the young man. "Some female friend a yours been walkin' 'round after dark by her ownsef an' ain't turned up, you best be headin' fo' the Vieux Carre station." His input on Julienne's disappearance was frightening, but he did provide directions to the police department, which had a branch near the corner of Royal and Conti, a little over a block from our hotel. Perhaps the advice of a native convinced Jason, who had not previously been much inclined to make a fuss about Julienne's strange absence.

At any rate, he agreed to make the long walk back to our hotel, although he would have saved himself steps by going to the area of the convention center instead. Fortunately, Jason is not averse to exercise, whereas I, had I not felt that Julienne's well-being was at stake, might have preferred to explore the river area. Back we trudged along South Peters, Canal, and Chartres, past our hotel to the corner of Conti and Chartres, then left on Conti to Royal.

The station proved to be an impressive sight: cream stucco with two-story columns holding up an elaborate roofline, trees and shrubs growing green and healthy outside, and a black wrought-iron fence behind which sleek white police motorcycles were parked on the flagstones surrounding the coche portiere. I found the handsome building reassuring, but once inside, both the decor and our reception were less so. The desk sergeant wanted to know what our relation to the missing person was, and he took the news that we were simply friends as no cause to leap into action. Further questioning elicited the information that Julienne Magnussen had a husband in town. The sergeant wanted to know why the husband hadn't reported her missing. The final blow to our case was the admission that our friend, whose husband hadn't seen fit to come in himself, had been missing less than twenty-four hours.

"Ma'am," drawled the sergeant, "we don' go lookin' for no adults 'less they been missin' forty-eight hours. Likely this lady jus' run off from her husband an' don' wanna be found. No use us lookin' for a woman don' wanna be found."

"You're not going to do anything?" I cried.

"Well, when she been gone forty-eight hours, y'all send in the lady's husband. Then we might —"

"But she disappeared between Etienne's and the Hotel de la Poste," I protested as Jason tugged at my arm. "She must have been kidnapped."

The sergeant picked up his ringing telephone and turned his back on me. And to think my mother always told me that policemen were my friends! I scowled at his back and allowed Jason to escort me out the door, through the lines of motorcycles, and out onto the sidewalk. Where, I wondered, were the policemen who were supposed to be riding the motorcycles and protecting the public from the dangers of the Big Easy? The only policeman I had seen was that recalcitrant sergeant.

"How about a hurricane at Pat O'Brien's?" Jason asked.

"A what?"

"It's a famous New Orleans rum drink." He steered me resolutely along Royal Street toward Saint Peter Street and O'Brien's, which was housed in a delightful, late eighteenth-century brick building with tall windows and a wrought-iron balcony but marked only with a discreet round, green sign. By the time we arrived, I had discovered in my guidebook that the building had originally been a theater built by a Spanish military officer.

Perhaps foolishly, I wanted to sit on the patio, which, even with the ever-impending rain, was crowded with noisy young people. Our waiter, an ancient black man wearing a green jacket with white piping and a black bow tie large enough to dwarf the back of a lady's head, wiped off two seats and served us the largest alcoholic drinks I have ever seen — and the pinkest. However, they were very tasty and just what I needed.

Now searching for information on the drink, I discovered as I sipped that the hurricane was reputedly the result of an imprudent overbuying of rum and glasses in the shape of hurricane lamps by the owner in the 1930s. What fun! I made notes and told Jason I might just order a second. Jason replied that he thought the four ounces of rum in the drink I had ought to be enough for one afternoon. I think he was afraid eight ounces of rum might disable me to the extent that I wouldn't be in any condition to walk out of the bar on my own, and he was probably right, although at the time I thought he was exaggerating the alcohol content.

Fortunately, I took his advice and managed to exit Pat O'Brien's in a ladylike fashion, even remembering to claim the deposits on the glasses. What a strange custom that is. Of course, the management wanted to sell us the glasses as souvenirs, but I didn't want a souvenir of a day when the police refused to assist in finding my best friend. Furthermore, tourists evidently used the glasses to hold beads they acquired during Mardi Gras parades. No Mardi Gras parades would be held during our visit, so we didn't need bead receptacles.

Pat O'Brien's
Hurricane Punch

Mix *4 oz. of dark rum* with *2 to 4 oz. of*

Pat O'Brien's Hurricane Mix. (Buy the passion fruit cocktail mix in New Orleans; then try to duplicate it at home — good luck!)

Serve in a hurricane glass filled with crushed ice. (The glass resembles the lamp of the same name, but without lighting apparatus, and is available at Pat O'Brien's, but you won't get your deposit back if you don't return it. Any very large, 12- to 16-oz. glass will do.)

Garnish with an *orange slice* and a *maraschino cherry.*

Because the police had not been at all obliging, I decided to investigate Julienne's disappearance on my own, beginning with Professor Linus Torelli, who Nils seemed to believe was Julienne's lover. Therefore, I went to the convention center with Jason, another long walk, and while he was registering at the table that included people whose names begin with B, I sidled over to the T table. Rendered ultragregarious and none too truthful by the hurricane, I breezily informed a pleasant and helpful young lady wearing a convention badge that I was looking for my friend Linus

Torelli. Had she seen him?

Much more obliging than the police, she ascertained that he had already registered; she even provided the name and telephone number of the hotel at which he was staying, the same nearby high-rise where Miranda and Lester Abbott were registered. With any luck I wouldn't run into them. No doubt, they would have disapproved of my mission, as I suspected Jason would, had he been aware of my intentions.

I ventured out with Jason's umbrella raised against a slanting new rainstorm that soaked my shoes and spattered my raincoat. Thank goodness for my New Orleans guidebook, which had advised carrying an umbrella at all times in this season. Jason had read it ahead of time. Otherwise, I would have been soaking wet instead of just damp and squishy of foot when I arrived at the reception desk and asked for Dr. Torelli. The clerk should have taken helpfulness lessons from the T registration lady at the convention center. He would not give me a room number; he would and did call the chemist in question, which is how I came to interview Julienne's colleague in the lobby of his hotel.

Linus Torelli was a slender man of medium height with olive skin and tightly curled black hair without a trace of gray, a good ten years younger than my friend, if I was any judge of age. More convinced than ever that he could not be her lover, I blurted out, immediately after the introductions and not long enough after the hurricane, "What's your relationship to Julienne, Dr. Torelli?"

Not surprisingly, the man was taken aback to be so addressed by a mature female, who was somewhat the worse for rain and totally unknown to him. He coughed and stammered and finally managed to tell me that they ran a combined seminar for their graduate students. Then he seemed to reconsider this innocuous explanation and added, "Of course it goes without saying that Julienne and I are good friends."

What does that mean? I wondered testily. Was he her lover or not? "When did you last see her?" I demanded.

"Madam," he snapped, but got no further for I repeated my question more aggressively. Normally, I am a very low-key person; alcohol and worry seem to have caused an unfortunate personality change. Was I, by any chance, experiencing a testosterone surge? Could menopause be creeping up on me? And did menopause actually trigger the production of testosterone in women? Probably not. While I was worrying about my uncharacteristic aggressiveness, Dr. Torelli was mumbling that he had not seen "Julie" — he called her Julie! Surely that was significant! — since Friday, the day before she left for New Orleans. Did that mean he hadn't left until this morning?

"She's missing," I told him. "She hasn't been seen since 7:30 last night — unless you've seen her." I thought I saw alarm on his face. "Have you? Seen her?" He was taking much too long to answer a simple question.

"No. No, I told you," he stammered. "Not since — ah — at the department. Last Friday."

I didn't believe him, and he seemed to realize as much, for he hastened to add, a slight sneer in his voice, "Why don't you ask Nils? Her husband." With that, Dr. Torelli walked out the front door. Into the rain. Without a raincoat. I'm sure *that* was significant! I just didn't know of what. Or exactly how he had lied to me, although I was convinced that he had. And I didn't like the man. There was something sneaky about him. Not Julienne's type at all. So nothing made sense.

I plopped down onto a deep-cushioned sofa, inexcusably indifferent to the damage my damp clothing might be doing to the expensive upholstery, and tried to reason my way through the evidence I had. Julienne and Nils had been quarreling. She had left the dinner because of his unpleasant attitude. And disappeared. Kidnapped? Off to see the man her husband claimed was her lover, a man who denied having seen her? Before I could carry my thought processes further, Linus Torelli reappeared, brushing rain from his curls and sports jacket.

He planted himself in front of my sofa and said, "She's chairing a session, you know. And giving a paper. No matter where she is, she'll be back for those."

Spoken like a true scientist, I thought as he strode toward the elevators. Evidently, he had changed his mind about escaping from me by going for a walk. Two other people got on with him, but I noted all the floors where that particular elevator stopped: seven, fifteen, and twenty-two. That narrowed down the location of his room, but not much. What if Julienne was up there? I should have rushed after him and boarded the same elevator. Not very subtle, but wouldn't he have been surprised?

Instead, I fished my wallet from my handbag and looked through the pictures until I found an old one of Julienne, her brother Philippe, and myself, taken at least fifteen years ago on the lakeshore when we had been visiting her family's summer cottage. It was the only picture of her that I had with me, so I slipped it from its protective plastic envelope and went to the reception desk where, after waiting through six check-ins and one check-out, I arrived at the head of the line and showed my photo to the clerk.

The woman nodded. "I remember her. At least I think it was her. She was wearing a red dress."

"Yes!" I agreed enthusiastically. "She was. When did you see her?"

"Last night. I worked a double shift yesterday."

"When last night?"

"Oh, eight-thirty or nine. Somewhere around then. She had me call one of our guests."

"What floor?" I asked breathlessly.

The clerk gave me a narrow glance. "I wouldn't remember that. Why do you want to know?"

"She's missing." I'm sure I looked as worried as I felt. "And the police won't do a thing."

"Really?" The young woman's eyes went wide. "Well, he came down —"

"What did he look like?"

"I don't know. Dark-haired. Cute. I figured he was her brother. I mean he was younger and had the same color hair."

I shook my head. "What happened then?"

"They went out and came back after midnight. She went upstairs with him. That's when I got curious because I was sure there was only one person registered to that room. The management doesn't like people having nonguests staying overnight. Still, I thought she was his sister, so I didn't . . . Well, you mean she wasn't?"

I didn't answer, embarrassed that Julienne might have been staying with a lover. I wouldn't have believed it. And maybe she wasn't. "Did you see her leave?" I asked hopefully. Maybe she had come right back down.

"I didn't," said the clerk, "but I went off shift at six this morning. Not his sister? Well, that's New Orleans for you." She still refused to tell me on what floor the dark-haired man had his room. That would be "against company policy."

I turned away, thinking hard. If the man with the dark hair was Linus Torelli and the woman in the red dress was Julienne, she hadn't been kidnapped at the restaurant or off the street, which was a relief. But why had he lied? And what had he done with her? Or was she still upstairs? If so, on which of the three floors? I glanced at my watch and realized that I had to get back to my own hotel and dress for the welcome mixer at the aquarium. The hurricane seemed to be wearing off just in time for the next round of alcohol. Maybe Julienne would attend the mixer.

7

Jug Wine and Tidbits

"Very piquant," said my husband judiciously as he sipped his white wine in a plastic glass. *Very piquant* is our wine code for *vinegary but overpriced.* We were attending the welcome mixer at the Aquarium of the Americas with Nils. Since we had run into him in the lobby at the hotel, I could hardly refuse to walk to the foot of Canal Street in his company, especially since Jason did not seem averse to doing so. Fortunately, the rain had abated, and I said nothing more about Julienne after Nils snarled at my first question. I was tempted to mention the desk clerk who had sighted a woman in a red dress in the company of a man at Linus Torelli's hotel, but I held my tongue.

As I kept my eyes firmly on the aquarium's distinctive round structure with its slanted, flat roof, which the three of us were approaching in virtual silence, it occurred to me that Nils himself might have found Julienne at Torelli's hotel. Could he have gone there looking for her the very night she left the dinner at Etienne's? Then, infuriated by her infidelity, real or imagined, he might have attacked her. But if so, where was she?

I resolved to begin calling hospitals as soon as we returned to our room, for I was imagining scenarios in which Nils knocked Julienne unconscious after catching her in Torelli's company. Although the softening process of middle age has begun, Nils is a big man. If he hit his slender wife, he would do great damage. After hitting her, perhaps he stuffed her into one of those taxis that lurk in front of large hotels. Then he gave the driver some excuse (perhaps that she had passed out in a diabetic coma), asked to be taken to a hospital, and left her there in the emergency room while he escaped the consequences of his jealous rage.

All this had passed through my mind as we reached the aquarium and joined the mob of scientists and their significant others attempting to reach the refreshment tables. The frustrations involved were enough to turn my imagination off for the time being.

"Might as well enjoy what we've got," Jason was saying of the hors d'oeuvres. "I, for one, don't intend to wait through any more long lines."

We'd waited fifteen minutes for the wine and even longer for the food offerings, which were not at all up to New Orleans standards, certainly not as exotic as the alligator puffs I had chosen for the reunion dinner. But then the American Chemical Society organizers had probably decided on this menu and were more interested in economy than culinary adventure.

"I'd planned to substitute this for dinner," said Nils morosely. He hadn't even mentioned his wife since refusing to answer questions on the walk over. All the more reason to suspect him of foul play, I decided.

"Jason! And the delightful Carolyn!" The newcomer looked more closely at Nils and came up with his name, too, although Nils is not a chemist. "Dr. Magnussen."

We all shook hands with Corbin Bunster, the eminent theoretician from Cal Tech, a man who has the amazing ability to remember every person to whom he has ever been introduced. For those of us less memory-endowed, Dr. Bunster is not to be forgotten because of his scientific renown and a set of eyebrows that flare from his forehead like the mustachios of an aging Mexican bandido.

"And where is your dear childhood friend, Carolyn?" he asked me. He remembers not only one's name and face but past conversations, no matter how mundane. "Since Dr. Magnussen is here, I presume the brilliant Julienne is as well, especially as she's scheduled to present a very interesting paper at the conference."

"She's missing," I replied, glancing at Nils to see how he'd react when a famous scientist learned of the disappearance.

"Missing the wine, is she? A sensible decision," said Bunster.

"Missing, period. None of us has seen her since last night, not even Nils."

Bunster looked alarmed. "Missing in New Orleans! Good God, man," he exclaimed, turning to Nils, "I hope you've reported this to the police."

Nils gave him a fulminating glance, then turned it on me, and left in a huff. This seemed to be his only method of departure since arriving in New Orleans.

"Irritable fellow," Bunster remarked and strode off to display his phenomenal memory elsewhere. Jason and I went to sample the beer after discreetly placing our half-full wine cups on a table of aquarium literature. Then, beer in hand, we began to wander the Caribbean Reef and Gulf of Mexico exhibits on the first floor. They included towering glass tanks inhabited by multitudes of aquatic creatures. As Jason greeted colleagues, talked of bonds, molecules, and heats of formation, scribbled little pictures of compounds on the program, and generally acted like a scientist, I tuned out the chemical chatter and admired the scene. There were vicious-looking, beaked turtles making rushes at lettuce bundles carried by divers and, my favorites, giant rays, rippling their sueded, winglike bodies, trailing stingers, and looking much more impressive than those who undulated lazily across the aquarium screen saver on my computer.

On the second floor in a humid rain forest with suspended walkways that allowed one to stroll amid lush vegetation and swooping tropical birds, we came across the McAvees and Nils. Carlene was quizzing him about Julienne, surprised that she was still among the missing but convinced that she would reappear the next day for Carlene's plenary address to the conference. Broder interrupted to say that, in such a dangerous and sinful city, Julienne might have been kidnapped by white slavers.

Because that was exactly the scenario I had envisioned the night before when I went to look for her in the Etienne's rest room, that particular set of fears was revived. I turned to Nils and asked if he had checked her belongings to ascertain whether anything was missing.

"I didn't notice anything," he muttered reluctantly, which I took to mean that he had at least looked. "Ask Torelli. He'd know what, if anything, she took with her."

"He says he hasn't seen her," I replied, without thinking. After all, I hadn't mentioned to Nils that I had pursued Torelli to his hotel.

"Well, if you believe that, you're more naive than I'd have thought," Nils snarled.

Actually, I hadn't believed Torelli, not after talking to the hotel clerk, but again I didn't mention that, preferring not to feed Nils's anger about the supposed liaison. On the other hand, when I reviewed Nils's response, I realized that, one, he hadn't commented on my having talked to Torelli, and, two, he'd seemed quite sure that Torelli had seen Julienne. *Had* he caught them together at the hotel? And if so, what had he done about it? I shivered, remembering the violent scenario I had concocted on the way to the aquarium.

"You must be wrong, Nils," said Carlene. "I can't imagine Julienne having an affair. Goodness, I've never had one — well, with Broder — but I married him." Having revealed something that shocked none of us, she went off, long, multicolored skirt swishing, to find another glass of the abominable wine; perhaps her foolhardy acceptance came from a misplaced loyalty to California vineyards. At any rate, she left in her wake a red-faced husband. No doubt, Broder was embarrassed to have revealed, even to friends, his premarital indiscretion. He immediately changed the subject to Calvinist theology.

Within three minutes even we long-time friends were shifting restlessly, so I rescued us all by murmuring, "As a point of historical interest, Broder, didn't the early Calvinists bury those they considered heretics up to the neck and then roll large stones at their heads?" Before he could answer, I turned to Nils and asked him to let me look over Julienne's belongings, explaining that anything found missing would at least reassure us that she had made it as far as the Hotel de la Poste safely. Sulky to the end, Nils refused, exacerbating my suspicions that he himself might be responsible for the disappearance of his wife.

"In that case, I intend to go looking for her tomorrow in all the places we planned to visit," I announced. "I think you ought to come with me, Nils. Since you aren't involved in the conference, you don't have anything better to do, and you might show some concern for —"

"I've already said that I don't intend to chase after her. Go by yourself if you're so set on finding a woman who obviously doesn't want to be found," he replied.

"Perhaps I'd better accompany you, Carolyn," said Broder.

"And miss my paper?" demanded his wife, who had returned with her wine refill in record time. Presumably, after one glass, other attendees had opted for beer.

"Of course not," said Broder. "We'll go after your address. But you'll agree that in a city this dangerous, a woman should not be wandering about unaccompanied by a protective male."

Dear Broder. It wasn't as if I'd be searching the city at night. I wanted to know if anyone had seen Julienne this morning or this afternoon. Still, I made arrangements to meet Broder after lunch on Monday. With any luck, Julienne might have come back before then. I certainly hoped so, not only because I loved her dearly, but because I didn't see Broder, no matter how well meaning, as someone who would help in wheedling information from denizens of the French Quarter.

When we finally left the aquarium, which was still packed with scientists taking advantage of free food and drink, and returned to our hotel, Jason went to the bar in Bacco, the hotel restaurant. He wanted to have a nightcap and draw more chemical structures on napkins with an environmental toxicologist from the University of South Florida who had followed us home. I went straight to our room, gumbo delivered from Etienne's in hand, and ate it while I called all the hospitals and the police stations to see if there had been any reports about Julienne. There hadn't, and I anticipated another night of worry and restless tossing.

How could my best friend have disappeared? When I'd spent less than an hour in her company. Was her marriage to Nils so terrible that she couldn't have stayed for my sake? Admittedly, I'd have been angry had Jason treated me the way Nils treated her at the dinner party, but then Jason would never do that. He may be devoted to his work and distracted from time to time, in fact, a good deal of the time, but he's always a sweet man when he returns from the realms of scientific thought. He proved as much when he arrived in our room, pockets stuffed with napkins written over with brilliant ideas and a libido inspired by the sight of me in my see-through lace nightgown. I may be forty-something, but my husband still thinks I'm the perfect amalgamation of physical desirability and culinary expertise.

Poor man. It hasn't yet penetrated his consciousness that, although I still enjoy our marital trysts in the bedroom, I am much less interested in kitchen adventures. I could write a book extolling the joys of other people's cooking. In fact, I am.

8

Beignets and Chicory Coffee

In New Orleans, café au lait means chicory coffee with milk. Among other things that the original French settlers learned from the Choctaw and Chickasaw Indians was the use of a peppery syrup made from the root of a dandelion cousin whose new leaves appear in your salad as endive. The chicory syrup in coffee may seem bitter to outlanders, but to New Orleans natives and other aficionados of the blend, it produces a rich beverage with half the caffeine of undoctored coffee. That may explain why citizens of New Orleans can drink more than twice as much coffee a day as the average American and still contribute to the laid-back ambiance of the Big Easy.

Carolyn Blue,
Eating Out in the Big Easy

I truly did mean to attend Carlene's lecture Monday morning but reminded myself that Julienne and I had planned breakfast at the Café du Monde on Jackson Square. Having missed yesterday's rendezvous, I had to be there today and hope that she would, too. Jason was very understanding about it and consoled me by saying that he wasn't expecting to understand a good deal of the science in Carlene's lecture himself. If *he* didn't know that much about leading-edge biochemistry, why should I? Therefore, with a clear conscience, I set off, raincoat-clad, newly purchased umbrella in hand, for Jackson Square, which was just over three blocks from the hotel.

The skies were gray, the streets wet as I chose a green plastic chair from among many placed on flagstones under the green and white striped awnings of the famous coffeehouse. Naturally, I ordered chicory coffee and beignets, those hot, delicious squares of fried dough lavishly dusted with powdered sugar. The chicory was a research impulse gone wrong. Even generous splashes of cream and multiple packets of sugar couldn't cut the bitter taste enough to suit me. For once I, the typical Midwestern, north-of-the-Mason-Dixon-Line Yankee, felt sympathy for the benighted Southerners that had been reduced to drinking chicory with little or no coffee during the Civil War. In their place, I think I would have surrendered years earlier just to get a less off-putting caffeine fix with breakfast.

As I devoured my beignets and brushed the resulting rain of powdered sugar from my black raincoat (Café du Monde would do well to provide bibs for its patrons), I watched the square for Julienne. I had already cased the café both inside and out before sitting down. The stones were bright with rain, and the trees blew in a gentle wind beyond the iron fence. Old-fashioned lampposts were mirrored on the wet street, as were the trailing images of cars and tourist buses. Across the street, a tiny mule with a bouquet inserted in its bridle turned its head to inspect the heaped blossoms of pink and purple inside the fence, while an egg-shaped woman tried to keep her excited toddler calm as she negotiated for a ride in the little red mule carriage. The vehicle had small wheels in front, larger behind, for all the world like an old-fashioned bicycle.

A man in a yellow raincoat played "St. Louis Blues" on his trumpet, and the sad, mellow notes met scattered applause and the tiger growl of thunder as the sky darkened and a fine rain began to fall. Laughing tourists in hooded jackets and stoic natives, umbrella-topped, passed by. As the rain grew heavier, young people with backpacks ducked under the awnings, and hungry, sheltering pigeons waddled under my table, but amid all this activity, Julienne did not arrive, and my disappointment burgeoned. What should I do? I stared miserably at the three white, shingle-capped steeples of the Saint Louis Cathedral, lifting simple crosses to the sky as if pointing out what a sad, dark day it was.

My waitress, an Asian woman wearing a white cap and long white apron over her black trousers, stopped to ask if I wanted anything else. Having taken up space at her table for over an hour, I felt obliged to order again, a frothy cappuccino this time and another beignet. When she brought them, I showed her the picture of Julienne from my wallet. "I'm waiting for this woman. Have you, by any chance, seen her? Either today or yesterday?"

Obligingly, the waitress peered at the picture. "That's you, isn't it?" she asked, pointing to me on the left. "Must have been years ago."

Had I aged so much? I wondered. Or did I appear dated because of the waist-length hair? "My friend looks a lot the same," I replied. "Have you seen her?"

"Not today," she replied, "and I wasn't working yesterday." She peered at the snapshot again. I must have looked as disappointed as I felt, for she added helpfully, "You want me to show it around?"

I hated to let the picture out of my possession; it was the only photo of Julienne, no matter how outdated, that I had with me. However, I released it, and off she went. *It's really very good of her to bother,* I told myself. And my search was rewarded, for she returned with a young black man, wearing the same apron, cap, and bow-tie costume. "Seen her yesterday morning," he said, handing back the photo. "Couldn't hardly miss her. Wearing a fancy red dress. Stayed about an hour. Left me a fine tip."

Almost limp with relief, I finished my delicious coffee, dusted away more beignet sugar, left my waitress a "fine tip," and then set off toward the convention center. Of course, Julienne hadn't been on Jackson Square to meet me this morning! She had gone to hear Carlene talking about computational biochemistry. I had to get there before the end of the lecture. By dint of more jogging than I had done in years, which earned me odd glances from natives, I did arrive while Carlene was still talking, no thanks to the New Orleans Police. At the corner of South Front and Poydras, when I was still blocks from my destination and completely breathless, a motorcycle officer stopped me, evidently under the impression that a pedestrian moving on foot at any pace faster than a saunter must be up to no good. The phrase, "Where are the police when you need them?" hardly applied here. I didn't *want* to be delayed, but I decided to make the best of his mistake.

Before he could arrest me or strip search me or whatever he had in mind, I gasped, "Could you give me a ride to the convention center? I'm late for a lecture on computational biochemistry."

He must have thought my statement eccentric enough to eliminate me from his list of possible wrongdoers. Instead of arresting me, he said, with no little sarcasm, "The N'Awlins Police ain't in business to give rides to tourists, ma'am. You see an extra helmet here? Any place for you to ride *on*?"

"Well then, thanks anyway," I called over my shoulder as I ran off. He didn't pursue. Lafayette, Girod, Notre Dame, Julia — I crossed them all before reaching even the corner of the huge center. If only I'd known about the Riverfront Streetcar, I could have saved myself such a traumatic overexposure to aerobic exercise. Surely it can't be good for one. I arrived with my heart thundering noisily in my chest and my lungs burning, but I did hear the last five minutes of the lecture and congratulated Carlene with proper enthusiasm on her presentation when it was over.

Fortunately, she didn't expect comments from me on the science. She got plenty of those from actual scientists. We hugged one another, Carlene asked after Julienne, but then took offense that our friend had not shown up. Given her attitude, I didn't mention that Julienne had been seen at Café du Monde yesterday. "She's missing, Carlene," I said firmly. I was only then beginning to realize that the waiter's identification on the basis of an old picture might

116

not be accurate, although he had mentioned a red dress. How many women went to breakfast in a fancy red dress? Well, in New Orleans, there might be quite a few, I had to admit to myself but not to Carlene.

"Don't you think she'd be here if she could?" I asked reasonably. But why couldn't she? That was the question. And why couldn't she meet me as we'd planned? Didn't she know I'd be beside myself with worry? Of course, she knew that.

I saw Linus Torelli at the same time he saw me. He tried to skulk away, but I left Carlene without so much as an "excuse me," which was very rude although necessary under the circumstances, and chased him into a small lecture room where chemists were beginning to assemble for a panel on something or other. "You lied to me," I said.

Torelli flushed with embarrassment, glanced nervously at three or four men who turned to stare at us, and then hustled me out into the hall.

"You said you hadn't seen her, but the desk clerk at your hotel says you two went out together Saturday night, and that she went upstairs with you when you returned."

"Sh-sh-sh," hissed Torelli. "If this gets

back to my . . . to her . . . husband, he'll . . . he'll . . . he's really paranoid about the two of us."

"Small wonder," I snapped. "Where is she?"

"I don't know."

"You do, too."

"Listen, Mrs. —"

"Blue."

"Julienne and I are not lovers." He was whispering, glancing nervously from side to side. "We're colleagues. We run a combined seminar for our graduate students."

"Then why was she spending the night with you?"

"Sh-sh-sh. She didn't. I mean, after she quarreled with Nils, we went out wandering in the Quarter. She wanted to take pictures."

"Did she have her camera?" She hadn't had a camera at Etienne's. She'd forgotten it, probably because she and Nils had been quarreling before dinner.

"Of course. She always has it."

"Fine. But she went up to your room afterward."

Torelli looked downright desperate as a skinny, redheaded man, eyeing us curiously, greeted him and slipped around us into the room. "Please keep your voice down,"

Torelli begged. "If you don't care about me, you might think of Julie's repu—"

"No one saw her leave your room or the hotel," I persisted angrily. If Torelli was worried about her reputation, why had he started something with her in the first place? If he had. "And no one knows where she is now." I glared at him accusingly. "She didn't even come to the plenary addresses."

"Well, it's not my fault!" Torelli sighed and admitted in a voice almost inaudible, "There are two beds in my room. She asked to sleep in one of them . . . because she was so furious with Nils, she refused to go back to their hotel. She said since he believed we were having an affair, she'd just spend the night with me."

"And initiate an affair?" I gasped. Oh Julienne! And Nils — this was all *his* fault!

"*No!*" exclaimed Torelli. Then, more calmly, "No. But she did say it would serve him right if, when she returned Sunday night —"

"But she didn't!"

"Are you sure? She said she was going to tell him that she'd spent the night with me. Jesus, can you imagine what would have happened if she'd done that? He'd kill me."

Or her, I thought with a shudder. Had she

119

carried out that crazy plan, and Nils —"

"I told her that was a really bad idea," Torelli assured me.

"And then what happened?"

"And then she came up with another crazy idea — that we should rent a boat. As if I'd do that. I don't like boats. I don't know how to drive a boat, and she expected me to . . . to run it while she took pictures."

He turned pale at the very thought. Aquaphobia, I deduced, wondering if he knew how to swim. Julienne swam with the ease and grace of a dolphin. We'd had wonderful times at the lake when we were children. Even Philippe had deigned to join us occasionally, although he wasn't nearly the swimmer Julienne was.

"That's crazy, don't you agree? I mean, she's a beautiful woman, and a brilliant chemist, but you couldn't get me into a boat in the daytime much less at night, and certainly not to take pictures on the river or in the swamp. And I hadn't had any sleep. I can't afford to skip the meeting and go dashing off —"

"Do you think she went?" I interrupted. It would be just like Julienne. When it came to photography, I'd seen her hang off cliffs and approach scary looking bikers.

Taking pictures from a boat would be no big deal for Julienne. I could imagine her photographing the river, the docks, the riverboats, the — good grief. What if her little boat had been run down by some huge riverboat or barge, and no one even noticed? Had she gone out and rented the boat right after waiting for me at Café du Monde on Sunday morning? After all, she hadn't known of the arrangement to meet for brunch at Praline Connection. It was made after she left. She probably wanted Jason and me to take charge of the boating while she took pictures, and when we hadn't been there to help, she'd —

"With who?" Torelli was asking disdainfully. "She couldn't handle both a boat and a camera at the same time. And who'd want to go boating in a swamp?"

That's right; he had mentioned the swamp. Surely she hadn't gone into the swamp by herself when she couldn't find anyone to go with her. I was conscience stricken to have failed her. Not that I'd have wanted to go boating in a swamp, except maybe on a tour. We'd talked about taking a swamp tour, which sounded safe enough. But alone? Well, if we'd met Sunday morning, I could have talked her out of that idea. "So you don't think she

121

actually went?" I asked hopefully.

"Of course not. But we did part on an unpleasant note."

"Did she have any extra clothes with her?" I asked, subdued. She wouldn't have gone boating in that red dress. Would she?

"I don't think so. All she had was her camera and one of those big shoulder bags. They look like pouches. I don't know what she thought she was going to wear to bed. Maybe one of my shirts. And that's a good point. If she hasn't been back there yet, she's probably in her hotel room right now. She can't still be wearing that red dress, even if she did look amazingly sexy in it."

Ah ha! It was obvious to me that Linus Torelli was or had been in love with Julienne, no matter how platonic and colleague-oriented he claimed his feelings were. Therefore, I didn't know how much of his tale to believe, and I couldn't very well demand that he let me look in his hotel room to see if she was still there. Still . . . "Can I look in your hotel room?"

"Why?" He glared at me. "Oh hell, why not? I have to attend this meeting, but . . ."

Attendees had been streaming past as we hissed discreetly at one another. Now a man at the door was giving Torelli an are-you-coming-in-or-not look. "Room 2210.

Here's the key. Leave it at the desk." He scooted through the door, which closed behind him, and I was left with his key, in which I was no longer interested. If he'd give it to me, obviously he wasn't hiding Julienne in his room. I did check and found nothing to indicate that she'd even been there, so I went back to my own hotel and knocked at the Magnussens' door, hoping fervently that Julienne would answer, that she had either returned to her husband or was at least packing her clothes in order to move somewhere else. If she'd had clothes in the shoulder bag Torelli mentioned, there couldn't have been many, not enough to last her into a second day.

What a disappointment when Nils opened the door. Still, I barged right in and insisted on looking through her belongings. There was no way to tell whether she'd taken clothes away, and Nils claimed not to know what she had packed.

"She came back last night, didn't she? Why didn't you tell me?" I was watching closely to see what he'd say, whether he'd lie.

"I've already told you. I haven't seen her since she walked out at Etienne's," he retorted.

He seemed more angry than guilty. "Her

camera's gone," I said, trying a new tactic.

He shrugged.

"And there's no laptop computer here. She must have brought one. You all bring them with you." I even carry one myself, now that I am a paid writer. Not that I bought it: I haven't earned that much. My laptop was Jason's before he upgraded.

Nils shrugged again. "*I* don't bring a computer with me," he said, as if this was a point in his favor. "Why don't you look in Torelli's room?"

"I did."

Nils gaped at me.

"Nothing of hers, including her, was in his room. But this means that, at the least, she came back here from the dinner at Etienne's to get her camera and computer." It then occurred to me that someone might have killed her on the street to get the electronic equipment. Julienne would have resisted, and then . . . Oh God! "You don't even care, do you?" I asked angrily. "You don't care what's happened to her."

"Nothing's happened to her," Nils replied. "She's run out on me, and she doesn't care who she worries or —"

"Oh, do be quiet, Nils," I retorted. "I don't for a minute think she was having an affair, but I can certainly see why she wouldn't want to spend the week with you. You're treating her abominably."

I left the room and went to the hotel desk. If Julienne had, in fact, meant to leave Nils, she would have turned in her key card, as any responsible person would. But she hadn't. The desk clerk assured me that both Magnussens had their cards, and if they'd lost them, they should report it.

What should I do next? I asked myself. Have lunch? Or visit the police station?

9

Muffulettas

You haven't experienced the ultimate in sandwiches until you have tried that New Orleans delicacy, the muffuletta. First, it is huge — big enough to feed two men or four women. Second, it contains generous piles of ham, salami, and mozzarella. Third and most important, it is garnished with a piquant, garlic-infused salad made of chopped green olives, capers, celery, and pickled carrots. All of this is encased between the two halves of a round, eight- to ten-inch, seed-covered loaf of soft white bread. Ah, heaven!

The muffuletta is messy to eat; bits of the olive salad may find their way onto your clothing. If you delay too long in devouring your muffuletta, the bun will become soggy. But even soggy, it is a treat. The only serious fault I can find with this treat is that it tastes so good, you'll be tempted to eat it all. Then, unless you're a very large person with a very large appetite, you'll feel in need of a tummy tuck or a girdle for hours to come. Still, what's a little discomfort when the cause is so yummy?

So walk over to the Central Grocery or the Progressive Grocery on Decatur Street and, as you devour your muffuletta, spare a thought for the many Sicilian immigrants who flooded into a crumbling French Quarter in the late nineteenth century, bringing with them new and delicious additions to the pantheon of New Orleans delicacies.

Hint: You can buy a half or quarter sandwich, something I didn't know when I purchased my first muffuletta.

Carolyn Blue,
Eating Out in the Big Easy

I sat down dejectedly on one of the antique chairs in the hotel lobby, thinking of Julienne, who might have been seen Sunday morning but not since then, maybe not since the previous night. And the bottom line was that no one was looking for her.

Not her husband, not her terrified-of-water colleague/lover, and not the police. Just me. And what did I know about finding a missing person? Deciding that I was more worried than hungry, I donned my raincoat, picked up my umbrella, and headed for the Vieux Carre Police Station. I was so upset that I actually found myself looking over my shoulder, responding to that eerie sensation one gets at the back of the neck when convinced that an unseen person is stalking one. Paranoia! At the station, before entering, I turned resolutely, scanned the street, and saw not a single suspicious individual. *Well, Carolyn,* I said to myself, *aren't you embarrassed? After all, you are not the person who is missing.*

Having rescued myself from silly timidity, I marched into the station. There was a different officer at the desk, but he was no more helpful than the sergeant who had sent Jason and me packing early Sunday afternoon. I tried to remain pleasant, remembering my grandmother's advice that more flies are to be caught with honey than vinegar. In this case "honey" did me no good. Perhaps it was my Yankee accent that offended the officer.

Finally, abandoning the gentle and ladylike persuasion I customarily espouse when not overcome by the effects of rum and Pat O'Brien's hurricane mix, I said forcefully, "I thought this was supposed to be a city that welcomed tourists. I do not consider your lack of concern for a missing professor, a very prestigious professor I might add, either friendly or helpful, and believe me, if anything has happened to Dr. Magnussen, I intend to start writing letters to every newspaper and travel magazine in the country to warn tourists of exactly how little protection they can expect from the New Orleans Police Department. In fact, I'm here to write a book about the city, a book for which I've already received an advance, I might add — just in case you think I'm some deluded nincompoop who couldn't get a book published if —"

"Ma'am." My tirade was interrupted by one of those deep, drawling Southern voices that are guaranteed to send a shiver down a female spine. I looked up to see, standing beside me, a very tall, very handsome man of a certain age, which is to say about my age. If I hadn't been a happily married woman, I might have melted into an adoring puddle at his feet. As it was, I simply stammered into stillness.

"Lieutenant Alphonse Boudreaux, ma'am." He smiled at me as if I was the woman he'd been looking for all his life.

I swallowed and steeled myself against such charm. I had Julienne to find. I didn't have the time or lack of wifely propriety to let myself be sidetracked by a man, even a police lieutenant, who undoubtedly left swarms of swooning females in his wake. "My friend, Dr. Julienne Magnussen, is missing," I said, "and this is the second time that I have reported as much without arousing the slightest interest among the officers of your department."

"Reckon they must be blind then," said the lieutenant. "Ah sure do find you mighty interestin'." Before I could reproach him for flirting with me when I had a pressing problem to solve, he said, "Why don't you step this way, Miz . . ." He glanced at my ring finger. "Ah don't think Ah caught your name, ma'am."

He put his hand under my elbow and gently shepherded me toward a door that led to an inner part of the station I had not been able to access before. "B-blue," I stammered.

"Beg pardon?" He pulled out a chair for me in his utilitarian office and seated me with a courtly flourish.

"My name is Blue. Carolyn Blue."

"Yes, ma'am. Ah thought for a minute

there, you were referrin' to your state of mind. Well, now, Miz Blue, why don't you tell me about your missin' friend. Whatever impression you might have got, Ah wouldn't want you to think N'Awlins doesn't care about the safety an' happiness of her visitors."

I stared at him. He really was a fine-looking man, dark-haired with a hint of gray at the temples, nicely weathered skin, and a physique that flattered his uniform rather than the other way around. Of course, he wasn't any better looking or built than Jason, just eight or so inches taller. And there was no chance that he was anywhere near as intelligent, or humorous, or sweet-tempered, or —

"Miz Blue?" he prodded, evidently realizing that he'd lost my attention to distracting inner thoughts. Good thing he couldn't read them. He'd either be amused at my interest or irritated that he had come off second best in comparison to my husband. "Could you tell me when the lady disappeared? She one of those tooth-straighteners we got in town this week?"

"I beg your pardon?"

"The orthodontists at the Superior Inn."

"Dr. Magnussen is a chemist. Here for the American Chemical Society meeting."

"Oh, sure. At the convention center. They're a lot less rowdy than the dentists."

"I'm delighted to hear it," I replied. "Now, having established my friend's credentials, could we —"

"Talk about her bein' missin'? Yes, ma'am. When did she —"

"She disappeared Saturday night . . . well, actually she was seen Sunday morning. By a Professor Torelli, but that was really in the middle of the night, depending on the hours one keeps, I suppose. And possibly Sunday morning around breakfast time, although that's not —"

"Why don't you just start right at the beginnin' an' tell me the whole story," he suggested. "Plus anythin' you can think of that might help me."

Help him? He was really going to investigate Julienne's disappearance? I felt as if a suffocating veil had been lifted from my spirit. Finally, someone who saw what a dangerous situation this might be! I smiled at Lieutenant Boudreaux and began to talk. And I told him everything, my suspicions about Nils, about Linus Torelli, about white slavers and muggers and camera thieves, about the possibility of Julienne being run down while boating on the river or becoming lost in the swamp.

The lieutenant nodded with a serious expression and even made some notes. By the time I got to Julienne sightings at Torelli's high-rise hotel and at Café du Monde, the lieutenant interrupted me to say that he'd had no lunch and was getting "mighty peckish."

I was quite hungry myself, so I could imagine how famished a man his size might be. Therefore, I agreed to walk over to an establishment famous for its muffulettas (the lieutenant pronounced it moofalottah), a New Orleans treat of which I had read and on which I would certainly need to write in my book. Seeing no harm in combining sleuthing and culinary research, I rose with alacrity and off we went, although I had to stop talking because it took all my breath to keep up with him. I couldn't even pause to look over my shoulder, although I again had that unsettling sensation of being followed. But who would be following me? And why? If there were a stalker, he certainly wouldn't be practicing his avocation while I was in the company of a very large policeman. So again I was being silly, experiencing a psychological discomfort induced by my friend's disappearance, no doubt.

Much to my surprise, we entered a place

called the Central Grocery on Decatur Street in the Quarter, hardly the milieu where I expected to find gourmet food, although it had that mouth-watering bouquet of aromas common to good Italian groceries. There we waited in a long line among milling crowds and ever-increasing noise to buy — and I, of course, insisted on paying for my own — two immense sandwiches. We carried those in paper bags to a bench on the Moonwalk, a charming, landscaped area on the levee by Jackson Square. The area's name derives from the nickname, Moon, of a former mayor. Perhaps he had been a moon-shaped politician as a result of eating too many muffulettas. I certainly felt moon-shaped after we had removed the voluminous wrappings and devoured the contents. But they were wonderful! Also much too big for me to eat. However, the lieutenant was only too glad to finish mine while I finished the story of Julienne's disappearance and my theories of what might have happened.

Once Lieutenant Boudreaux had disposed of the bags and wrappings, he sat down beside me again, and we watched traffic on the river for a time while he considered all the implications of my tale. "You may not know it, ma'am, but we're not supposed to look for adults until they're gone forty-eight hours," he began.

I'm afraid that the look I gave him was not only disappointed but also somewhat unfriendly.

"An' your friend's been spotted, so that runs the forty-eight-hour time period to at least tomorrow mornin'."

I positively scowled at him.

"Still an' all, Ah hate to disappoint a pretty lady who likes muffulettas almost as much as Ah do."

I began to feel hopeful again. "So you'll —"

"Ah'll check the police reports, an' the hospitals, an' call some friends Ah got on the river patrols."

"But —"

"An' Ah'll do it mahself — the callin' that is. Then, if that don' turn up your friend, an' maybe in this case, no news is good news; better an inconsiderate friend than a dead one; that's mah feelin'. Still an' all, if she don' turn up, then tomorrow, if you can get her husband to report her missin', Ah'll put out an APB on her so every cop in the city'll be lookin' for her."

"But what if he's the reason she's missing?" I protested. "He thinks she's unfaithful."

"Lots a that goin' 'round these days. Not too many husbands doin' away with their wives because of it, 'specially not professors with professor wives. Mos' smart folks would consider killin' a wife a bad career move."

"I suppose so," I had to admit.

"Don' mean it might not be the case. Happens he won't come in, Ah'll have to consider that suspicious. Might be Ah'll have to talk to him mahself. Would you say this Dr. Magnussen is a violent man?"

Was he? Until lately I wouldn't have thought so. "He spoke to her very angrily, even cruelly. And in public as well as in the privacy of their room. The housekeeper told me about a terrible argument they had at the hotel before dinner."

"Lotsa mean-mouthed folks around. Don' mean they take to hittin' or shootin'. He got a gun?"

"If he does, he couldn't have brought it with him. They came by plane. Wouldn't he have been arrested for carrying a weapon on an airplane?"

The lieutenant ran a large hand through that thick, black hair. "If security turned it up. Wouldn't be smart to chance takin' one on a plane. You know what kinda camera an' laptop the lady was carryin' when she ran off?"

I searched my mind desperately. As for the laptop, I was simply assuming its existence and had to tell him so, but I finally dredged up the name of the camera Julienne favored.

The lieutenant nodded, took out a notepad, and scribbled a few lines. "That's an expensive one, for sure. Can't hurt to put it on the pawnshop lists. Thief took it off her, he's gonna try to get money for it. It'll turn up. Then we'll have somethin' to go on."

I shivered when I actually had to face the implications of what we were discussing so theoretically.

"You sure you want to pursue this?" he asked kindly.

"Yes." I had to interrupt our discussion because I had actually been observing, while we talked, someone who looked suspicious, a bearded man sitting on the opposite bench and watching us over his copy of the *Times-Picayune*. I put my hand on the lieutenant's sleeve and whispered urgently, "Don't stare, but do you see that man across the way wearing the cap and rumpled tweed jacket?"

"Uh-huh," said the lieutenant.

"He's been staring at us," I whispered. Of course, the man wasn't staring at us now, but he certainly had been. During my conversation with Alphonse Boudreaux I had taken several peeks to confirm my suspicion.

"Could be," the lieutenant agreed.

"Don't you find that suspicious under the circumstances?" I asked.

"No ma'am. Likely he thinks you're pretty — Ah sure do — or he's someone Ah arrested sometime or other."

"A criminal?" I whispered.

"City's full of 'em," the lieutenant agreed casually. "Also full a men starin' at pretty women. Don' let it bother you, Miz Blue. If he's lookin' at you, he's not gonna come over an' invite you to have a drink with him, not when Ah'm here, 'cause Ah'm bigger'n he is. An' if he was lookin' at me . . . Well, there he goes, headin' off toward the street. Most likely he was lookin' at the cathedral. Got a good view of it from his bench."

I breathed a sigh of relief as the man in the cap disappeared into the crowd. I was being a ninny, and it occurred to me that this sudden attack of paranoia would not impress the lieutenant. He might think I'd imagined the whole thing about Julienne. I gave him my most earnest look and said, "I do appreciate your offer to make inquiries about Julienne. We're so worried about her. Well, not Nils, but then he's not thinking straight, or else he's —" I stopped, chary of continuing to accuse a man, whom I had known for years, of doing goodness knows what to his wife.

"Glad to do it, Miz Blue." He glanced at his watch and I glanced at mine, noting that I had only twenty minutes to get back to the hotel where I was to meet Broder for our search of the quarter.

"Well," I said, standing up, "I, for one, intend to put the afternoon to good use."

"What good use?" the lieutenant asked, looking worried. "Hope you're not plannin' any foolish —"

I had to laugh. "Believe me, Lieutenant, I'm not given to foolish ventures. Faculty wives are notoriously sedate." I smiled reassuringly at him. "I'm just rushing off to meet a professor of Calvinist theology. What could be more innocuous? I'm going to show him the Quarter."

"Well, y'all have fun," said lieutenant, looking as if he doubted that would be possible, given the companion with whom I planned to spend the afternoon.

10

Cajun Bloody Mary

Poor Broder was in shock. We'd passed The Unisex World Famous Love Acts/Men and Women, where the male and female genitalia in the drawings were discreetly screened by black patches, and then a place called The Orgy. Now we were standing in front of Wash the Girl of Your Choice, one of the choices being a merry-looking damsel with pancake breasts and wet hair. She was standing under a shower, laughing. Presumably, the customer was invited to join her there. Photos of other naked females in various poses surrounded her. Most were wearing high heels. Did the customer wash the lady of his choice while she was still shod? Did the establishment or the performers have to pay for soggy shoe replacement?

I didn't share these speculations with Broder, who was stammering and red-faced. I heard him mutter something about Sodom and Gomorrah. Fortunately, Julienne had not mentioned showing me any of these particular clubs in the city of her birth. I did take pictures (which I knew Jason would find amusing; Broder didn't) before hustling my protector away toward less bawdy surroundings, if I could find them. As I scouted out the Absinthe House, a favorite of Julienne's, Broder went on and on about the decadence of New Orleans and all the horrible fates that could have befallen our old friend: rape, murder, rape and murder, kidnapping by white slavers and incarceration in a house of ill repute where debauched customers might even now be . . . I had to stop listening and vowed never again to go anywhere with Broder McAvee. I'm sure he is a well-meaning man, but he was herding me in the direction of a nervous breakdown. How could he think of nothing but sin when all around us were marvelous old brick buildings with their lusciously ornate grillwork balconies? How did Carlene stand living with him? Maybe she took Prozac.

The Absinthe House, which Julienne had mentioned, has two incarnations, one in an 1806 building, the second down the street. The second has "Bar" tacked on its name and features the original marble-topped bar on which rests the original brass water-dripper, once used to add water to absinthe, no doubt to slow the progress of poisoning the absinthe drinkers. Broder warned me about the dangers of absinthe, but I assured him that no one in this country served it any longer. The bar top, dripper, and other fixtures had been spirited away during prohibition when the historic drinking establishment, then a speakeasy, was raided by federal agents. Both Absinthe Houses encourage customers to tack their business cards on the wall.

In Lafitte's Old Absinthe House, on the corner of Bourbon and Bienville, I did so. Imagine me with a business card! I'd ordered them the very day I signed my contract with the publisher. "Carolyn Blue, Writer," they said in a very discreet format. Black on white. Raised type. They even give my E-mail address, about which I still feel amazed — that I have one. My husband and children may have used computers for years, but not I. I more or less edged into the computer age. First, I wrote a letter to my father on Chris's computer and at Chris's insistence. He was a sophomore in high school at the time and perhaps embarrassed to have a mother as backward as I. I was so enchanted with revision capabilities that did not involve erasures or bottles of White-Out that I continued to use the computers in the house for letter writing and even for that first article on eating goat.

Then Gwen, my daughter, called long distance to announce that she had found a web site called "Medieval Feminists." Well, I could hardly pass that up, so I ventured out on my first www adventure. And finally, my agent, on hearing that I had no E-mail address, insisted that I get one. Jason added me as a second user on his home computer. Gwen is now saying that I need my own web page and has threatened to set one up for me.

Young people are amazing, aren't they? I can remember thinking that an old-fashioned, manual typewriter was a magical device. Of course, I was four years old at the time, and my father, when he caught me adding letters to a manuscript page of his, forbade me to enter his study again. By the time I was once more allowed in, to dust the furniture after my mother's death, he had an electric typewriter, which I was still forbidden to touch. A psychiatrist would probably say that my reluctance to use computers is the result of psychological damage done to me at an early age by my father. My father, of course, would say, "Rubbish," and I rather imagine he'd be right.

Well, I put my card on the wall, hoping Julienne might see it.

Broder refused to produce his, but who can blame him? I didn't find any business cards identifying Calvinist theologians. I did find a few cards from Roman Catholic priests, and I found Julienne's card, but couldn't tell whether it was new or old. I also found a bartender who, on studying her picture, thought he might have seen her sometime Sunday. She had been wearing jeans and a jean jacket.

Since the bartender asked me three times during the interrogation what I'd have to drink, I studied the menu and ordered a Cajun Bloody Mary, prepared to take notes for my book. However, I wondered wistfully what the bar's most popular drink in the nineteenth century, the absinthe frappé, would have tasted like. It sounded too delicious to be poisonous. Broder, after some prodding, ordered Jell-O shots. Evidently, he thought he was getting dessert. My drink was amazingly spicy and filling. Even though I have become accustomed to the chili peppers that imbue the Mexican food in El Paso with its unique flavor, my tongue was burning after the first sip, no doubt from Tabasco sauce, that staple seasoning of Cajun cooking.

Legend has it that Louisiana boys off fighting the mid–nineteenth-century war in Mexico were mustered out with renewed enthusiasm for hot peppers. One such soldier named McIlhenny brought special Mexican pepper seeds home to Avery Island, where Tabasco sauce was born as a result. I suppose one could say that some good comes out of a war, but I'd just as soon my son Chris didn't have to fight in any, no matter what seeds he might bring home to improve our various national cuisines.

Cajun Bloody Mary

*1¹/₂ oz. vodka
3 oz. tomato juice
1 dash ea. steak sauce and
    Worcestershire sauce
1 tsp. canned beef bouillon
1 tsp. horseradish
2 dashes Tabasco
¹/₂ tsp. ea. black pepper and celery salt*

Combine in a mixer and shake.

Serve over crushed ice in an old-fashioned glass.

Garnish with *a slice of lime and pickled okra or pickled green bean.*

With my tongue still tingling, I left Broder to have a second helping of Jell-O while I went to the telephone to call Linus Torelli and Nils. I wanted to ask if Linus was sure that Julienne had left wearing the red dress and Nils if she had brought a jean jacket with her. Neither was in his room, and I doubted that having Torelli paged at the conference would be productive or, if productive, a welcome interruption. But a jean jacket didn't sound like Julienne. I couldn't remember her wearing any such thing. Her Southern-belle mother, Fannie Delacroix, would never have approved. Was the bartender mistaken in his identification? If not, could Julienne have fitted both jeans and jacket into the shoulder bag Torelli had said she was carrying when she came to his room?

When I rejoined Broder to finish my Bloody Mary, he told me that Jean Lafitte, the notorious pirate/patriot, had used a secret room upstairs, now a restaurant, for meetings.

"Shall we go up for a snack?" I asked eagerly. Maybe Julienne had eaten there. If not, I was, after all, researching a book on

New Orleans food. Did they have authentic pirate food upstairs? I took a picture just in case I located any recipes for pirate cuisine.

Broder gave me a reproachful look and reminded me that we had to find Julienne. I must say, he was more cheerful and less likely to terrify me with dire predictions of Julienne's fate in Sin City after his second helping of "dessert." In fact, while we were looking for the voodoo museum, another favorite of Julienne's, we stopped to listen to a black street band that featured a tuba player in shorts, two men on trombone and drums, and a portly woman in a white dress who sang and played several instruments herself. Along with haunting blues songs, she did some gospel, after which Broder actually hopped the street barriers that surrounded the group and shook the woman's hand.

"Finally!" he exclaimed. "A good Christian woman!"

I was afraid she or her companions might take him to be some kind of dangerous religious fanatic. The men were certainly scowling suspiciously. The singer, however, beamed at Broder and asked, "You a man a' God, brothah?"

Before he could launch into a convoluted academic explanation of his calling, I, too, slipped between the barriers and whipped out Julienne's photo. "We're looking for a friend," I said quickly. "She's been missing since Sunday." Even the bartender couldn't place her after Sunday.

"Why you think we seen her?" demanded the tuba player, towering over my shoulder.

"Well, I . . ." Had I somehow offended them? "We're asking everyone."

The drummer abandoned his stool, and the trombone player ambled over to look at my photograph. "Das you," said the tuba player belligerently.

"Yes," I agreed, glancing backward apprehensively. "Taken about ten years ago."

"Honey," said the woman, "Ah don' notice folks when we on da street playin'. You oughta try da po-lice."

"Like sayin' you oughta try da mob," muttered the drummer.

"The Mafia's here, too?" gasped Broder.

"Excuse me," said a paunchy tourist in an embroidered shirt. He was in the act of dropping a five dollar bill into the open trombone case on the street. "Could you play 'The Saints' for my wife and me? We always wanted to hear it played in New Orleans. Somehow it's not the same, hearing it on TV or in Indianapolis."

"Sure we can, honey," said the singer. She smoothed down her tight, white dress and began to sing even before the instrumentalists could play any introductory music. Evidently she wasn't interested in staring at Julienne's picture any longer. So much for one Christian coming to the aid of another.

"Come on, Broder, let's find the voodoo museum." He did not look pleased to hear our next destination and told me it was once thought that white children were captured and sacrificed in voodoo ceremonies

"What luck our children aren't with us," I replied. I, too, was feeling the effects of alcohol. Unfortunately, Broder's Jell-O shots seemed to be wearing off as new anxieties overwhelmed him. He lectured me on the evils of combining pagan African rituals and snake gods with Roman Catholicism, of which he also seemed to have a horror. I, in my pretrip reading, had found the whole subject fascinating, although not something I took very seriously.

The museum itself proved to be — well, there's no other word for it — spooky. It was dark and smelled like old houses that need a good airing . . . very atmospheric, I suppose. The entrance fee almost caused

Broder to rethink his offer to protect me from evil. However, Christian knightliness spirited the five dollars from his pocket, and in we went, but not with any luck, initially. The attendants could hardly see the photograph in the gloom but were anxious to offer us appointments for cemetery tours, voodoo ceremonies, psychic readings, even voodoo tours that included visits to voodoo pharmacies, a prospect that moved Broder to nudge me and hiss, "Absolutely not. Absinthe was bad enough."

As if we had any absinthe, I thought. I'd had vodka; he'd had tequila in Jell-O.

I was worried enough about Julienne to ask if a psychic reading could locate a lost person, whereupon Broder dragged me away from the helpful attendant and into the gift shop, which had, at least, a higher level of light, not to mention an interesting selection of gris-gris potions and voodoo dolls. I bought, over Broder's objections, a love potion for my son Chris who, in his last phone call from school, had complained that the object of his affection had just dumped him for a marketing major. There's nothing like a joke, which I considered the love potion, to cure a minorly broken heart.

Then I selected a voodoo doll for my

daughter. I thought she might find it thera-
peutic to name it after her American government professor and stick pins in it. He
had thrown a blackboard eraser at her in
front of some two hundred students when
she dozed off during an unusually boring
lecture. I hadn't cared much for government myself, except as it applied to things
medieval. The organization of the English
court system under Henry II, for instance,
had once been a matter of great interest to
me when I was a young medieval history
major.

As the clerk in the voodoo gift shop was
wrapping my purchases and Broder hovered
nervously, as if to protect me from spells
and charms and other unchristian dangers,
I fished out the photograph of Julienne,
Philippe, and me. "Has this lady visited
your shop?" I asked, pointing to Julienne.

"Looks familiar," the girl allowed,
passing me my wrapped love potion and
pincushion doll. "Looks like a lady came in
— Sunday, I think. Some time in the afternoon. Before dusk, anyways. We close at
dusk."

Broder muttered to himself. He seemed
to find something ominous in closing at
dusk instead of, say, 5:30 or 7:00. In fact,
he found the dusk closing so ominous that

he decided he'd wait for me outside.

"What was she wearing?" I asked, hardly noticing Broder's departure now that I was on the trail of information about Julienne.

"Nothin' fancy," said the clerk. "Don' really remember. Nice curly hair, though. Well, jeans. Yeah, I think jeans."

"And a jean jacket?" If so, her observation would support the bartender's at Lafitte's Absinthe House.

The clerk pulled thoughtfully at one of many long, thin braids. "Didn' notice a jacket, ma'am."

I must have looked disappointed.

"Mighta been over her arm."

I nodded encouragingly.

"Bought a voodoo doll." She pointed to a male doll.

Was Julienne going to stick pins into a representation of Nils? Or even Linus, who hadn't been willing to forgo a night's sleep to accompany her on another photographic session? "Was she carrying a camera?"

"Everybody's carrying a camera." She nodded at mine as a case in point. "Well, except that fella who left just now. You want a book about Marie Laveau? She was the most famous voodoo queen of New Orleans."

"Does it contain recipes?" I asked. That would make a wonderful chapter. Voodoo recipes. If they happened to be tasty. The clerk was giving me a peculiar look. I imagined what Broder would think if he could hear me asking about voodoo recipes. He'd assume I was interested in gris-gris type things, scary potions, while I, practical woman that I am, had been wondering what Marie Laveau had cooked for breakfast. If it was grits, the Marie Laveau chapter was gone!

Still, I took a picture when I got outside, then looked around for my escort. Goodness! He was nowhere in sight. Could Broder, imagining that I had sold my soul to souvenir-dispensing devil worshipers, have deserted me? Instead of Broder, I was approached by a stocky woman wearing a turban, a bunchy, many-colored, ankle-length skirt, and a black knitted shawl. *A freelance voodoo tour guide?* I asked myself. She grabbed my arm and thrust her face, a remarkably ugly face, into mine.

In a raspy, threatening voice, she whispered, "Bad luck you stay heah in N'Awlins, missus. I got da second sight."

"Really?" I pulled back to try for a better look at her, but she had me by both arms now, and her grip was bruising.

"Bettah you go away, missus. Bad things come to you, you keep walkin' dese streets."

It occurred to me that she meant to steal my camera or my handbag. Why else would this peculiar person be trying to frighten me with spurious prophecies?

"Danger. Ah see danger," she intoned in a loud, hollow voice.

"Me, too," I replied as I jerked away from her hands and got a firm grip on both my purse and my camera. "If you don't go away, I intend to summon a policeman."

"You be callin' dem po-lice, you nevah leave N'Awlins alive."

"You stole that outfit from the museum, didn't you?" I retorted, feeling braver each minute because, after all, there were other tourists I could call out to. "I saw one just like it on a mannequin inside." Still clutching my handbag to deter theft, if that was her game, I reached behind me to turn the gift shop doorknob, then flung the door open, stumbled over the sill, and cried, "This woman has stolen your . . . your artifacts."

The clerk who had sold me the voodoo doll and several customers, who must have entered the shop from the museum, gaped at me. The turbaned woman gave me a baleful look over her shoulder as she fled, running down the street and colliding with Broder at the corner. Being a Christian gentleman, he helped her up. Being a rude criminal, she shoved him aside and disappeared around the corner.

It wasn't until I returned to my hotel room that I realized I had lost the gifts for the children. Had she taken them? Or had I simply dropped them on the sidewalk or in the shop during the hullabaloo that followed her departure: Broder's fussing, official apologies from the staff of the museum, and a brief spate of note-taking from a policeman who arrived to investigate the incident.

He told me that the city was full of "nut cases" and I shouldn't let the incident worry me since I was none the worse for it.

11

Risotto Mille e Una Notte (Thousand and One Nights Risotto)

Before I collapsed on the cabbage rose bedspread in our room at Hotel de la Poste, I
called Linus Torelli again and, for a
wonder, found him in. "Did Julienne have
jeans with her when she left your room?" I
demanded, not even bothering to identify
myself.

Torelli did not sound happy to hear from
me. "I told you she was still wearing the
red dress. She had no other clothes with
her except some sort of shawl thing and
the purse."

Perhaps it was another woman, not Julienne, seen yesterday by the bartender and
the voodoo sales clerk. "I hope you're
telling me the truth, Professor. It's only
fair to warn you that I've already talked to
a police lieutenant at the Vieux Carre station, and I mentioned your name."

"I can't believe this!" His voice had gone high with anxiety or exasperation; I wasn't sure which. "All I did was befriend her. That's all! You must be a crazy woman to harass me like this." He hung up before I could pursue the conversation.

Sighing, I propped a pillow against the French headboard on my bed and picked up my New Orleans guide. Where else had Julienne suggested we go together? I thumbed through the book and came upon two more places: the French Market and the swamp tour boats. Julienne loved the swamps; she had always said they were unearthly, eerie, and mysterious. Oh, how I hoped that she'd return to accompany me on a swamp tour. And go shopping for souvenirs with me at the French Market. I'd already missed sharing the Historic Voodoo Museum with her and hated to think of paying another five dollars should she insist on returning to point out things that I might have missed. Of course, I probably had missed everything of interest, now that I thought of it. I'd been focused on finding someone who had seen her, not to mention inhibited by all Broder's carping and the unfortunate confrontation with the pseudoseer outside. With such thoughts spiraling through my mind, I drifted into a light sleep from which I was awakened by the telephone bringing me Lieutenant Alphonse Boudreaux's sexy, drawling voice.

"No news is good news, Miz Blue," he said. "We got no unidentified Caucasian women in our hospitals, jails, morgue, or fished outa the river, so Ah don't know where your friend is, but it don' seem like she's dead or injured in N'Awlins."

"I guess that is good news," I said doubtfully. "I found two people who may have seen her yesterday afternoon in the Quarter."

"Well, that's good news, too. Means she was OK twenty-four hours ago. Ah hafta say it sounds to me like she left of her own free will. That bein' the case, this isn't really police business. Country's full of runaway wives, ma'am. They got a right if that's what they want to do. Like you said, her husband hasn't been treatin' her kindly."

"But Lieutenant, believe me, if she were OK, she would have called me, no matter how angry she is with Nils."

"Maybe. But an angry woman, she don' always think about anything but what's botherin' her. Could be that way with your friend. Like as not, she'll be gettin' in touch when she cools down. Meantime, Ah believe Ah did see your name on a police report came in the end of the shift. You the Miz Carolyn Blue got accosted outside the Historic Voodoo Museum?"

"Oh well, it was nothing," I assured him.

"You weren't hurt?"

I looked down at my forearms, which were beginning to ache, and there I saw the fingerprint bruises made by the strange woman who had warned me of danger. "Did you catch her?" I asked, realizing that I would have to wear long sleeves for several weeks. It was no problem here in cool and rainy New Orleans, but when I got home to El Paso, the temperatures could well be nudging the short-sleeve range. We don't really have much of a winter, except at night. Temperatures do tend to plummet then, but not below zero, as had been the case when I was growing up in Michigan. In El Paso, we're lucky to see temperatures near freezing, and then the local weathermen issue all sorts of plant and pet warnings. What weather wimps Southwesterners are!

"We haven't caught the lady who bothered you, no, ma'am, an' Ah'm sorry to say we likely won't. The museum isn't even sure she stole a dress from them like you thought."

I sighed. A familiar police refrain. Two porch chairs had been stolen from my courtyard at home, and the police had said the same thing, adding that my chairs were probably on their way to Mexico. If my assailant had stolen that outfit or the gifts for my children, those articles would, no doubt, stay in New Orleans, but that didn't do me any good. "I do thank you for your efforts, Lieutenant," I said and bade him good-bye.

"What lieutenant has been making efforts on your behalf?" my husband asked, entering the room and dropping his briefcase on the bed.

"I was accosted in front of the voodoo museum by some crazy woman," I replied, holding out my bruised arms for his inspection.

"Good lord!" Jason exclaimed and dropped down beside me, all concern.

"But I fended her off and managed to keep both my purse and camera."

"Where was Broder during all this?" Jason asked, loosening his tie. "I thought he was supposed to be protecting you from sin and sinners."

"More like protecting himself," I muttered. "He left, horrified, when I asked about Marie Laveau voodoo cookery."

Jason grinned. "I won't even ask you what voodoo cookery is, unless it's something you plan to practice on me."

"You know I don't cook if I can help it now that I'm semiretired in the domestic venue."

"More's the pity," he replied sadly. Then he informed me that Lester and Miranda wanted to meet us at Bacco for dinner. They'd read about the restaurant in some gourmet magazine. Since Bacco was in our hotel, I didn't see any way to avoid the dinner, although the prospect of listening to Miranda talk about the $350 an hour she billed while defending greedy and amoral corporate clients didn't give me much joy.

Nonetheless, I smiled at my husband and ducked into the bathroom to shower and put on something less casual. Maybe the very rich Miranda and the very eminent Lester would pick up the bill. And I could certainly make cuisine notes for my book.

While I was waiting for Jason to fiddle the knot of his tie into a configuration that pleased him, I thumbed through my *Louisiana New Garde* cookbook because the restaurant at which we were destined to eat rang a bell with me. Indeed, I found a number of recipes in the book that were attributed to Ristorante Bacco. What luck! I hadn't previously noticed that such luscious-looking dishes came from our very own hotel. When I pointed out items to Jason, he found several he wanted to try.

Bacco was charming in a number of ways: the wood-fired ovens (I was almost tempted to order pizza), the lessons in Italian piped into the ladies' room (Miranda complained about hearing the same thing when she was put on hold while calling for a reservation), the charming ambiance, the elegant curved ceilings, but particularly the food. Once I had tasted it, I was sorry to have stuffed myself with the muffuletta at lunch, not that the sandwich wasn't wonderful, too — but the food at Bacco — *Viva la Italia!* It almost made Miranda's company bearable and Lester's news less disturbing.

Because I was still suffering from lunch overload, I chose a salad and the oyster and roasted eggplant ravioli (a first course hearty enough to be an entrée). I myself have been known to make a memorable lobster ravioli, so complicated that I hope never to make it again. Therefore, I choose these time-consuming seafood raviolis when I have the chance. And this one was lovely. I believe I detected in the filling, besides the minced oyster and eggplant, hints of garlic, green onion, breadcrumbs, oregano, and a dash of something spicy. And the sauce — which I confess to finishing with my bread when I had consumed the ravioli — cream, butter, wine, shallots, garlic, the oyster flavor and then the surprise — the taste of some licorice liqueur. I checked when we returned to the room and discovered that it was a favorite of New Orleans chefs: herbsaint. What a charming name! I wondered what saint might have favored anise. My reference books don't say.

While I was eating my salad, Jason and Lester were feasting on polenta topped with squid that had been sautéed in garlic olive oil, highly seasoned, then cooked in wine. I'm not really a fan of polenta, but I sampled a bite of Jason's squid. Delicious! I made notes. I don't remember what Miranda ordered as a first course because she didn't offer me a taste. She did complain about my making notes on the food. The waiter, however, seemed pleased and happily discussed ingredients with me.

While we were waiting for our entrées, Lester said, "Julienne is really causing a stir with this puzzling disappearance.

Carlene was highly insulted, as were several scientists whose presentations she'd promised to attend. Of course, I assume that she will stop sulking and reappear tomorrow, since she's responsible for chairing a session."

"Am I the only one who's worried about her?" I asked as I sipped Chardonnay.

"From what Lester's told me, I don't think we need to worry," said Miranda with an insufferable air of superiority and disdain.

How could I have liked the woman so much when we were young? I wondered. She'd changed out of all comprehension. Lester I could understand. His jolly personality had evidently been the result of alcohol, which he no longer consumed. According to Miranda, he also had a cholesterol problem, which had not been ameliorated by his drinking problem. How unfortunate for Lester! Although the gourmet world was celebrating the health benefits of red wine, those benefits had not worked for him. Miranda insisted that he order a risotto dish, which she described as well reviewed and cholesterol-free. Poor Lester acquiesced but looked sadly envious when Jason chose veal chops in a chicken liver–balsamic sauce, a dish he had seen in my New Orleans cuisine book.

"Maybe you wouldn't mind explaining that remark, Miranda," I said. "If there's news of Julienne, I'd like to hear it."

"I doubt that it's the news you were hoping for," said Miranda smugly. "Tell her, Lester."

The waiter had begun to serve our entrées when Lester responded to his wife's command. "There's quite a contingent here from Julienne's university," he said. "As I'm on the organizing committee, I was, naturally, aware of that, so I took the trouble to look some of them up." He shook his head dolefully and dug into his rice, then chewed with an enthusiastic smile. "This is very good!" he exclaimed. Miranda looked smugger than ever. "Here, Carolyn, try it," Lester offered.

Naturally, I did, and goodness! It was heavenly! How hard was it to make? I wondered. It seemed like an excellent choice to pass on to my readers if the chef would give me the recipe, which I didn't remember seeing in the book. Later I discovered that I had missed the recipe, probably because of its long Italian name. "What is it called?" I asked, even as I waved to the waiter.

Lester didn't remember. "Risotto Mille e

165

Una Notte," said Miranda.

She would remember, I thought, feeling rather grumpy at the thought that Miranda probably spoke Italian fluently, whereas I knew only the few words I had picked up from operas. Being able to exclaim, "Oh, *ciel!*" which means "Oh, heaven!" isn't really very helpful when reading a menu.

"Here, let me try it," Miranda said to her husband. "I don't know why you'd ask Carolyn's opinion. I'm the one who suggested the risotto."

"Carolyn's the expert," said Lester somewhat plaintively, if a man could sound plaintive while he was eating as fast as he could. And I noticed that he didn't provide his wife any, even when ordered to.

With the waiter heading in my direction, all smiles, Miranda whispered urgently, "For heaven's sake, Carolyn, you're not going to go into another long food discussion with the help, are you?"

I ignored her and told the waiter I was interested in procuring a recipe for a book I was writing on New Orleans cuisine. I mentioned my publisher, in case he thought I was some charlatan trying to gain special attention with little white lies. However, he was delighted. Evidently, the chef and the restaurant owners liked publicity. Miranda would have been horrified had she been able to see the ingredients, which included, as one might expect of a good risotto, a lot of butter and cheese, not to mention all the lovely prosciutto. I didn't show the ingredients to her. Lester was enjoying his meal, and I'd have felt terrible if she made him stop eating. Surely his cholesterol wasn't so high that one meal would kill him. Maybe she was primarily worried about his calorie intake.

Risotto Mille e Una Notte

Wash and pat dry leaves from *1 bunch spinach,* blanch in boiling water 2 to 3 minutes, transfer with slotted spoon to bowl of cold water, drain, puree in blender or food processor.

In a large saucepan, bring *12 cups chicken stock* to simmer

In a large, heavy sauce pan, melt $^3/_4$ *cup unsalted butter* over medium heat and sauté $^1/_2$ *cup chopped onion* 3 to 4 minutes or until pale golden.

Add *2$^1/_4$ cups (1 lb.) Arborio rice* and stir 1 minute.

Add *1 cup dry white wine* and cook until almost evaporated, 5 to 6 minutes.

Add $^2/_3$ *cup peeled and diced carrots,* $^2/_3$ *cup chopped prosciutto,* $^1/_2$ *cup diced fresh porcini mushrooms,* and $^1/_2$ cup of the hot chicken stock. Cook, stirring with wooden spoon, until broth has evaporated. Repeat, adding $^1/_2$ cup hot stock at a time until rice is tender, but slightly chewy.

Fifteen minutes into broth addition, stir in $^1/_3$ *cup green peas* and spinach puree.

When rice is done, stir in $^1/_2$ *cup unsalted butter, 1 cup (4 oz.) grated Parmesan cheese, salt, and pepper to taste.*

Garnish six wide, rimmed soup bowls with 12 whole slices prosciutto (2 to a bowl), and serve risotto warm.

Having taken care of my professional duties and tucked the recipe in my handbag, Miranda scowling all the while, I turned again to Lester. "Now, what's this bad news about Julienne?"

"Scandal," said Lester around a mouthful of rice, vegetables, and prosciutto. "It seems that Nils's accusations have a basis in fact. Several professors in her department are under the impression that she and this Italian fellow are having an affair."

"Why? Because they share a seminar for their students? That's hardly grounds for sexual gossip," I retorted defensively.

"Because Torelli has all but told them so."

"But he denies it. I asked him."

"You asked him!" Jason looked astounded. "When did you ask him?"

"I tracked him down at his hotel and asked him straight out, and he denied it. Then, and on the telephone today, he said there's nothing to the rumors. That their relationship was strictly —" Well, I couldn't really say "professional" since he had taken her in the night she left the dinner and her husband. "Strictly platonic," I finished somewhat lamely.

"That's not what he's hinting to his male colleagues," said Lester, "and you shouldn't be surprised that he'd deny it to you. After all, he wouldn't want to tarnish her reputation with her female friends, who might tell her what he was saying about her."

"But he wouldn't care if she was being slandered in every locker room in town?"

"I've met Torelli," said Jason mildly. "I'd be surprised if the man has been in a locker room since he got out of high school."

He smiled at me sweetly and offered me some of his veal, which was excellent. Especially the sauce. I detected not only the flavor of chicken livers (very finely chopped) and balsamic vinegar (a flavorful addition to anything from a salad, vegetable, or fruit, to a soup or meat sauce), but also red pepper and sage. I assumed that a meat stock was added as well.

"Wonderful choice," I said to Jason. If I hadn't lost my taste for cooking, I'd have tried to reproduce it when we got home. Maybe I could interest my husband in conducting a sauce experiment. Instead of looking at the recipe, we'd wing it. How much different could it be from the excitement of creating some new compound in a lab or trying to reproduce some other chemist's work? Except, of course, that in the kitchen you could eat the result of the experiment. Since Jason is mainly interested in toxins, no one would want to eat anything produced in his lab.

"I don't believe a word of it," I told Lester.

"Then why did she run away?" Lester asked. He was waving the waiter over.

Did he want a recipe, too? I couldn't imagine that Miranda devoted much of her $350-an-hour time to cooking. However, Lester didn't want a recipe. He wanted the dessert menu.

"The last thing you need is a dessert, Lester," said Miranda.

Jason evidently saw an argument coming on because Lester looked both stubborn and petulant. "My poor wife, in her search for Julienne, was accosted this afternoon and bruised by some crazy woman," said Jason as he cut and provided me with another bite of his veal. I'd rather have had a bit of the sauce mopped up with bread, but we'd eaten all the bread.

"Yes," I agreed cooperatively. "She said, among other things, that I'd never leave New Orleans alive unless I left immediately."

"You didn't tell me *that!*" Jason exclaimed.

I shrugged. "She really had another agenda; to wit, my purse or camera or both, neither of which she got," I added with excusable satisfaction. "But I do think she stole the love potion and the voodoo doll I bought as presents for the children."

"I consider those very peculiar gift choices," said Miranda.

171

"No more peculiar than you and Lester giving your son toy guns when he was a toddler," I retorted. "My gift selections were jokes. Were the weapons jokes, as well?"

"Goodness, Carolyn, I certainly didn't mean to offend you. I was going to point out that beliefs in illogical things like love potions and astrology are all too prevalent these days."

Miranda sounded definitely huffy. *Too bad!* I thought.

"Amen to that," Jason agreed. "Just this year I discovered that over fifty percent of a junior-level chemistry class claimed to believe in astrology."

"If you go back far enough, even the Catholic Church acknowledged the uses of astrology," I pointed out.

"Oh, well, the Church," said Miranda dismissively.

"And in Padua, there are astrological signs above the seats of judges, so lawyers weren't immune, either," I added.

"When was that?" she retorted. "The Middle Ages?"

"Of course."

"Back when I was teaching, I certainly uncovered some peculiar superstitions among my students," said Lester.

"You don't teach anymore?" Jason asked, surprised. "All *our* deans teach."

"Perhaps they don't have enough administrative functions to keep them busy," said Lester.

Since I knew he was about to launch into denigrating remarks on Jason's new university, I said quickly, "Before you get into that, could I have the dessert menu, Lester?" The waiter had slipped it to him discreetly.

"Lester!" screeched Miranda.

No more was said about Jason's decision to change his place of employment or my run-in with the ugly, turbaned lady. And the Abbotts did *not* offer to pay for any dinners but their own.

12

Po'boys and Café Brûlot

Another favorite sandwich in New Orleans is the po'boy, which once cost a nickel. These days, the price has gone up and might be too steep for the pockets of poor boys; however, no one, rich or poor, can find fault with the ingredients. In a long, slender French loaf, one can order meatballs, roast beef and gravy, oysters, shrimp, soft-shelled crab, or even plain old ham and cheese. A dressed po'boy adds mayonnaise, lettuce, and tomatoes. Like the muffuletta, the po'boy is a meal in itself.

Carolyn Blue,
Eating Out in the Big Easy

I awoke on Tuesday morning feeling depressed. Julienne had now been missing since Saturday night and had not, as far as I knew, been seen by anyone since Sunday. Where was she yesterday? Why, if she was safe, had she not called me? And now I had to contend with the rumors passed on by Lester: People in Julienne's department thought that she had, indeed, been the lover of Linus Torelli, who had hinted of the affair to various men friends, although he had vehemently denied it to me.

Well, what else would he have said when I was, in essence, accusing him of being responsible for her disappearance? Was he responsible? The man admitted to quarreling with her early Sunday morning, but he claimed that she had stormed off alone. That part of it could be a lie. A man who tells one lie may tell another, and in his conflicting stories about their relationship, one of the versions had to be a lie.

And there was Nils, who wouldn't report her missing to the police. Even if the Sunday Julienne sightings were accurate, today would see the passing of the necessary forty-eight hours, but Lieutenant Boudreaux insisted that Nils had to make the report, not I. And Nils refused, believing his wife unfaithful, believing her to be with Torelli, no matter what Linus said. Was Nils so certain because Julienne had done what she'd threatened — returned to their room on Sunday night, claiming to have slept with Torelli? And now her husband was refusing to report her missing because he had caused her disappearance, the result of a fit of rage and jealousy. But when had he attacked her? She'd been seen Sunday, and he attended the mixer Sunday night. Had he returned to find her waiting for him? All primed to hurt him by claiming to have fulfilled his suspicions? And then he, furious, had — what?

I stifled further disturbing speculation, rolled out of bed, and padded barefoot to the bathroom. Jason had left earlier to breakfast with colleagues. I would return to Café du Monde in the hope that Julienne, still alive, would take pity on a worried friend and meet me there. She didn't. I made a solitary meal of beignets and café au lait, this time without chicory, while I considered my next stop. Obviously I had to check the convention first. Everyone else thought she'd show up to chair her session. I thought that, if she were able to do that, she'd have called me. And I knew her better than the rest of them.

At the conference information desk I managed to extract, from the young woman answering questions, the location of Julienne Magnussen's session, although

Jeanne Rae, as her name tag identified her, took great pains to assure me that, as an accompanying person, I was welcome only to the social events, not the lectures. As if I wanted to hear people going on and on about arcane scientific topics. Much as I love my husband, I am no more enamoured of chemistry than I was when he was the graduate assistant in my chemistry class. I did point out to Jeanne Rae that, in fact, accompanying persons were invited to plenary lectures, which were, essentially, public events. Then, having wasted precious time, I had to jog through the corridors of the convention center to reach the appointed room before the session attendees had dispersed for lack of a chairwoman, my second, and no less distressing, attempt at jogging in twenty or more years.

I needn't have run so fast, for the attendees were clustered outside the door of the meeting room with Lester at the center of the group, in midtirade upon the unconscionable, irresponsible, inconsiderate . . . Julienne had not arrived to chair the session, and Lester was appalled. I was appalled as well, but for wildly different reasons. Now I was convinced that my childhood friend had come to grief.

Nils was there, too, although he, being a mathematician and no ACS member, had no more right to attend the session than I did. "Have you heard from her?" I whispered to him. If he was innocent in the matter of her disappearance, surely he was now as worried as I.

"No," he replied curtly.

"You have to report her missing," I said pleadingly.

"Why should I?"

He killed her. The thought flashed through my mind like a tornado warning.

"She's obviously run off with Torelli. You'll notice he's not here, either. Since they're such *close colleagues,* he wouldn't have missed her session."

Misdirection or innocence on Nils's part? I wondered.

"Nils isn't required by law to report Julienne missing," said Miranda, who had joined our whispered conversation unexpectedly.

What was *she* doing here? She wasn't a conference participant, either. And she wasn't whispering. Lester and the several men around him turned when she spoke in that authoritative, courtroom voice. "The police don't want to hear about runaway wives," said Miranda. "They have their hands full with genuine disappearances. And don't give me that reproachful look, Carolyn. Have a little pity on poor Nils. Think of how embarrassing this is for him — to have his wife run off with a younger, more attractive man." Miranda looked almost pleased at the notion of a woman running off with a younger man. Nils did not look at all gratified by her defense of his cuckolded sensibilities.

"Torelli isn't better looking," I mumbled. How could these people, who had known Julienne for years, think so badly of her and show so little concern for her well-being?

"Thanks for that, Carolyn," said Nils sarcastically. "It's nice to know that my wife's best friend thinks I'm more attractive than my wife's lover. Too bad Julie wasn't of your opinion." He turned and walked away.

My impulse was to run after him and beg him to accompany me to the Vieux Carre station, but in my heart I knew it was hopeless. For whatever reason, guilt or male ego, Nils wasn't going to change his mind. "I guess your unkind remarks mean that neither you nor Lester has seen Julienne since last night?" I murmured to Miranda.

"We're not likely to see someone who doesn't want to be seen," said Miranda briskly. "Lester, I find that I'm free for lunch. Would you like to meet me at the hotel?"

Looking officious, Lester said, "I'm afraid that won't be possible, my dear. I am now forced to contend with the possibility that Julienne may fail to show up for her paper, having disappointed us today as she has."

I spotted Jason coming down the hall and walked quickly toward him. "I know. She's still missing," he said quietly. "I've been asking around. No one's seen her. Carlene's worried, too, and feeling badly that she made such a fuss about Julienne not attending her lecture. She told me Broder says you two may have found people who saw Julienne Sunday?"

I nodded.

"Unfortunately, that doesn't explain her absence yesterday, and certainly not today."

"Nils still won't go to the police."

"The man's a fool," said Jason.

I could have hugged him for his support and his good sense.

"Even if she's having affairs with ten different men, she wouldn't abrogate her responsibilities here and risk her scientific reputation."

"Exactly," I agreed. "And I don't think she's having an affair. I didn't even like that Torelli. Julienne wouldn't be interested in him. Not in a romantic way. He's just some emotionally retarded, would-be Lothario. He probably can't get a date, much less a wife, so he's trying to make himself look sexy at Julienne's expense. That's . . . that's disgusting behavior. He should be drummed out of the American Chemical Society."

Jason grinned at me, and that reaction took some of the furious wind out of my sails. "I don't know of any case in which a member was drummed out of the society for his sexual exploits, real or imaginary." He thought a moment. "Well, maybe if he raped a student and got sent to jail for it, but then he'd be drummed out of his university and . . . well, you see my point, Caro. What are you going to do now?"

Jason knew me well enough to know that I wasn't going to go home and have the vapors. I considered my options, then said, "I'm going to start making calls, first to her house and her department, in case she went back. Maybe she was so furious with Nils that she got the first plane home in order to file for divorce."

"Maybe," said Jason dubiously, "but it

doesn't sound like her."

I sighed, admitting that it didn't. She'd have contacted me. She'd have warned conference officials that she was going to miss the sessions in which she was chair and lecturer. In fact, she'd have stayed for those and then gone home. "Well, I'll start telephoning hotels to see if she's registered somewhere else. If only that . . . that husband of hers would call the police, I wouldn't have to do any of this." Although Lieutenant Boudreaux had told me that no one of Julienne's description had turned up at a hospital or morgue, I wanted to know where she was and that she was safe. What if she'd been hit on the head by her supposed lover, her husband, or a mugger and was suffering from amnesia?

"That sounds like a sensible plan," said Jason, giving me a little hug.

I returned Jason's hug, an unexpected pleasure since he wasn't given to physical displays of affection in front of colleagues. Then I went back to our room in the hotel, sat myself down on the rose-covered bedspread with my address book and the New Orleans phone book at hand, and began to make calls. No one answered at Julienne's house. Her departmental secretary told me that Julienne was at the American Chemical Society meeting in New Orleans and wasn't expected home until the weekend, and, no, she hadn't returned early. Why would she? Dr. Magnussen was a distinguished scientist whose presence at the meeting was important to her department, to her, and to the other attendees. Some secretaries are so officious. The woman sounded like Lester. Then I began calling hotels in New Orleans asking if Julienne had registered under either her married or maiden name. She hadn't.

What now? Julienne had wanted to take the swamp tour. Both to introduce me to the wonders of the swamp and to take pictures. I telephoned swamp tour numbers in the Yellow Pages. No one of her name or description could be recalled by any of the bookers. Fine! That was a long shot, anyway, I consoled myself. She wouldn't have gone without me. We'd had extensive E-mail correspondence about the grotesque vegetation I'd see, the little above-ground cemeteries on the shores, and the alligators and snakes that would be swimming in the bayous and sunning themselves on the mud flats. If she had actually gone without me, I might have better luck interviewing boat captains, who would be more likely to remember her than would some ticket agent for a tour operator. Should I try to go this afternoon?

I rose to glance out the long windows that overlooked the street below. It was raining again, a light, mistlike rain, but still not good weather for a boat excursion or even for walking from boat to boat on some wooden pier surrounded by dripping vegetation that might well harbor nasty creatures, leeches, or something equally distasteful.

And I really needed a more recent picture of Julienne. And of Linus Torelli and Nils. But how? If I had an Internet connection, I could access the departmental web sites at their university, where there would be pictures of the professors that I could print out if I had a printer. But although Jason and I both have laptops, and his has a modem, neither of us has a portable printer. I called the desk, but the hotel did not offer that service. The desk clerk suggested that I try a computer bar.

Computer bar? People sat around drinking and playing with computers in New Orleans? That didn't sound very Creole to me, not very Cajun, not very French Quarter. Nonetheless, I again used the Yellow Pages and made yet more phone calls. A CompuCoffee representative informed me that his customers came to play computer games and didn't ask for printers, which he didn't provide, but that I'd undoubtedly enjoy CompuCoffee's chicory coffee and their newest game. It had some horrible name like Demise of the Bloody Death Planet. On my fourth call, I found an establishment called Po'Boy Computer Café that provided delicious drinks, sandwiches, and Internet access with printer facilities.

I took a cab and ordered, from a young man who told me that he was a computer science major at the University of New Orleans, a "loaf," which consisted of spicy fried shrimp on buttered, heated French bread. Delicious. I was starving after all those telephone calls. Given my appetite and my new profession, it's more than fortunate that I have an active metabolism.

With my shrimp loaf, I had café brûlot, a strong coffee in which are steeped cinnamon, lemon, clove, orange, and sugar. I asked the waiter and wrote down the ingredients after the first lovely sip. He had poured in brandy and set it afire right at my computer table — well, actually, at the eating and drinking ell on the table. The management discouraged endangering their computers with the food and drink and, in fact, asked us not to take the protective cover off the computer until we had finished the repast.

I was only too happy to comply. After devouring my shrimp loaf and my coffee, which was served in a charming cup on a pedestal, I turned to the computer, whipped off the cover, surfed the web, and printed out, with only two emergency visits from their computer techs, pictures of Linus, Julienne, and Nils — five by seven pictures. Ah, the wonders of modern science.

The whole experience was rather expensive, but the food was deductible; in fact, I used the Po'Boy computer to type up notes on the sandwich and brûlot. Even given the cost, I felt quite merry after my Internet success and my brandied coffee. Imagine! A computer establishment with a liquor license! Only in New Orleans! Or perhaps I am showing my lack of sophistication. Such places may exist all over the country without my being aware because I have never traveled in the circles where one would hear of such a thing. Most of my friends tend to look on computers as technological tools rather than gourmet experiences. How fortunate I am to have become a food writer instead of a scientist. Not that there was ever any chance of my becoming a scientist.

13

Mugging a Mugger

Before leaving the Po'Boy Computer Café, I folded the pictures of Julienne, Nils, and Linus Torelli and slipped them into my handbag, then scanned the street for transportation back to the hotel. As you might expect, there wasn't a cab in sight, but I was not downcast. Cognac will do that for you. Instead of fretting, I set off in the direction of the Quarter with the intention of flagging down a taxi when one appeared. In the meantime, I would simply plot out my next move.

Unfortunately, my next move was, of necessity, the defense of my person and purse. A scruffy little man with wild red hair and sunglasses slithered out of an alley and grabbed my purse. I, in turn, managed to snag the strap before it whipped off my shoulder. "Help! Thief!" I screamed.

"Shut up, bitch!" he snarled and gave my

purse, which was clutched in his large, hairy hand, a mighty tug.

"Help!" I screamed and tugged back for all I was worth. Imagine calling me "bitch." Bad enough he was trying to purloin my handbag. "Help! Help!" I yanked harder on the strap.

"You dumb broad. Don' you see dis here pigsticker?" The redheaded criminal swung his left arm, and I felt, simultaneously, a burning on my hand and the departure of the purse strap through my fingers. The scoundrel had cut the purse from my grasp, cutting me in the process, while I, intent on saving my belongings, hadn't even noticed the knife in his hand until the blade was flashing in my direction. Was that what he had meant by *pigsticker?* Thoroughly incensed, I swung my umbrella at his head. I'm not sure what injury I did him, and I really don't much care, but he did cry out, drop my purse, and disappear back into his alley.

"Don't let him get away!" I cried to a male passerby. The man gave me a blank look. "He injured me!" Indeed he had. My hand was bleeding, and the passerby was scuttling away, as were two ladies who had been behind him on the sidewalk. No wonder there are so many criminals. Citizens no longer feel obliged to come to the aid of their fellows, and the police are never there when you need them. However, a cab had finally appeared. I waved my bloody hand, and the driver pulled to the curb. Then a man in a vested suit, dark blue with a fine pinstripe, tried to slip into the backseat ahead of me. I gave him a rap with my umbrella and climbed in.

"Way to go, lady!" said the cabby and asked where I wanted to be taken.

"The Vieux Carre Police Station," I replied. "I've been mugged."

"Tryin' to snag a cab from someone ain't da same as muggin', ma'am."

"I was accosted by a purse snatcher," I replied. "As it happens, I can tell the difference between rudeness and crime, although I imagine criminals are often rude as well as unprincipled. The purse snatcher certainly was."

"Sorry to hear it, ma'am. Makes da city look bad, dat's what Ah say."

"You're quite right," I agreed. "I am not finding New Orleans a friendly place."

"Ain't da same place as when Ah was a chile," said the cab driver, nodding mournfully. He was a black man who looked, given the scar on his cheek, as if someone had taken a knife to him, too.

"Were you mugged?" I asked.

"Me? No, ma'am." He glanced into his rearview mirror and caught me examining his cheek. "Oh, dis here? Mah ole lady done dat. She be as red hot as good gumbo." The man actually sounded overcome with admiration for the violent propensities of his wife, or had he meant his mother? *My old lady* could mean either.

"Um-m," I murmured. I had pulled off the scarf that tied my hair back so that I could knot it around my hand. But what a shame to get blood on that lovely periwinkle blue print, I thought as I pulled the knot tight with teeth and free hand. The color exactly matched my linen shirt and slacks. Then I considered the attack. No doubt, my conduct would be considered foolhardy. Well, it was, and had it not been for the cognac, I would probably have acted in a more sensible manner.

On the other hand, I had saved not only my handbag, a very nice leather envelope with shoulder strap that Jason had given me for Christmas, but also my money, credit cards, driver's license and, equally important to my mission, the pictures I had printed out at the café. And I thought that I had injured the man with the knife, which he richly deserved. Now I intended to file a complaint against him. I was prepared to give quite a detailed description of my assailant.

"Here you are, ma'am," said the cabby. I climbed out in front of the police station on Royal Street and paid him, including a generous tip.

"Now you take care, ma'am," he said as he pulled away. It had begun to rain, so I put up my umbrella. It was then that I discovered I had broken several of the ribs while belaboring the purse snatcher, or possibly the man who had tried to commandeer my cab. *Bother,* I thought as I raced under the portico with my umbrella at half-mast around my head. It was the umbrella I had purchased here in New Orleans, perhaps an inferior product produced for hapless tourists.

"Let me guess," said the sergeant at the desk. "You wanna see the lieutenant."

"I want to report a mugging," I retorted severely. I could see that he was already pressing a buzzer to summon Alphonse Boudreaux.

"Who'd you mug?" muttered the sergeant.

"I heard that," I snapped back.

"Miz Blue?" The lieutenant escorted me to his office and listened sympathetically to my story. When I told him that I had hit the attacker with my umbrella, he began to grin. When I showed him my hand, wrapped in the now blood-spotted scarf, he made soothing sounds and came around his desk to unwrap the injury and inspect it. Did lieutenants customarily devote this much attention to female complainants? Somehow I doubted it.

"Well, Miz Blue, Ah don' think it needs stitchin', but Ah can surely have one of mah men drive you over to the hospital —"

"No, no," I replied quickly. "I'm sure a bit of disinfectant and a Band-Aid will do the trick. No functional damage seems to have occurred." I wiggled my fingers to show that they still worked. "However, I do want to describe the mugger for you."

He nodded and returned to his desk chair, from which he made notes as I talked.

"Perhaps you could call in a police artist." I had seen that done on TV. "Then you can put up posters of my assailant in the various substations."

"Happens we don' have a police artist handy," he said as apologetically as if he were personally responsible for that deficiency. He made a few more notes, then looked up. "Miz Blue, you sure do get yourself in a soup pot a trouble."

"Believe me, Lieutenant, nothing like this ever happens to me at home. It's New Orleans. I don't want to hurt your feelings, but I have to consider this a dangerous city."

"Most cities are, ma'am. Now, what were you doin' at Po'Boy Computer? That is a known drug hangout. We have raided that establishment more than once."

"Drug hangout?" I was nonplused. "But it looked perfectly respectable, and their computer facilities are excellent."

"That may be, but those computer geeks sure do like cocaine. Ah wouldn't be surprised to hear they're refinin' it in the back room. On the other hand, the sandwiches are mighty good."

"Indeed. I had the spicy shrimp, which was delicious. And the café brûlot!" I sighed with remembered pleasure.

"Tut tut," he said, grinning. "Drinkin' cognac in yo' coffee in the middle of the day?"

"It's part of my research," I explained defensively. "Café brûlot is considered a New Orleans specialty. I did take notes, you know. In fact, I typed them up and printed them out, along with the pictures."

"Now, what pictures would those be?"

"Of my friend, her husband, and the

man she stayed with during part of Saturday night. I can't find her if I can't show the pictures around."

"Seems to me, seein' as trouble jus' follows in your footsteps, maybe you should try stickin' to ordinary tourist activities."

"Perhaps I shall," I agreed cunningly. "I think I'll go on a swamp tour tomorrow."

"Good idea." The lieutenant rose. "Wish I could go with you." He had circled the desk and now touched a finger to my hair, which was no doubt tumbled messily around my face now that the restraining scarf wrapped my latest injury. "Yo' hair sure does look pretty hangin' loose like that, Miz Blue. Mighty pretty."

"Thank you," I replied and left hurriedly. I certainly didn't want to give the lieutenant any mistaken ideas about my availability. Did he think, because I had visited the police station daily, that I was smitten with him? Surely not.

Having walked the short distance back to the hotel, I took out the small first aid kit I always carry on trips, disinfected my cut, and covered it up with three Band-Aids. Then I inspected my handbag and umbrella. The three bent umbrella ribs straightened out reasonably well when I pounded them with the heel of my shoe.

As for the handbag, its strap had been cut just above the buckle, so I unhooked and discarded the cut end and gouged a hole two inches above the remainder of the strap with my manicure scissors. Pleased with my makeshift repairs, I then took a well-earned rest on the bed while I studied the pictures of my dear friend, her hard-hearted husband, and Professor Torelli, whatever he was to her. Perhaps I should make one last call — to his hotel.

I did that, and you can imagine my dismay when I was told that he had checked out that morning. The clerk assured me that Dr. Torelli had left the hotel alone after having the concierge book him an early return flight on Delta Airlines and requesting that a cab to the airport be called.

Julienne was still missing, and Torelli had fled! Oh God. In a panic, I called Lieutenant Boudreaux, but he had left to attend a meeting at police headquarters. I was forced to leave a message with the derisive sergeant, the one who had acted as if I was the mugger rather than the muggee. Disheartened, I collapsed onto the cabbage roses and worried myself into a restless sleep. I find that even a troubled nap is better for the nerves than no nap at all, especially when one is exposed to the rigors of travel.

At five, the lieutenant called to say that Julienne had not been on the Delta flight with Torelli. It seems that policemen can get any information they seek. Delta Airlines would certainly have refused any request I made to check their passenger lists. But was that good news? That Julienne hadn't departed with Torelli? I thought not.

At five-thirty, Jason returned from the convention center and sat down beside me on the bed to give sympathetic ear to my findings and my fears. I didn't mention my little brush with the would-be robber, and he didn't notice the Band-Aids on my hand. Sometimes having a husband whose mind tends to be taken up with things scientific can be a boon; one doesn't have to worry him with the little things.

"The fact that she didn't leave with Torelli doesn't mean she's dead, Caro," he assured me. "We'll take the pictures you got and show them around the Quarter. Maybe someone has seen her."

Thank God for my dear husband. Although he understood my dismay and sympathized, he did not give way to panic. Instead, he proposed a course of action, and action is always both more reassuring and more productive than fruitless lamentation. I got up to shower and change. Fortunately, the hotel provided a shower cap, which I wrapped around my hand, while my own shower cap protected my hair.

We would search the Quarter from one end to the other with these new pictures, I told myself as I used the perfumed soap provided by the hotel. At home I buy less exotic soap products. I was feeling particularly good-humored because Jason had mentioned how very clever it was of me to think of the university web site as a source of pictures. He had also been most interested in my description of the Po'Boy Computer Café. I didn't mention the drug connection. Since neither of us would be going back, there was no need to bring that up.

14

Crawfish Etouffee

The two historic cuisines of New Orleans are Cajun and Creole, the first the child of Arcadian farmers and fishermen immigrating to the Louisiana swamps and bayous from Canada in the eighteenth century. Why any group of sensible people would travel so far to settle in a swamp is certainly a puzzle, but we do owe them a vote of thanks for their contribution to traditional New Orleans menus. Cajun food is hearty and rustic, spicy and rich in lard, while its cousin, Creole cooking (Creole means native of Louisiana), is more urban, more sophisticated, more delicate, and more likely to employ cream and butter in the French fashion. The original settlers were French, although the charms of French cooking and its innovations had to be reintroduced to the population of New

Orleans by the Ursuline sisters who ar-
rived in 1727.
Carolyn Blue,
Eating Out in the Big Easy

We set out with the idea of eating Cajun
and finding Julienne. My first thought was
to try K-Paul's Louisiana Kitchen for the
food part of our mission. It was just down
the street from our hotel, but the line was
far too long. Jason was amenable to by-
passing Chef Paul Prudhomme's establishment because it was listed as "expensive" in
the guidebook. Bacco's, the previous night,
had been expensive as well, especially to
two people becoming used to the lower
eating-out prices in El Paso, Texas. Of
course, the self-proclaimed well-to-do
Abbotts had not sprung for dinner. Why
had I thought they would?

Therefore, in the interest of economy in
research, we next headed for the Père
Antoine Restaurant on Royal Street, which
was also recommended by our guidebook
and listed in the "inexpensive" section.

Before we got there, however, we de-
toured to watch a marvelous street show
that featured two hip-high puppets in sunglasses and suits. One played a small piano

while the second sang into a microphone — with the help of a sound track. Puppet lip-synching, if you will. When the show was over and the crowd dispersing, having deposited donations in a box, Jason approached the puppeteer, a person in baseball cap, T-shirt, and unlaced, high-top tennis shoes. "Have you seen any of these people?" Jason showed him, or her, the new photo of Julienne, then the old one, then those of Linus and Nils.

"You 'ave not contributed to the box, monsieur," said the piano-player puppet, who was dangling from the hand of the puppet master.

Jason looked embarrassed, whether at the oversight or because he was being admonished by a puppet I couldn't say, but he did drop all the change from his pocket into the box. It made a respectable waterfall of tinkling sounds, but the puppeteer didn't look impressed. Perhaps he/she detected the fall of pennies. Jason hadn't checked to see what he was contributing.

"Don't recognize them," said the puppeteer with hardly a glance at the photos.

I flourished the old photo and asked dryly, "Not even this one?" I pointed to the picture of myself.

"Nope," said the puppeteer and, walking

the piano player over to the piano bench, began a spiel for the next performance.

I was disappointed. Julienne would have appreciated that show and would probably have given generously enough to be remembered had she seen it and had the puppeteer been willing to search his/her memory. We had almost reached Père Antoine's when, at the corner of Royal and Saint Peter, I stopped to admire an all-silver figure standing, statuelike, on the sidewalk. In fact, at first glance I took him for a statue but was almost immediately disabused of that notion when we resumed our stroll and he leapt toward us with a shriek. Startled, I shrieked in return. Perhaps I had been more traumatized by the mugging that afternoon than I realized.

Jason seemed not at all taken aback, as if being attacked by a silver-painted man on a city street was an everyday event. He whipped out the photos and presented them to the antic statue, who seemed very disappointed with that reaction. Mine had caused him to grin; Jason's was obviously unexpected. "Have you seen any of these people?" Jason asked.

"Why?" retorted the statue.

"We're looking for this lady." Jason displayed the computer printout of Julienne's university photo.

The statue examined each of the photos carefully while I fretted lest he leave silver paint on the only pictures I had. Finally, he passed back the three computer printouts but held onto my precious snapshot. "That's you," he said, smirking as he looked from me to my image on the picture. I said nothing. "And her I seen, too." He pointed to Julienne. "Same woman as in the other picture but even more of a babe. Younger, right?"

My heart speeded up. "When?" I asked eagerly. "When did you see her?"

"Shit if I know. It was like . . . on the weekend." He still held the old photograph, and I had to restrain the desire to wrest it from him.

"And him. She was with him," said silver skin.

Who? I looked eagerly to see whether he had identified Nils or Torelli. "Saturday? Sunday?" asked Jason.

"I dunno. Saturday?"

I tried to keep the disappointment off my face. The person he was pointing to, as having been with Julienne, was Philippe Delacroix, her brother, who was in the Midwest, not New Orleans. And if the puppeteer had seen Julienne on Saturday, it would have been late at night with Linus Torelli.

"What time?" I asked.

"Afternoon? Early evening?"

"Impossible," I snapped, turning away. Julienne had been arguing with Nils at the hotel or at Etienne's Saturday afternoon and early evening.

"So maybe it was Sunday." The fellow shrugged. "What I know is, I was in my pose — an' by the way you're supposed to show your appreciation with a tip — an' I jumped out at them just like I done with you, an' this guy . . ." He stabbed his finger at Philippe. ". . . he called me an asshole an' pushed me off the curb. If you know the bastard, just tell me where he is, an' I'll —"

"I'm afraid you're mistaken," said Jason calmly and tucked a dollar bill into the silver man's hand.

The statue held it up and muttered, "Damn cheap tourists," but we were already on our way down the street toward Père Antoine's and a dinner that was much more satisfying than the interviews we'd had thus far.

We both agreed that the silver statue had not seen Philippe and, therefore, had probably not seen Julienne either, especially since he couldn't even tell us on what day the alleged encounter had occurred. "He was just looking for a big tip, so he told us what he thought we wanted to hear," Jason guessed. I felt very discouraged. It was more disheartening to be lied to than to get no information at all.

After our disappointment, Père Antoine's was a pleasant surprise, featuring, as it did, a charming decor with flowers in front, large mirrors in back, and modest prices. I had crawfish étouffée, a thick stew made with roux, lard or some other artery-clogging fat, crawfish tails, and spices. Jason had the seafood platter, which included everything: scallops, catfish, shrimp, crab, and an item called Cajun popcorn (seasoned shrimp, deep-fried). It was a feast to which I helped myself — in the interests of my research, of course. We split an order of red beans and rice to round out our Cajun experience. One wonders if all Cajuns are fat. I certainly felt fat when we staggered out of Père Antoine. If I'd been wearing a belt, I'd have loosened it.

15

Mint Juleps

After our Cajun feast, we wandered up and down Bourbon Street. Even in this unwelcoming weather and on a Tuesday night, it was mobbed. I knew that people lived in the French Quarter, but I couldn't imagine how they endured the noise. Then I saw pictures that rang a bell. Julienne had said I had to see the tassel twirlers, and there they were, or their pictures at least. Presumably, the real performers were inside. I tugged at Jason's arm, pointed to the establishment, and shouted above the crowd noise that I wanted to go in.

"No, you don't," Jason assured me, looking embarrassed.

"Julienne mentioned it."

"But Carolyn . . ."

I ignored his reluctance and urged him inside. The place — whose name I hadn't even noticed, but surely there couldn't be two dens of tassel twirlers in the city —

was mobbed, mostly with men. A seedy looking person tried to lead us to a table, but Jason was immediately hailed by a large group of men who had that scientific look about them: rumpled clothes, suede-patched elbows, beards, ACS badges. Voices accustomed to lecturing in large halls to hordes of students roared over the cacophony, inviting my husband to join them in male camaraderie.

Then they saw me behind Jason and looked dismayed, like small boys caught looking at dirty photographs. Julienne and I had once caught our fifth-grade male schoolmates perusing such items. Julienne grabbed a few, and we dashed off, giggling hilariously. Once we had looked at our booty, we were rather puzzled and threw the pictures away, but those boys viewed us with fear and trembling for months, afraid we'd tattle, I suppose.

Having invited Jason, the table of scientists couldn't very well change their minds when they learned that I was part of the package, so I was duly introduced to a number of mighty intellects out on the town. The man by whom I was seated, a professor from Purdue, assured me that their presence here was in the nature of a research project. While Jason ordered a beer and I chose a mint julep, another of the New Orleans favorite cocktails on my must-try list, our table mates proved their scientific acumen with a learned discussion of the physics of tassel twirling. I sipped the mint julep and asked the waiter how it was made, taking notes for my book as he described the process.

Mint Julep

Make simple syrup by combining *1 cup sugar* with *2 cups water* in a medium saucepan. Bring to a boil, stirring. Reduce heat and simmer 5 to 10 minutes. Cool and store in the refrigerator in a covered jar.

For one cocktail, combine *3 tablespoons of simple syrup* and *6 fresh mint leaves* in an old-fashioned glass. Crush leaves with a wooden pestle.

Add crushed or cubed ice.

Add *1½ ounces of bourbon,* stir, and serve.

Then I turned my attention to the performer, a curvaceous young woman wearing only tassels, which were attached to strategic portions of her anatomy. While noisy men shouted their approval of her talents and the professors discussed, for my benefit I imagine, the rotational forces involved in tassel twirling, I marveled that the young woman seemed to have developed muscles in parts of the breast that I would have assumed to be without muscles, had I ever given the matter any thought.

She could twirl her tassels clockwise, counterclockwise, and both at once: left breast counterclockwise, right breast clockwise. Amazing! She could also execute similar tricks with her buttock tassels. It certainly wasn't as entertaining as the American Ballet Theatre doing *Giselle*, but the performance was unusual. Also, she was a very pretty girl and evidently quite athletic. I, for one, clapped enthusiastically at the end of her number while my husband's colleagues joined me, casting surreptitious glances in my direction all the while.

Then an intermission was announced and the bill presented. My drink cost $20! "Did you see this, Jason?" I asked, horrified.

"Yer payin' fer the entertainment, lady," said the waiter. "Ya thinkin' about not payin', I'll have to call the manager."

"She wasn't *that* good!" I muttered as Jason paid the bill. Fortunately, I didn't say it loudly, for the young lady herself appeared just then at our table and posed seductively as she asked if any of the gentlemen would care to buy her a drink.

The august members of the American Chemical Society looked flummoxed, but Jason, always considerate of the feelings of others, said that we would be delighted to. I must admit that I looked at him askance. The young woman sidled over, pulled up a chair from another table, and pushed in between us, giving me a challenging look. She had the most amazing eyelashes when you saw her up close: so thick and long that one had to anticipate them tearing loose from their anchors at any moment and taking her natural eyelashes with them. I winced to think of how painful that would be.

Poor girl. She was obviously in a profession with dangers beyond the obvious: breast sprains, lascivious men, and the health hazards of dancing practically naked in the cold and damp of a New Orleans winter. Would they let her work if she had the sniffles? A woman, no matter how pretty, is not very seductive with a runny nose. Julienne's mother had always advised us to break a date rather than appear in public with a red nose and a handkerchief at the ready.

The tassel twirler was batting those eye fans at Jason as he asked what she would like to drink. She opted for champagne. I said, "I doubt that the champagne is very good here, but this drink is nice — a mint julep." I gestured to my glass. "I even have the recipe, if you're interested."

The young woman looked flabbergasted. "Well . . . OK," she responded.

"She'll have champagne," said the waiter.

"Nonsense," I retorted. "Since my husband and I are paying for her drink, she can have whatever she wants." I turned to her. "Maybe you'd rather try a hot buttered rum. It *is* a nasty night."

"Tell me about it. I slipped and fell on my butt walkin' over for the first show."

I nodded sympathetically. "That's very painful. I did that once at Disneyland. We were taking our children to see that silly It's a Small World After All thing."

"I seen that," said the young woman. "I liked it."

"I did, too," Jason agreed. "It was the only time our children stopped whining to go on the roller coaster, but poor Carolyn was in agony sitting through that ride. This is my wife, Carolyn, by the way, and I'm Jason, Jason Blue."

"Desiree," said the young woman, who then turned pugnaciously to the waiter and announced that maybe she would have that hot buttered rum. "I ain't never had one," she said to me.

"Oh, they're delicious," I assured her. "And you must be chilly." Although the room was warm with the presence of so many people, the door to the street opened repeatedly to admit new customers and damp, cold drafts. Desiree had goose bumps surrounding her tassels.

"You're very talented," I added, trying to make her feel at ease socially since she seemed to be rather out of her element. Perhaps she wasn't used to being bought a drink by couples. The other professors certainly seemed to be visibly astounded at the situation.

"Say, you two ain't into any kinky three-some stuff, are you?" Desiree asked suspiciously. I presume that was her stage name; what mother would actually name her daughter Desiree? "I'm an exotic dancer. I'm not no whore."

"Of course not," I agreed.

"We wanted you to look at some pictures," said Jason hastily.

"Dirty pictures?" She scowled.

"Hot buttered rum." The waiter slapped it down on the table and presented Jason with the bill.

"Why am I paying for entertainment?" he asked. "Miss Desiree *is* the entertainment, not the entertainee."

"Oh, pay the man, Jason," I said and took the pictures from my purse. "We're looking for my friend." I pointed to Julienne. "And anyone she might have been seen with." I pointed to Nils, then to Linus.

"Well, I got a memory for faces. Men, they only look at tits. Women look at faces." She was gulping the hot buttered rum with obvious relish. "Now this is more like it," she said and bent over the pictures. "Him!" she said quickly. "Saw him here last night." She pointed at Nils.

"With Julienne?" I asked eagerly. That damn Nils. He knew where she was; he'd actually seen her and wouldn't even tell me. No wonder he refused to report her missing.

"Nah. He was with a bunch of guys," said Desiree. "They all had two drinks each, watched my set, didn't want to buy me a drink, but this guy —" She pointed to Nils again. "He said he liked my hair an' give me ten bucks."

Nils had liked Desiree's hair? That was sad. It was black and curly like Julienne's, only much longer, possibly a wig.

"Big blond guy," Desiree continued. "Over the hill, but I'll bet he was cute ten years ago. He coulda put his shoes under my bed. Ya know what I mean? Least he din' sound like none a these mush-mouthed Southerners. Now me, I'm from New Jersey. Workin' the exotic dance circuit an' ended up here 'cause I had a boyfriend wanted to . . ."

I'm afraid I stopped listening to Desiree, who was pouring her heart out to me. Probably she didn't get much attention from mother figures, although it was hard to think of myself as the mother of an exotic dancer. Still, the disappointment in finding out that she had not seen Julienne, just Nils, was overwhelming. As was my anger that Nils would be out ogling twirling tassels on young breasts when his wife was missing and in God knows what sort of trouble.

Desiree wound down and announced that she had to get back and change for her next set. Change? Did she have different tassels for each appearance? Different colors? Longer or shorter? Maybe they operated on batteries, and the batteries had to be changed. I could understand that. Tassels that suddenly refused to twirl would not be conducive to the sexual titillation inherent in her performance. I was dying to ask but didn't want to embarrass her, so I stood up and offered my hand. "It's been so nice to meet you, my dear," I said. "I do wish you continued success in your career." I was ready to go home and give up for tonight. Jason, angry that he'd been levied a cover charge on Desiree's drink, paid the bill, and left the waiter a two-cent tip.

"I've always wanted to do that to a rude waiter," Jason murmured with satisfaction as we threaded our way through the crowd of tassel-twirling aficionados and out into the street.

16

A Salad from Hell

I woke up Wednesday with the sinking realization that Julienne had now been missing since Saturday night. Others might have seen her Sunday, but I hadn't, and I had no idea why she hadn't called and no reassurance that she was safe. Therefore, I had to entertain the suspicion that she wasn't, although that suspicion did not mean I would stop looking.

When my mother died during my eleventh year after an eighteen-month fight against cancer, I had run from the house, grief-stricken and terrified of what the future might hold. Who would look after me now that she was gone? I knew that my father loved me, but his interests were academic, not nurturing. And so I had, in essence, run away from my fears, hidden from them, secreting my afflicted self in a little half cave on the banks of a nearby creek where I sometimes went to be alone.

I fled to the place where I had occasionally found comfort in solitude.

And Julienne had found me there. She had not said, "Oh well, Caro's run away. We'll just have to wait until she shows up again." Julienne had come looking for me because she was my friend. And she had found me and taken me home to her own house and her own mother, who was warm and comforting and quite willing to adopt a half orphan into the family. From then on, although I lived in the same house with my father, my comfort lay in Julienne's house with my surrogate mother. Fannie Delacroix was a Southern belle who was as affectionate as my own mother had been but in all other ways so different that her love was not a reminder of what I had lost.

So Julienne had rescued me from grief, and I intended to do the same for her: rescue her from grief, or anger, or humiliation, or whatever emotion had driven her from the dinner party. Since she hadn't flown home, she must still be here in New Orleans. And I intended to find her.

As my first step on this new day of the search, I spent yet another hour waiting at Café du Monde and considering where, if she did not reappear, I should look next. It seemed to me that the swamp was my best choice. We had planned to take one of the boats. She had picked up her camera after leaving the dinner party — a shoulder bag, possibly containing a change of clothes, and the camera — and she had expressed a desire to Torelli to photograph the swamp. Remembering that, I paid my bill, dusted the sugar from my jacket, tucked my damaged umbrella under my arm and, map in hand, set out to purchase a ticket on a Louisiana Swamp Tour van. Jean Lafitte Swamp Tours, Captain Terry's, Magnificent Alligator Adventures, Cajun Cap'n — there were many to choose from.

Once on the docks, which were out at the end of a rural road, I went from booth to booth, waiting through lines so that I could show Julienne's picture to the ticket sellers. I alternated ticket sellers with boat captains, a weathered lot, many with barely decipherable Cajun accents. No one remembered Julienne. One captain, who had a stuffed alligator head mounted behind the wheel of his boat, asked me why I thought he ever looked at the tourists when he had "snakes, an' snags, an' gators" to keep his eye peeled for. The last ticket taker, a woman less patient than the rest, glared at me through the wooden frame of her booth. She had dark, rough skin and a crooked nose and wore a raveling cardigan sweater buttoned over a flowered dress. "You come to my window, you buy a ticket," she said, a look of ferocious determination on her face. Obviously, anyone taking up space in her line was expected to come up with swamp fare. I bought a ticket and went back to tour with the alligator captain.

I was here; Julienne wasn't, so I might as well see this swamp about which she had talked so much. I stationed myself at the rail adjacent to the wheel as we pulled slowly away from the dock. The captain had already begun his spiel over the loud-speaker system as he piloted his boat, the *Gator Belle*, out upon the brown waters.

You may think of a swamp as suffocatingly green. Not in winter, not near New Orleans. The vegetation was abundant on the shores but ranged in color from bone white to a brown green that reminded me of desert bushes. Some of the trees appeared full and healthy; some bare of leaves with thin branches haloing the trunks like ghost thickets. Some thrust up black and dead from the water's edge, raising twisted limbs to a white sky, and many hung heavy with the mysterious, killing moss that blanketed and stifled life.

Occasionally, there was a white, bony skeleton of a tree, leaning precariously toward extinction, still weighted down with its burden of moss, and the moss was white, too, having sucked the life out of its host before dying itself. No wonder Julienne had wanted to photograph this. I took pictures myself as we cut through the water, leaving a wide, white wake behind us that washed into the bushes where the banks narrowed toward one another.

Our captain pointed out a cemetery on the shore, its pure white box graves and crosses overhung by great moss-laden trees. A rough barricade of rocks separated the graveyard from the bayou. The greenest sight in the swamp was the grass in this cemetery, but that grass was not fertilized by the bodies of the dead, for corpses had to be buried aboveground here because the water level was just below the surface. While the captain explained this, I screwed up my courage for a question, afraid that my inquiry would meet with the same brusque retort as the last I had made to him. He was an off-putting sight with his alligator trophy, his mirrored dark glasses, and his camouflage fatigues — more like a mercenary or right-wing, backcountry militia person than a Cajun boat captain.

"Do these boats run at night?" I asked timidly, after tapping him on the arm.

He ignored me and pointed out a small shack and tottering pier passing by on our right. I knew that he had heard me, so I waited for my answer. He pointed out a wide-nosed alligator, which looked as if it might slide into the water and head our way. The sight of such an ugly, dangerous creature sent a shiver up my spine.

As we passed a narrow outlet, clogged with fallen branches, I repeated my question about night tours. The captain turned slightly in my direction, mouth grim. "No ma'am. Da *Gator Belle* don't cruise at night."

"Do any of the swamp tour boats?" I persisted. How had Julienne planned to photograph the swamp at night if no boats ran and she could get no one to accompany her?

"Nothin' to see. It's dark," he muttered. Then he pointed out a snake undulating in our direction. As it was the same color as the water, it could only be detected by the path it cut.

"The boat could have a headlight," I pointed out.

He turned into a narrow passage where the river branched.

"Dis swamp is huge, lady. You live here all your life, you might not know all da passages. So you think someone's gonna take tourists in where dey cain't see nothin' an might git 'em lost an' . . ." He shrugged, disgruntled, and began to talk about the creatures, other than man, who lived in the swamps — alligators, egrets, black bear, feral hogs —

My imagination took off at the mention of feral hogs. Were they akin to wild boar? I could hardly forget the terrifying depictions of wild boar, snarling, viciously tusked, hair bristling, as they were pictured on medieval tapestries. And Julienne wanted to go out among such creatures? At night?

"Herons, beaver, deer, osprey —"

"What if someone wanted to take pictures here at night?' I asked him.

"Dey'd be a damn fool," he said shortly. Other tourists were beginning to mutter because I kept interrupting the lecture.

"But if someone did? How would they go about it?"

"Rent a boat, but don't do it, lady. You'd never come back. Only a tourist would think up such a damn fool —"

"This lady is a native," I said hurriedly. "And she wanted to. And now she's missing."

221

"Raised up in da swamp?" he asked after a few comments on swamp owls.

"In New Orleans."

"New Orleans don' make you're no swamp rat. If she's missin', she's pro'bly dead."

I must have looked distraught. Indeed, I was biting my lip to hold the tears back.

"Check da boat rental places," he advised reluctantly.

"Where are they?"

He gave me a few names and directions, which I scribbled on the back of the directions to my camera, the French version. "But if she's a native, she wouldn't be stupid enough to do it. She'd need someone to run da boat, someone who knew da swamp, an' still she'd be in trouble. Now go up front, will ya, lady?" And he began to lecture again as he took us deeper into territory that was more vegetation-choked and more sinister looking. Obediently, I strolled toward the front of the boat, from which I saw more alligators, one actually nosing the boat as we idled in a side channel while the captain talked about raccoons. Somehow or other, raccoons were a comfort to me. We'd had raccoons knocking over our garbage cans when Julienne, her family, and I vacationed at their cabin on the shores of a lake north of home.

Sweet days. Fishing from an old rowboat, gathering wildflowers, giggling over boys, setting off fireworks that burst in dazzling showers above the lake waters, taking home a bear cub. Oh lord, that had been Julienne's idea. Always chasing the wild and dangerous — that was Julienne. Her father had been furious when the equally furious mother bear had torn down his shed to retrieve the cub stowed there by Julienne. In fact, because he was in one of his fierce moods, Mrs. Delacroix had to talk her husband out of shooting the mother bear. If anyone had the audacity to penetrate these eerie swamps at night for photographs, Julienne would. She had taken pictures of the cub, and then of the mother bear battering the shed, and even of Mr. Delacroix, rifle in hand. I'd have to canvass renters of boats.

As I left the *Gator Belle* to catch the van back to the city, the captain called after me, "Your friend wouldna been dat dumb."

Dumb? No. But venturesome? I was afraid she might, or maybe not. Maybe she had been testing Torelli, seeing how far she could push him. That would be like her, too. I remember the Thanksgiving holiday when we were sophomores in college. She was after her father to raise her allowance and suggested that if he didn't have the money, maybe he should play the stock market and get rich. The first two times she made that suggestion, Mr. Delacroix ignored her. He'd been virtually silent during that vacation. The third time, after he'd begun to perk up, Mr. Delacroix got an unholy gleam in his eye and said, "Good idea, Twinkletoes."

Julienne and I had taken ballet lessons as children, and for years afterward she had to put up with that paternal nickname. Whereas, I don't think my father ever realized that I was about to put on toe shoes and become the next Maria Tallchief when my mother finally agreed to free me from the hated classes.

But I digress. Three months later, by dint of buying futures, taking out stock options, and other risky ventures, Mr. Delacroix was rich, and Mrs. Delacroix was on the verge of a nervous breakdown. I felt better for having remembered that incident. Julienne had tested her father's courage, with marvelously lucrative results. Perhaps she'd tested Torelli's courage, as well, found him wanting, and left. So who was she testing now by staying away? Me? I hoped not.

Because the van wasn't scheduled to leave for ten minutes and I didn't care to sample any of the uninteresting food offered by vendors in wharf shacks, I stood out of the crowd at the edge of the pier, leaning against a pole and studying the bayou. I could understand Julienne's fascination. There was an otherworldly quality to the brown landscape with its twisted, bearded trees. I had just raised my camera to take one last picture when I was so rudely jostled by a passing tourist that my desperate attempt to grab the pole did not serve to keep me on the boards. Down I plunged into the brown water, my panic-stricken mind conjuring up all the snakes and alligators I had seen on the tour. When I surfaced, slimy, rotting swamp greens, a salad from hell, trailed from my mouth, and I was still clutching my camera in one hand, flailing wildly as my clothing dragged me under again.

17

Potato Galettes

German immigrants, lured to New Orleans with promises of paradise by the financial scam artist John Law, settled down to farm and were soon feeding the less agriculturally inclined French settlers. Often they intermarried with the French or adapted their German names to the local language. One of the ironies of New Orleans cuisine is that its famed French bread and pastries were baked then and are now by German bakers. At La Madeleine, with a bite of luscious cream puff melting in my mouth, I found myself wondering whether Madeleine had once been Minna or Gretchen.

Carolyn Blue,
Eating Out in the Big Easy

I fought desperately to the surface, where I heard shrieks and a foghorn voice shouting,

"Tourist in the water." Then a life preserver splashed down beside me, and I was saved — at least if I could get out before the hungry swamp creatures attacked. I went under, bobbed up, spit out more slimy growths, and hooked an arm through the ring.

"Hang on," the foghorn roared. I clung for dear life and, trailing nasty, rotting fronds, was dragged through the water to rickety steps that had been nailed haphazardly to the wharf poles. Grasping the first crossbar with one hand, I maneuvered to stuff my camera into the handbag that hung from my arm. Now wasn't that foolish? Here I was trying to save a camera that would never function again, when an alligator might even now be cutting a path in my direction.

Arms and legs trembling, dripping liquid mud, I began to climb. When I felt a crossbar tilt under my foot, I almost fainted, but by then a sturdy Cajun on the wharf had grasped my arm. Not waiting for my clumsy efforts, he hauled me to safety, where he proceeded to lecture me in an angry voice. I assume he blamed me for my mishap, but his accent was very thick, so I couldn't be sure.

"I was shoved," I announced, incensed.

He paid no attention but dragged me toward the waiting van.

"I cain't take her. She'll ruin my seats," said the driver, a tough-looking woman wearing rolled socks and a skirt far too short for a woman with legs as burly as hers.

"I want the police called," I snapped.

A noisy argument erupted among captains, van driver, ticket sellers, po'boy vendors, and tourists, who didn't want to ride with anyone who looked and smelled as bad as I did. As they quarreled, I shivered. I was cold, and I was wet and miserable, and I wanted to go back to the hotel. In fact, I wanted to go back to my own house in El Paso and never return to this benighted state again. "If you don't take me home immediately, I'll sue."

A number of the combatants stopped talking, but not the tourists.

I narrowed my eyes at the van driver. "I'll get an attorney and just . . . just sue the socks off the lot of you."

She glanced uneasily at her socks, as if I planned to demand that she hand them over immediately in reparation.

"And I'll file police charges."

People began to back away from me.

"And write to the newspapers about the

dangers of this tour." A few more threats of that sort, which warmed me up and evidently alarmed the swamp entrepreneurs, earned me a solo ride to the door of my hotel. I didn't tip the sock lady, either. I was still furious.

And even more furious when the hotel personnel tried to keep me from going upstairs. They didn't believe anyone as disreputable looking as I could be a paying guest. Well, too bad about them. I'd probably caught some horrible disease from that disgusting swamp water, so I didn't care if I dripped mud on all their precious antiques as long as I got to my room and washed myself clean. I even called the desk and demanded that a bellhop come to carry away my sopping, muddy, swamp-rot-fronded clothes, which I threw out into the hall. I never wanted to see them again. I couldn't imagine that any washing machine would be equal to the task of making them clean enough to wear safely.

Then I spent perhaps an hour under hot water in the shower washing my body, my hair, even the inside of my mouth. Once sufficiently clean and dry, I considered whether or not I needed a preventive antibiotic to protect me from dangerous tropical diseases. It was then that I noticed my most immediate need: food. I was starving.

Forgetting the microbes and parasites that might be attacking me internally, I used the hotel hair dryer on my stringy hair, donned clean clothes, the wearing of which completely ruined my carefully planned wardrobe schedule, and set out for Jackson Square. There is nothing like a terrible fright to make one ravenous, and it took only a glance at my list of eateries that needed visiting to settle on La Madeleine.

It was a good choice. The ravishing French bakery smells were wonderfully comforting to a person in my traumatized state. Nonetheless, I knew that I needed something more nourishing than pastry, so having dragged myself away from the tempting breads, croissants, cream puffs, tarts, éclairs and so forth displayed in the glass cases up front, I bought a potato galette, a salad, and a glass of white wine. Then I sat down by a window to eat, regain my equilibrium, and consider my options.

My galette was unbelievably good — a crispy, thick pancake the likes of which I could eat every day for lunch if I had the opportunity. Unfortunately, I probably never shall. I liked it enough that I even tried to reproduce it at home, but the results were disastrous. I produced a galette that was deliciously brown and crispy on the outside, but inside an unappetizing combination of raw egg and crunchy, uncooked potato bits turned even my husband away from the table. Perhaps I'll find a recipe one day and overcome my aversion to cooking enough to try again. I may well have been so distracted by my terrible experience on the swamp tour that I completely misinterpreted how the dish had been made.

That's quite possible, but I did manage to calm down enough to reject the idea of going home with my tail, figuratively, between my legs. Also I had had an idea, an idea that should have occurred to me much earlier. I would call Diane, Julienne's daughter, at boarding school. If Julienne had contacted anyone, it would be her child. No matter what Nils said about my friend's lack of maternal instinct, I knew that she loved Diane and that Diane loved her. Perhaps Julienne had left New Orleans and flown to see her daughter. Oh, I hoped so. I could forgive her for having caused me so much anxiety if only she was safe.

And there was nothing dangerous about making one long-distance telephone call. I couldn't be mugged or drowned while doing so. I couldn't even be bruised by crazy voodoo priestesses. In fact it seemed to me, on reflection, that an undue number of dangerous situations had befallen me during my short stay in the Big Easy. Easy indeed. Easy to run afoul of the crazy, the rude, and the criminal! Should I call Lieutenant Boudreaux to tell him that I had been pushed off a pier?

Well, probably not. I didn't want him to think I was paranoid. Or disaster prone. People tend to avoid the disaster prone, and I might need his help if I ever uncovered any evidence of Julienne's whereabouts.

18

Chocolate Éclairs

I didn't resist that pastry counter after all. Before I left La Madeleine, I gazed longingly through the glass and decided that I might need more sustenance to get me through another afternoon of investigation. Therefore, I bought a chocolate éclair and carried it back to the hotel, where I put in the first of several calls that yielded surprising information.

A very Boston-sounding lady at the prep school attended by Julienne's adopted daughter reluctantly agreed to call Diane off the soccer field to take an "extremely important long-distance call." That's the way I put it to Ms. Ivy League. Where had she gone to school? Radcliffe? Mount Holyoke? She'd probably majored in something delightful like medieval history, as I had, but she'd been offered jobs while I'd been asked how many words a minute I could type and if I took shorthand. Medieval history wasn't seen as a marketable commodity in the Middle West when I graduated.

But then would I have wanted to teach in a girls' school instead of marrying Jason and raising Gwen and Chris, then beginning this new career to fill my "empty nest"? Career in mind, I took a bite of the chocolate éclair and made relevant notes while I waited: "real cream whipped to a thick, rich froth . . . smooth, dark chocolate shining on lighter-than-an-angel's-wing pastry . . ."

"Hi, Aunt Carolyn. What's up?"

My weight, I thought in silent answer to Diane's question. She sounded out of breath and cheerful. Hurriedly, I swallowed my second delectable bite (although it was a crime not to savor every smidgen) and greeted Julienne's child. "Is your mother visiting you, Diane?" I asked.

"No. Is she planning to?"

"Well, have you heard from her this week? Or anytime since Saturday?"

"Not a word, but she promised me a neat present from New Orleans before she left. Hey, I thought you were there, too."

What should I say to that? I didn't want to alarm Diane, and she didn't seem to have any information on Julienne, which was disappointing.

"Boy, everyone's looking for Mom. Is she hiding out or something? Did she meet some gorgeous hunk and elope?" Diane giggled.

I wondered if Julienne's daughter had suspicions about the relationship between Julienne and the missing Professor Torelli.

"Dad called Monday night asking if I'd heard from her, and I said, 'Like hey, Daddy, haven't *you* heard from her?' "

Like hey, Daddy? Was Diane rooming with some valley girl from California who was having an unfortunate influence on her speech patterns?

"And you know what? I don't think he answered. Aunt Caro, I hope you're not going to tell me they're fighting again. I told them I absolutely would not tolerate a divorce in the family. I mean it. I'll run away from home. Well, from school, and I've got a bunch of tests coming up, so that would really screw up my chances of getting into a good university and . . ."

It was interesting that Nils had called asking about his wife. Did that mean he wasn't responsible for Julienne's disappearance — at least in any physical way? Or was he concocting an alibi for himself? "I didn't do anything to her," he'd say. "Ask our daughter. I called trying to *find* Julienne."

"And then Uncle Philippe called," Diane was saying. "When was that? Saturday, I think. Weird as usual, of course."

Philippe had called? "What time?" I asked.

"What time what? Was he weird? He's always weird."

"Did he call?"

"I don't know. Afternoon. Before we drove over to Exeter for the dance at Phillips Academy."

So Philippe had called before Julienne disappeared. What for? Weird in what way? Just because he rarely spoke to me and never seemed to like me when we were young didn't make him weird — just not my favorite person.

"Actually, now that I think of it, I left a message for Mom at her hotel. I told her what he'd said. I'll bet she got a laugh out of that."

"When did you leave the message?"

"Saturday night," Diane replied. "Eight o'clock or so. Kind of pathetic, don't you think, that my date was so boring I could take time out to call my mom and never worry about missing a thing?"

Had Julienne received that message later? Obviously, she'd still been at Etienne's — or somewhere else — when Diane called. Or possibly she hadn't answered in the room because she thought that her husband was at the other end of the line. But Julienne might well have picked up the message when she left the hotel with the camera she'd come for. I'd have to check. "Tell me about Philippe," I suggested as I tried to put everything together.

"Oh, he's so grumpy and gloomy. You know?"

Well, that wasn't news. No one in the family had ever said so, but as I grew older, I'd begun to suspect that Philippe was subject to bouts of depression.

"He's decided — you won't believe this." She giggled. "He's decided that the laws of primogeniture entitle him to all of Gram's estate, instead of the half he got. Primogeniture? How screwy is that?"

I wanted to tell her what a difference primogeniture had made in the history of Europe, but I managed to restrain myself. As interesting a topic as it was (the accrual of land and power in fewer hands when only elder sons inherited), it didn't really relate to the disappearance of my friend in any way, aside from the effect it might have had on her brother's thinking. Because now I remembered how cavalierly I had dismissed the identification by the silver-statue man of Philippe as Julienne's companion on a street in the Quarter and his description of Philippe pushing him off the curb. Was that the action of someone who was depressed? I had no idea, since I'm not given to depression. And what was that fancy school teaching Diane if not the importance of primogeniture in the history of Western Europe?

"My nutty uncle has decided that Mom should just hand over everything she inherited from Gram. Can you imagine?"

I sighed. Julienne's mother had died just this year in an automobile accident — a matter of a pickup truck running a stop sign on a rural road. It was the second such death in the family, although Mr. Delacroix's accident, which occurred years ago, had involved only his car and been virtually inexplicable. The police had finally decided that he must have fallen asleep at the wheel. Both deaths had hit Julienne hard, and I, too, found her mother's death devastating.

When I went home to visit my father, I'd always ended up spending most of my time with Julienne's mother, even when my friend wasn't in town, although often she was. Such lovely visits those had been. I'd learned to love New Orleans cooking before I ever visited the city because Fannie Delacroix was a wonderful cook and showed off her talents when either of her "sweet girls," as she called us, came back.

"I told Uncle Philippe she was in New Orleans, and he'd have to take it up with her. Like she'd give him the money or Gram's silver or any of that stuff. No way. She's already promised a lot of it to me. Of course, I didn't say that to my uncle because I didn't want to send him into a funk. Anyway, he said he was heading straight for New Orleans to talk to Mom. Can you imagine? It's the middle of the semester, and he's not invited to the ACS meeting, I shouldn't think."

Probably not. Philippe was on the faculty at a medical school.

"So I gave him her address, and I left a message at her hotel warning her that he might show up. Or then again, he might take whatever medication he's supposed to take and get sensible. You never know with him."

And if he hadn't taken his medication and gotten sensible? Had he flown to New Orleans? Was Julienne with him? Maybe he'd arrived, met her, gone completely to pieces, and she'd had to commit him. It had happened before, at least I suspected as much. Her parents had never talked about Philippe's moods. But that scenario didn't explain why Julienne hadn't been in touch with me. It might be an embarrassing situation if her colleagues knew about it, but surely she wouldn't try to hide Philippe's problems from me if they had become her responsibility after her mother's death.

"Aunt Carolyn, you're not saying much." For the first time I heard a note of worry in Diane's voice. "Is something wrong?"

What could I tell her? That her mother was missing and I now had to try to find her uncle to see if he was involved? Or her father? Or her mother's alleged lover? This was not a situation one wanted to explain to a teenage girl. "Diane," I said, rather cunningly I thought, "Diane, I think your mother has skipped town."

"Skipped town?"

"Absolutely. She must have got your message and headed for the hills." Could that be true? I suppose there would be times when one got tired of dealing with the severely depressed, especially when everything else was going wrong.

Diane had started to giggle, which was better than panic.

"Thanks for the information, dear. I'll keep

in touch, and you study hard, you hear?" I gave it my best Southern accent, which all Delacroix family members agree is ludicrous.

Diane certainly found it so, for she replied, "Oh, Aunt Carolyn, you don't sound *anything* like my mother or Gram either. You'll just never make it as a Southern belle."

"I am deeply hurt," I retorted. "I thought I was improving."

I finished my chocolate éclair as I considered my next move. M-m-m. The stiffly whipped cream was delicious, and wasn't there a hint of vanilla? Or were my taste buds remembering the way my mother whipped cream before she became ill? With a little vanilla and sugar. Oh, those strawberry shortcakes she made! With wild strawberries we picked ourselves, laughing and eating as many as we picked, each of us in wide-brimmed straw hats to protect our fair skin. Mother had been blonde, too.

Had she used a biweekly rinse on her hair? I didn't know. That was something I'd probably have found out had she lived into my teens and beyond. *Well, enough of that,* I told myself sternly as I popped the last bit of chocolate éclair into my mouth. But still, I thought I'd ask at La Madeleine how they doctored their cream — if at all.

241

19

Missing Siblings

Having finished my chocolate éclair and dropped the doily and bag into a flowered wastebasket by the French provincial desk, I returned to the bed to think about Philippe and Julienne. If he hadn't come to New Orleans, it didn't much matter whether Julienne had picked up the message from her daughter. Or did it? On the off chance that he might make the trip, had Julienne disappeared in order to avoid an unpleasant interview with her brother? It was possible. I seldom saw Philippe these days, and Julienne didn't talk about him much, but when she did, it was with a sort of weary forbearance. She certainly didn't laugh about her brother as Diane had. But was she afraid of him?

After dialing the long-distance information operator, I asked for the number of the medical school where Philippe taught. Would Julienne skip her convention obligations to avoid a confrontation with her brother? I asked myself. For that matter, were depressed people dangerous? Logic told me that the only danger they posed would be to themselves.

Having obtained the number, I then called the medical school and asked to be connected to Dr. Delacroix's office. Three rings. Four. Soon I'd be transferred to an answering machine, and what would I say? Philippe's failure to answer his phone at the office didn't mean that he'd gone to New Orleans. He could be teaching a class, supervising students, taking a coffee break, gone home for the day. Should I try to get his home number?

"Dr. Delacroix appears to be out of his office," said a pleasant voice, surely the operator who had answered originally, not some recording. "Would you like to leave a message? Or be transferred to the chairman of his department?" the real female person asked.

I made a snap decision and opted to talk to the chair. If Philippe had left town, I'd find out. If he was at home, I could get a number, unless the number was unlisted. Maybe I'd use Julienne's name if the chairman proved unwilling to give me a home number. Maybe I'd even claim to be

Julienne. At this point, I was prepared to be shameless in my quest.

"Who's this?" a male voice demanded. "Is that you, Delacroix?"

"No," I replied, taken aback. "I'm Carolyn Blue, but I — I'm looking for Dr. Delacroix," I stammered. So much for impersonating Julienne. I'd never be a successful liar. "I'm a friend of his sister."

"Well, I'm looking for Dr. Delacroix myself," snapped the chairman, or so I presumed him to be.

"He's missing?" I asked, astounded. Both of them were missing? What in the world did that mean?

"As far as I can tell. The man's not in his office, not at home, and not showing up for his classes, his appointments, or his meetings."

"For how long?" I asked.

"Devil if I know. He didn't appear for his Monday class. You say his sister's looking for him, too?"

"Well, I —" Would the chairman be interested if I told him Julienne was missing and that I was looking for both of them?

"If she finds him, have her tell him for me that tenure isn't the guarantee of lifelong employment it once was."

That was definitely a threat. "Philippe

244

didn't mention that he would be absent?" I asked.

"Not a word. To anyone. And he'd damn well better have a good excuse. Just because he's brilliant but too weird to practice medicine doesn't mean we'll put up with this kind of behavior on the teaching end. What kind of example does this set for the students? They'll think they can just take off and leave their patients in the lurch."

I'd known a few doctors who obviously thought that anyway. A case in point was a pediatrician who had moved his office halfway across town without warning me. I discovered his defection when I rushed Chris in one day with his thumb, so I thought, half severed, and found a locked door from which the name had been removed. A janitor, exiting the men's room with mop and bucket, told me that my pediatrician had decamped, although he didn't know to what new address.

At that point I was so terrified that I took Chris to the emergency room — at considerably more expense, I might add, than it would have cost to visit his doctor, had the doctor been considerate enough to tell us he was moving. "Well, good luck trying to teach consideration and responsibility to a group of medical students," I said, an unfortunate remark that just slipped out on the heels of my angry recollections.

"What was that?" demanded the chairman. "Are you one of these ungrateful patients who think they should get unlimited time with their doctors for no money? Well, I can tell you what's going to come of that attitude. No doctors. Or only doctors who can't speak English. Maybe we real *American* doctors should go on strike. Close up the medical schools. Let disease . . ."

Pity the poor patient who looked to this man for sympathy and a kindly bedside manner, I thought. He had the personality of a porcupine. "If I can find Dr. Delacroix, I'll pass on your message about tenure," I said loudly enough to interrupt his tirade. "Do you have any suggestions about where he might be?"

"None," snapped the angry chairman. "If I knew, I'd have tracked him down myself."

And that was the end of our conversation. What had I learned? That Philippe might be in New Orleans. Now I needed to know if Julienne had received her daughter's message about Philippe when she came back Saturday night to pick up her camera.

Could Philippe have been in New Orleans even then? I called the front desk and explained that Mrs. Magnussen's daughter wanted to know if Mrs. Magnussen had received the telephone message left Saturday night. The clerk, somewhat dubious over the propriety of releasing such information, finally agreed to check when I assured her that I didn't want to know what the message was, just whether my friend had received it. Having decided to be helpful, the desk clerk informed me that Mrs. Magnussen had actually retrieved two voice-mail messages Saturday evening and made one phone call. The call had been made around nine o'clock.

Was the call she made local? I asked. The clerk didn't feel free to discuss that but suggested that Dr. Magnussen could look at the billing himself and tell me.

Given Nils's attitude toward any queries about his missing wife, I doubted that he would. In fact, it occurred to me that the desk clerk, looking at telephone records, would have no way of knowing which Magnussen had heard the messages and made the call. Still, nine o'clock, she'd said. It had to be Julienne. Nils was still at the restaurant at nine. Then I was reminded of all the calls I myself had made that evening, none of which Julienne had responded to. Oh well. I had to admit that I hadn't left messages. While tapping the telephone impatiently, thinking, I noticed that my index fingernail on the left hand needed filing.

So what did this information mean? I wondered as I fished a nail file from my toiletry bag. Two messages? Well, one was obviously the call from Diane. But who had left the second message? Philippe? Or Linus Torelli? And whom had Julienne called?

She could have ignored a message from her brother and fled to Torelli, arranging the safe harbor by phone. Or perhaps she had called Philippe and agreed to meet him the next day, then set out for Torelli's hotel. Her colleague hadn't mentioned whether her appearance that night was expected, and now I couldn't ask him. So if she had an appointment to meet her brother, it would have been sometime after she waited for me at Café du Monde. Of course, having left Etienne's before the plans were made, she didn't know that I would be preparing for the Gospel Brunch, not café au lait and beignets on Jackson Square with her. Had she been planning to tell me about Philippe's imminent arrival?

She might even have been angry when I didn't show up. That would explain why she'd never contacted me. Well, not really. Even angry, Julienne was a considerate friend, no matter what Nils said about her.

I shook off these speculations and returned to my plans. Torelli was gone. I knew that. But I could call around town trying to locate Philippe or at least find out if he had been here. A new telephone search was obviously my next move. I began calling New Orleans hotels, asking for Dr. Philippe Delacroix. Many hotels later and having exhausted French Quarter listings, I found him registered at the Superior Inn. My guidebook said it was "inexpensive" and "five minutes from the central business district."

The more-or-less helpful desk clerk told me that Dr. Delacroix had checked in Sunday at noon and was still registered. In answer to my question about a possible visit from his sister, she remembered a woman, wearing tight jeans, a form-fitting, low-necked knit top, and high heels. "She didn't look like a doctor's sister to me, honey," said the Superior Inn desk clerk. "Showed up Sunday night. I was thinkin' of callin' the house detective when the doctor fella came downstairs to meet her.

Jeans? Well that fit the other sightings, but high heels? Absolutely not. Julienne would never wear jeans and high heels or, for that matter, look like the kind of woman who would inspire a call to the house detective. Had Philippe called a prostitute? What a muddle! "Have you seen the woman since Sunday night?" I asked.

"No, Ah haven't, honey, but Ah'm not on duty all the time, you know. They went out together. Ah remember that. They were arguin'. An' he came back sometime aftah midnight."

"But she wasn't with him?"

"Well, honey, Ah just don't know. Mah shift was ovah at midnight, but mah guess would be she came back with him. She looked the type. He showed her a good time in the Quartah an' she showed him a good time in the room. Know what Ah mean?"

"They were planning to visit the French Quarter?" I asked.

"Where else would anyone go in N'Awlins?" the clerk asked, aggrieved. "We got us free shuttle service to the Quartah 'cause that's where folks want ta go of an evenin'."

"And they took the shuttle?"

"Now Ah wouldn't know that, would Ah?"

"Thank you," I said politely. "You've been very helpful." Actually, she'd been downright forthcoming. It's a wonder she managed to keep her job if she always talked so freely about the establishment's guests.

"Why don' you try callin' him, honey. He's bound to answer if he's in, an' Ah haven't seen him leave today."

That would depend on whether he was taking his medication, I thought. A depressed person might not answer his phone.

"Want me to try his room, honey?"

"Yes, please." Could Julienne be staying with him? Or somewhere else under an assumed name? At least she'd been all right Sunday evening, if peculiarly dressed. That is, if the woman in the jeans and high heels had been her, which I doubted. The only person who had ever accused Julienne of looking like a call girl had been her husband.

"Ah'm not getting' an answer, honey. Wanna leave him a message?"

"Yes, please. Ask him to call Carolyn Blue at the Hotel de la Poste." I gave her the number.

Well, it was back to the Po'Boy Computer Café. Even if they were, as Lieutenant Boudreaux had suggested, manufacturing cocaine on the premises, I needed an updated photo of Philippe, which I could print out from the web site of his university. If offered drugs, I would simply say, "No, thank you," as Nancy Reagan had advocated in her Just Say No campaign.

On the other hand, I'd just as soon not associate with drug dealers. What if the place was raided while I was there? Would the police arrest an innocent, semi–computer literate professor's wife? Would Lieutenant Boudreaux rescue me? If only Jason and I had a portable printer with us. Our room had a data port and Jason's computer had a modem, but no printer between us. We just weren't as up to date technologically as we liked to think.

Well, I would have to soothe my fears of drug dealers and raids with another sumptuous, flaming café brûlot while I was surfing the net for Philippe's photograph. I would forgo another of their tasty po'boys, however, since Jason would undoubtedly want to eat dinner out.

20

Pralines

Happily, I managed to make the trip to Po'Boy without incident. No New Orleans criminal so much as looked my way. Perhaps my crooked umbrella emitted an aura of menace. I obtained a printout of Philippe's university web site picture, plus copies of the pictures of Julienne, Linus, and Nils. The originals had become soggy along with the other contents of my purse during my recent fall into the bayou.

Fortunately, I had a backup handbag packed, although it did not match my walking shoes, but then they were too soggy for use, either. I had to wear the shoes I had brought for evening wear, which are not as comfortable as they might have been, and the matching bag, which doesn't hold as much. Still, I couldn't be fussy under the circumstances. I was lucky to have something in which to carry those things we females find necessary to keep at hand. Of course, some of my purse contents were still damp and had to be put in Baggies, of which I always carry a supply when traveling.

I did treat myself to two pralines on which to nibble while I waited for printouts and sipped my flambéed coffee, and I must say Po'Boy's pralines are delightful — rich and creamy, laden with pecans. I include a recipe, which I obtained from a friend, for those of you who may desire to make your own.

Joan's Pralines

Grease waxed paper.

Select a pot large enough to prevent boil-overs.

Pour into the pot *I cup of buttermilk, 2 cups granulated sugar,* and *1 tsp. baking soda.*

Stir until sugar is completely dissolved. Place pot on low to medium burner and, stirring constantly, let candy boil to the soft ball stage (when a half tsp. or so of the syrup forms a soft ball upon being dropped into a cup of cold water). The mixture will turn a brownish color.

Remove pot from heat, add *2 cups pecan halves, 1 tsp. vanilla,* and *1 tbs. butter.*

Beat mixture briskly until it becomes glossy and very thick.

Quickly spoon onto greased, waxed paper, making small patties.

Let candy completely cool before removing from paper.

Should the mixture harden before you have time to get it all onto the paper, return to the heat for a few seconds to restore the right consistency.

Once I had finished my computer business and my snack, the clerk at Po'Boy sniffed and wrinkled his nose when I extracted my credit card from my soggy wallet in its baggie. Was he sniffing because he was a cocaine addict or because my wallet smelled bad? The latter, I decided, having detected a whiff of swamp odor myself. How very embarrassing! Now I had to wonder whether I had managed to eradicate such odors from my person. I believe I blushed as he handed back the credit card. I couldn't use cash, of course. My dollar bills were drying in the bathroom at the Hotel de la Poste, and my traveler's checks would have to be replaced, the signatures having smeared.

I had taken a bus and had to return on one so that I could pay for my transportation with change, which I had washed off with the perfumed hotel soap and dried on a hand towel before leaving. But before I returned, I spotted a shoe store and stopped to buy myself a new pair of walking shoes. If my wallet retained the swamp scent, so would my shoes, and no one wants to be trailed at every step by unpleasant odors.

This was all extremely inconvenient. If I could find the rude person who bumped into me on the wharf, I would certainly give him a lecture on manners. It brought to mind an incident some years ago when Jason and I were attending a performance of Strauss's *Silent Woman* at the New York opera — a lovely theater but a dreadful opera, by the way. Very unmelodic.

Be that as it may, I was bumped from behind by a woman holding a champagne glass, which she spilled on the shoulder of a very pretty teal silk dress I was wearing. The impact unbalanced me, and I fell against a stout, red-faced man smoking a cigar. The cigar burned a hole on the other shoulder of the dress, completely ruining it, and then the two of them snarled at *me*, as if I had been at fault, although I was simply standing in the lobby chatting with Jason and a couple from New York University. We had been immersed in conversation about the soprano, who would probably have sounded wonderful had she been singing some other opera.

Because my attackers didn't hasten away, I got the chance, in that instance, to tell them exactly what I thought of their manners. In fact, I believe I was quite intemperate. I demanded names and addresses so that they could reimburse me for my dress. Unfortunately, the bell sounded, and they took that as an excuse to go to their seats without giving me any information other than their opinion of non–New Yorkers. Jason was vastly amused at my display of temper and chuckled all the way through the last act. However, his humor was subsequently tempered by my revelation of what it would cost to replace the dress. Jason is not a miserly man, but then again, he's not given to flinging his money around.

Consequently, he was taken aback when he returned from the ACS meeting to find his wife absent and his bathroom festooned with damp currency, not to mention the errant smear of mud and swamp vegetation that I had missed when I attempted to set the bathroom to rights after my long shower.

"Carolyn, what happened in here?" he asked when I came in.

I must admit that I hadn't been planning to tell him about my mishap on the swamp wharf, having expected to be back before he returned and to use the hair dryer on the money if it hadn't dried out.

"There's mud in the sink," he said. "And wet money everywhere."

I did wonder what he made of these two facts. He might explain the drying money by surmising that I had developed some eccentric fetish for money laundering, but that would hardly explain the mud. I sighed and told him the whole story, and Jason was horrified at my ordeal, except for my ill-considered comment that swamp vegetation tasted like *uni,* which happens to be one of Jason's favorite sushi choices. However, his sympathetic nature overcame gourmet pique as related to *uni,* and he consoled me over my traumatic experience. I felt much better for having confessed and received his sympathy.

Jason then, with some hesitation, told me that Julienne had not appeared to give her scheduled paper, nor had she been in touch with conference officials to cancel. "I must admit, Caro, that I'm very worried about her. Missing Carlene's lecture was a failure of friendship, and missing the session she was scheduled to chair a failure of responsibility, but failing, without explanation, to give her paper . . ." He shook his head. "I just can't imagine Julienne doing that unless something is very wrong."

"I've known all along that she was in trouble," I said. "Does Nils know that she —"

"I haven't seen him, but I believe he's to join us for dinner tonight, and I can't imagine that he'll take the news of his wife missing her own paper as anything but very alarming."

"Absolutely," I agreed. "He'll just have to contact the police now. Unless . . . unless . . ."

"What, Carolyn?" Jason asked.

"Unless he's responsible for her disappearance."

"Surely not," said Jason.

"You know that Torelli left the conference unexpectedly?"

He nodded.

"And I just found out this afternoon that Julienne's brother Philippe is trying to get in touch with her. In fact, he's in New Orleans."

"Well, that's good news. Philippe can insist that Nils contact the police. In fact, Philippe can do it himself, since he's a relative."

"I suppose," I said dubiously, "but I can't get hold of him, and he may have been seen with Julienne on Sunday, the last day anyone saw her. According to Diane, he's got some bee in his bonnet about being entitled to the whole of their mother's estate. You don't suppose —"

"He's her brother," said Jason. "He wouldn't . . . certainly not over money." My husband looked appalled at the very idea.

"Well, you know what they say: most murders are motivated by sex or money."

"Who says that?"

"Mystery writers," I admitted. "And policemen, I suppose."

"We don't know any policemen," said Jason reasonably.

I knew Lieutenant Boudreaux, but he hadn't said anything about motivations for murder.

"And we don't know that Julienne's been murdered. I wouldn't imagine that we know anyone who knows anyone who's been murdered. After all, it's not something that's common in academic circles."

"No," I had to agree. "Did you mean to say that we have to have dinner with Nils tonight?"

"Before we get into that, I was checking for messages at the desk downstairs when the clerk asked if I was aware that the hotel charges for local calls, and that we've made quite a few."

"How much per call?" I inquired, aghast. I had no idea how many I'd made. It could be hundreds.

"Seventy-five cents." Jason studied me, looking a bit puzzled. "It is rather steep, but you can't have made that many. Say you made ten. That would be $7.50."

Say I'd made a hundred; that would be seventy-five dollars. I was going to have to ask just how big a bill I had run up. "I'll try to limit the calls in the future," I promised, knowing that if my search for Julienne demanded more calls, I'd make them. Would they be tax deductible? No, of course they wouldn't. My search for Julienne had nothing to do with a book on New Orleans cuisine.

"Now, about the dinner you mentioned?" That, at least, would be deductible. Unless it was to be held at some restaurant so boring that I couldn't write about it. "Who's going? Not just Nils, I hope."

Jason smiled. "The whole alligator-dinner group."

"And I'm supposed to find them another alligator dish?" I wasn't ecstatic to think of sharing my evening meal with Nils or the Abbotts.

"No one mentioned alligators," he replied. "They're taking us to the Palace Café. In thanks for your time and effort on the reunion dinner."

"You mean they're paying our way?" *Had Broder agreed to that?* I wondered.

Jason grinned. "Reluctantly, in some cases. I believe Carlene had to nudge Broder into participating, but yes, we're the invited guests."

Isn't it amazing how often married people find themselves thinking the same thing? Both Jason and I had immediately realized that Broder would object to another expensive dinner, especially when he had to kick in for two extra people. The Palace Café? I thought I remembered it from my *Great Chefs* book. "Where is it? The restaurant?"

"The central business district, I think. Is that a problem for you? Were you planning on writing only about restaurants in the Quarter?"

"Oh, it's fine." The central business district? Was that near Philippe's hotel? If so, it wouldn't hurt to pop in and try to talk to him. Surely, he'd be in his room by the time we finished dinner.

21

Catfish Pecan with Meunière Sauce

The French and their New World cousins the Creoles are noted not only for gourmet cooking but also for thriftiness. Combine these traits with the periods of poverty that formerly rich Creoles experienced (after the Civil War, for instance) and several famous New Orleans dishes were the result. Gumbo is certainly one — a combination of garden vegetables, leftover meat and seafood, and, of course, roux. Bread pudding and *pain perdu* are two others. In New Orleans, day-old French bread is not wasted. It is used to make New Orleans style French toast (*pain perdu*) as well as the many delicious bread puddings to be found in French Quarter restaurants. Don't decide, as I did, that you dislike bread pudding until you sample one of the exotic New Orleans varieties.

Carolyn Blue,
Eating Out in the Big Easy

The Palace Café, which specializes in contemporary Creole menus, is another of the Brennan family ventures, and the Brennan family is synonymous with New Orleans cuisine. For a wonder, Carlene had chosen the restaurant. Maybe the "contemporary" label suggested California cookery. Perhaps it was a compromise with Broder, who would have chosen "inexpensive" from the guidebook and had to be satisfied with "moderate." (I had looked the restaurant up before we ventured out.) It was also blessedly close to our hotel, being on Canal Street.

At any rate, the ambiance was delightful. The dining area downstairs was given over to booths in green, cream, and brass with an impressive spiral staircase in the middle. We climbed the stairs. The second-floor dining room had a wonderful mural that depicted famous New Orleans musicians, reminding me that in my concentration on food and Julienne, I hadn't so much as visited Preservation Hall or any of the famous jazz clubs. The visit to the tassel-twirler establishment could hardly be counted as a musical experience, although the bands on the street, when I had the chance to listen, were wonderful, and outside our window at the hotel, we often heard the wail of trumpets and trombones.

At the end of the dining room, we could see the chefs working behind glass. Luckily, I spotted that feature before we were seated and asked if we could be moved closer. Miranda and Lester grumbled, but the maître d' was very gracious. He simply replaced the reserved sign on our table, bowed to me, and led us farther back, where he removed the reserved sign from another table and seated me facing the kitchen. "Madame is interested in the preparation of fine food?" he asked.

"Madame's writing a book," said Carlene, grinning. "So be sure to produce your most delicious dishes for her."

"Carlene," Miranda hissed.

"Our creations are always delicious," the maître d' assured her and then beamed at me. I beamed back. It really is fun to be a restaurant critic. I even got the first menu, which caused Miranda to frown. No doubt she felt that, being the most well-paid member of the group, she should be the diner most catered to.

Two appetizers had been recommended by the guidebook: red bean dip with homemade potato chips and oyster shooters. The shooters are raw oysters served in a shot glass, which did not appeal to me. Truth to tell, I like my oysters cooked and wanted to visit Antoine's for their oysters Rockefeller, a recipe that originated with the restaurant's founder. Rockefeller refers to the richness of the sauce, not some Rockefeller for whom the dish was created.

I chose the red bean dip, which was excellent, especially the homemade potato chips. I wondered, for just a moment, how hard it would be to make one's own potato chips and even walked to the glass wall to see if I could catch a glimpse of the potato chip chef at work (I didn't), but then I remembered that I really preferred other people's cooking and returned to my seat. Miranda glared at me.

Broder was saying, as I replaced my napkin in my lap and made a few notes on the red bean dip, that Julienne's failure to appear for her lecture was a cause of great worry to him. "Yes," Carlene agreed. "I think we all know her well enough to say that this last incident is ominous. Have you heard *anything* from her, Nils?"

"Torelli left. She probably went with him," Nils muttered.

"She didn't," I said. "The police checked that for me."

"You've been to the police?" Nils looked furious.

"Well, you wouldn't," I said coldly.

Nils didn't answer, but he looked upset, as well he might. Jason defused the situation by insisting that I try his crawfish cakes. Spicy, crispy, infused with Romano cheese and the delicious flavor of crawfish — they were wonderful. The waiter and I had a quick, whispered conversation about the flavors; Worcestershire and Louisiana hot sauce were responsible for the extra tang. I had two bites, one to savor the cakes by themselves, the second to appreciate them as they were served, with a lemon butter sauce in which I also detected white wine. I nodded to Jason and whispered, "Superb choice." My husband does have a wonderful way with a menu. Of course, I invited him to try my selection, as well.

"I can't imagine what's going on with Julienne," said Lester. "No matter what your marital problems, Nils, she shouldn't have failed to fulfill her conference responsibilities."

"Don't blame me for that," snapped Nils, "and I couldn't agree with you more. When I go to a conference, I give the paper I'm scheduled to give."

"Have you ever known Julienne not to show up for her lecture?" I demanded. Nils was silent. "Which means something is dreadfully wrong, and you're refusing to do anything about it. Now, Diane says that Philippe is looking for Julienne."

"You called Diane about this?" Nils was obviously infuriated at my interference. "The last thing she needs during midterms is to be worried about her mother."

"She's worried that you and Julienne might divorce," I replied, "and I can only assume that's because she's picked up on your attitude and your unfounded suspicions." At least, I hoped they were unfounded. Why else would Torelli have left so hurriedly? A man who was in love with Julienne wouldn't have left like that. Unless she'd sent him away. Oh dear, I just wanted to stop thinking about it. I wanted Julienne to appear and be fine and have some logical explanation for her disappearance, preferably one that would show Nils to have been unfairly suspicious of her.

Lips pressed together angrily, I turned to my entrée, which had just been served. I had been lured away from guide selections by a dish called catfish pecan with meunière sauce. My anger and worry fled, at least temporarily, as I gazed at my beautiful entrée: a six-ounce catfish fillet, brown and crispy in its pecan crust and topped with pecan halves, parsley, and a lovely, spicy meunière sauce. It tasted as good as it looked.

Since catfish farming developed into a lucrative industry in the United States, I have become very fond of this firm, sweet fish. It is not only tasty, but also low in calories and cholesterol, for those who worry about their weight and their arteries, and best of all, it's available in markets all year round, filleted so that the fish lover doesn't have to deal with all those tiny, dangerous bones.

Catfish Pecan with Meunière Sauce

Preheat oven to 450°. Trim all fat from *six 5- to 7-oz. catfish fillets.*

Grind *3 cups roasted pecans* and *1 cup dried breadcrumbs* in a blender or food processor until fine. Pour into a pie pan.

Place *1 cup all-purpose flour* in another

pie pan and stir in $\frac{1}{2}$ *tsp. pepper* and *1 tsp. salt.*

Beat together *3 eggs* and $\frac{1}{2}$ *cup milk* in a medium bowl.

Season catfish with seafood seasoning. (Mix together *6 tsp. paprika, 4 tsp. ground garlic, 4 tsp. black pepper, 2$\frac{1}{2}$ tsp. ground onion, 1$\frac{1}{2}$ tsp. fine thyme, 1$\frac{1}{4}$ tsp. fine oregano, 1$\frac{1}{4}$ tsp. basil, 1 tsp. cayenne,* and *salt to taste.* Can be stored in a cool, dry place, tightly sealed.)

Dredge catfish fillets in flour, dip in egg mixture, and coat with pecan mixture. Film bottom of large, ovenproof sauté pan or skillet with *olive oil* over medium heat.

Add fish and brown on both sides.

Bake in oven for about 5 minutes.

Meunière Sauce
Cook *2 cups fish stock or bottled clam juice, juice of* $\frac{1}{2}$ *lemon, 1 tsp. Worcestershire sauce, dash of Louisiana hot sauce* in medium saucepan.

Add *1 tbs. heavy cream* and cook to reduce for 1 to 2 minutes.

Remove from heat and whisk $\frac{1}{2}$ *cup (1 stick) unsalted butter* into liquid.

Serve over cooked fish fillets and sprinkle with *roasted whole pecan halves* and (if desired) *chopped parsley.*

Carlene ordered a marvelous crabmeat cheesecake and offered me a bite, on which I made copious notes, and Jason had the seafood boil, which was served on a raised platter. The waiter told me that Paris cafés served in that fashion, and Jason pronounced his seafood so fresh that it must have been pulled from the sea that very day, which the waiter assured him it was. Nils and Miranda didn't offer me any of their entrees, and Miranda and Lester had rather sharp words when his selection arrived, a double pork chop, rotisseried and served with candied sweet potatoes.

Midway through the meal, someone from Julienne's department, evidently someone who disliked Nils, stopped to tell him the latest news. "Just got a call from home," he said. "The dean is in a real snit.

In fact, our chair is pissed off, too, because your wife's using departmental funds to attend this meeting and then isn't —"

"Oh, Brad," said his wife, tugging on his arm, "do be quiet and come on. They're holding our table."

"How did the dean hear about Julienne not showing up for her meetings?" Nils asked. When the young professor shrugged, Nils said, "Won't do *you* any good, Forrester." His tone was just as nasty as Brad's had been. "She's the one with tenure. You're the one who hasn't got it yet, and she'll still have a vote on yours, no matter how many papers she does or doesn't present at national meetings."

"Brad," hissed his wife.

Brad yanked his arm loose from the cautioning marital hand, shook a hank of dishwater blond hair away from his eyeglasses, and continued, "You haven't heard the best of it, Magnussen. Torelli took off for Sweden today or last night. No one's sure exactly when. Didn't even get administrative permission. Makes you wonder what's going on, doesn't it?" The young assistant professor then scuttled away with his wife talking to him angrily all the way from our table to theirs, which was back near the stairs and not at all convenient for visiting us. Nils had turned red, then pale.

"Whatever you're thinking, Nils," I said hastily, "Julienne has not run off to Sweden with Linus Torelli."

"You don't know what I'm thinking," he responded.

"You should be worried about her safety. Why is Torelli fleeing the country? That's the question we should be asking. Does he have tenure? Can he afford to —"

"He doesn't," said Nils.

"There. So the question is, what's he done to Julienne that he has to run away?"

"Really, Carolyn, don't you think you're letting your imagination run wild?" cautioned Broder. "Professors don't murder one another and then skip the country."

"Murder?" Nils's voice was faint, his lips trembling. "Is that what you think, Carolyn? That someone murdered her? Did you think I had? Before you heard this latest news about Torelli?"

"I don't know what to think," I admitted. "I'm scared to death. And why shouldn't I be? You've been acting as if Julienne has been unfaithful to you. Torelli's denying any relationship with her and starting rumors about them at the same time."

"What rumors?" Nils demanded.

"And suddenly he's left the country under suspicious circumstances when Julienne's been missing since Sunday, and he's probably the last person we know to see her."

"When was this?" Nils practically shouted his last question at me.

Carlene said, "Sh-sh-sh, Nils."

The waiter came rushing over to ask if there was a problem.

"No problem," Nils snarled. "Go away." Then he turned back to me. "When did Torelli see her?"

How I wish I hadn't said that! "And then there's Philippe," I responded hastily.

"Good heavens," said Miranda. "I remember him. The world's glummest sibling."

"Forget Philippe," said Nils. "When did Julienne see Torelli? Sunday? After she left me?"

"Philippe is a professor in a medical school now," I said, choosing to respond to Miranda rather than Nils. "And he's decided that he should have the complete inheritance from their mother, both his portion and Julienne's."

"So what? He's not here," said Nils. "I want to know —"

"But he is," I interrupted. "He's been here since Sunday, and he won't answer his telephone at the hotel. For all I know, he's disappeared, too."

"Good grief," said Carlene, "I don't like the sound of that at all. I always thought Philippe was somehow off kilter."

"He's all right," said Nils, but he was beginning to look more worried than angry. "As long as he takes his meds, he's —"

"But Diane said he sounded weird — her words — when she talked to him."

"He went to see my daughter?" Now Nils looked thoroughly upset.

"No, he called to find out where Julienne was, and Diane told him. He's not in New Hampshire, he's here in New Orleans, so Nils, you've got to report her appearance to the police."

"Jesus." Fingers clenched in thinning blond hair, Nils bowed his head over his empty plate.

"Why is Philippe thinking about challenging his mother's will?" asked Miranda, ever the lawyer. "I wouldn't imagine that Julienne's mother was so wealthy it would be worth the expense."

"Oh, the father made a lot of money on the stock exchange. I remember that. It was when we were in college," said Carlene. "Maybe Mrs. Delacroix still had it when she died. Did Julienne inherit a lot of money, Nils?"

"It's none of your business," he muttered.

Carlene looked highly offended. Some people didn't like to talk about money, but Carlene obviously wasn't one of them.

"When did Julienne's father make all this money?" Lester asked. "I thought he killed himself."

"I don't know why you'd think that," I replied. "He did die not too long after his big bonanza on the stock exchange, but his death was an accident."

"Still, it's peculiar when you think about it," said Miranda. "If they were rich, I mean. Both of them dying in car accidents."

All of us stared at our bread pudding. Were the deaths of Julienne's parents connected to the money? I wondered, then decided that was a silly idea. Mr. Delacroix had gone to sleep at the wheel. No problems had been found with his car and no indication that anyone had run him off the road. And Mrs. Delacroix had been killed by that pickup truck. The driver was in jail for vehicular manslaughter. So whether or not they still had the money, it hadn't killed them.

But what about Julienne? If she inherited a lot, had she died because of it? I thought about Philippe, who allegedly wanted her share. Killing her wouldn't get it for him. Nils would be her heir, Nils and Diane. I looked at Nils, who was still looking stricken. He hadn't eaten a bite of his white chocolate bread pudding, which had been served during our discussion.

We'd all ordered the same dessert, for which the Palace Café was famous, and it was excellent. Had you asked me a month ago if it was likely that I'd order bread pudding twice in one week, I'd have laughed, but both the banana rum and the white chocolate bread puddings were amazingly good. Only in New Orleans, I thought as I scooped up another bite.

"I'll go to the police tomorrow," said Nils.

His sudden acquiescence only increased my confusion. And fear. Did he think that Philippe was a threat to Julienne? Or had he realized that Torelli, having fled the country, might be implicated in her disappearance? Or was he now worrying that by refusing to report her missing after all this time, he himself would look that much more guilty of whatever had happened to his wife? "I'll go with you," I announced.

The group broke up on a glum note. Jason and I thanked the others for the lovely meal to which they had treated us, and then we lost sight of them when the maître d' stopped me to inquire about, first, whether I had enjoyed my dinner, and, second, the nature of the book I was writing. Having reassured him on both counts and now being free of the rest of the group, I talked Jason into paying a visit to Philippe at the Superior Inn.

Once there, we had the desk call his room, but no one answered. Then — and it embarrasses me to say what I did next — I asked the desk clerk to try one more time in case Dr. Delacroix had been in the bathroom. While she was punching in the numbers, I craned my neck to make them out: 214.

"Why don't we have a drink, Jason?" I said when the clerk had announced, rather brusquely, that the room still did not answer.

Jason looked puzzled but allowed me to drag him out of the clerk's view and then over to the elevator. "Where are we going?" he asked as I rushed inside.

"To Philippe's room," I replied.

"But she didn't tell us his room number."

"It will be the same as the number she dialed," I explained, exiting on the second floor.

"Carolyn!" my husband exclaimed. But his disappointment in me did not stop me from knocking at the door of room 214. And knocking. And knocking. No one answered.

22

Eggs Sardou

I was a fetus in a womb of amniotic gumbo, my attempts to move thwarted by the murky soup that enclosed me. Blind to anything but brown swamp water, I could see no hint of light pointing the way up. If I lifted a hand to my eyes, the fingers and wrist were ghostly, and they trailed supple bonds that lapped around all my limbs and slid as sinuously as snakes into my mouth and around my neck. My frenzied mind told me I was being sucked down, but that nowhere would my feet touch a firm surface against which I could push off toward safety. All was mud, above and below, and my lungs burned for lack of air. The muscles of my chest trembled with the desire to suck in something. I was dying.

"Carolyn! Carolyn!" I felt a hand clutching mine and heard a voice, so muffled that I couldn't recognize it. The hand drew me upward as, trailing the clutching fronds, I sought to help in my own rescue. When I burst at last into the air, I saw Julienne leaning over the low edge of a boat. She was smiling at me, camera dangling from her neck. Happiness exploded like light in my heart because she was safe.

Then I opened my eyes, and Jason said, "That must have been one hell of a nightmare, Caro." I looked around for Julienne, but I was in my bed at the Hotel de la Poste. Only Jason and I were in the room, and I was trembling, he patting my arm consolingly in the way of men, who never know quite what to do with their wives' tears or terrors.

"It was just a nightmare," he murmured.

A nightmare? Perhaps. But Julienne had been alive. And in the swamp. I hoped it was an omen. Illogically perhaps, I determined right then that the next search I made would include the people who rented boats on the bayous, boats with sides that were low to the water and had motors in the back. I remembered the motor, although I had had only that one glimpse of Julienne and her boat as, in my dream, she saved me from drowning.

I pictured her living in a wooden shack, raised above the mud on stilts. She would be fishing and taking photos, lounging and listening to music on a portable radio, enjoying a respite from the pressures of her job and her husband's unconcealed enmity, thinking today might be the day she went back to it all, or maybe not. Maybe tomorrow. Cajun men in pirogues would stop by her retreat to drop off supplies and news of the world beyond the swamp. Or just to pass the time of day with a lovely woman who made friends wherever she went.

And I would find her. I could almost hear her laughter as we talked of her latest escapade and compared it to the time she had taken her father's boat and set up camp on an island in the lake. From her hideout, she'd watched as summer neighbors rowed about and shouted her name. She'd listened as her father promised at the top of his lungs to return her bicycle if she, in turn, promised not to hitch rides by hanging onto the back of the postman's truck and coasting with her feet stuck out. Her delighted laughter had given her away one afternoon when Postmaster Boggis stopped at a rural box to drop off newspapers, catalogues for winter woolens, and utility bills. How could I have forgotten that incident?

"You'd better get up," my husband said.

"Remember? You said you'd go to the police with Nils this morning."

"Rats," I muttered, getting out of bed and reaching for my robe.

"Rats?" Jason couldn't have looked more astonished. I'd been hounding Nils since Saturday night to report Julienne missing, and after all this time, he'd agreed. Under the circumstances, I could hardly go running off to follow a clue that had come to me in a dream; I had to be on hand to introduce Nils to Lieutenant Boudreaux and to be sure that Nils actually filed the missing persons report.

But Julienne had looked so real. I was now sure that she was alive. Should I tell the lieutenant where to look for her? Policemen probably didn't put much stock in dreams, although there was certainly a lot to be said for this one. It wasn't just an omen. It was my subconscious searching through the information I had and telling me what course to take.

Hadn't I always found that, before an exam at college, a good review of the subject material and then a good night's sleep were the surest path to a high grade? I had always awakened with the subject much clearer in my mind and with new insights ready to pour out onto my blue-book pages. And that was just what had happened with this dream.

"Seven-thirty," Jason prompted. He had come out of the bathroom to remind me, a bit of shaving cream still clinging to his throat where he had given his beard an edging. Jason always said that if he were rich, the first thing he'd do would be to find a beard barber and patronize him regularly. Which was a modest enough ambition, surely. Not that either of us expected to be rich. I tried to imagine sales of *Eating Out in the Big Easy* running into the millions, making us disgustingly affluent, but it didn't seem likely. How many people would want to read my opinions of New Orleans restaurants and try the recipes I included? Not millions, certainly.

At eight-thirty Nils and I were waiting in line at Brennan's, although I *had* made a reservation. The restaurant was, conveniently, on Royal Street, a block from the police station. What culinary writer could justify missing breakfast at an establishment that reputedly sells 750,000 poached eggs a year? From their menu I chose eggs Sardou, that delicious dish that nests artichoke bottoms topped by poached eggs on a bed of creamed spinach and bathes the whole in hollandaise sauce. The anchovies are optional, and I opted out.

In 1908, Victorien Sardou, the renowned French dramatist, had breakfast at Antoine's, where the owner, Antoine Alciatore, created this dish in his honor. Since Sardou wrote *La Tosca*, whose operatic embodiment I adore, I naturally ordered Sardou's eggs.

As I savored my choice — sometimes I think I could eat a poached Gila monster if it was served in hollandaise sauce — I worried because I would not be returning that morning to Café du Monde, but that was silly. Julienne wasn't going to return from the swamp for beignets and café au lait. It was much too far. In fact, I would probably have to rent a car to begin my canvass of boat rental facilities.

I told Nils about my dream and my plans, suggesting that he might come with me. Truthfully, I don't like driving around strange cities, much less backcountry swamp areas. I was hoping that Nils would drive. Also I've found, although it is a situation I deplore, that men respond more readily to questions from other men. Oops! I was assuming that most of the boat owners would be men. For all our efforts to effect equality between the sexes in fact and in attitude, I was making sexist assumptions. And I had only caught myself as an afterthought. Progress certainly wasn't impinging much on my thinking.

"You want to rent a car and have me drive you around asking questions on the basis of a *dream?*" Nils demanded in response to my story and suggestion. "I thought that's why we were going to the police — to get professionals hunting for Julienne and Torelli."

"You still think she's with Linus Torelli?" I couldn't believe my ears. "You were told last night that he's gone to Sweden."

Nils shrugged. "Maybe she went with him. Maybe he's lying, and he hasn't gone to Sweden at all. The police can find out. Then you can stop worrying. You'll know she's run away."

I glared at him. There are some men whose opinions can't be changed with a large rock to the back of the head, much less a combination of fact and logic.

"Obviously, it's going to take a professional to track her down," Nils continued. "You certainly haven't accomplished anything."

"At least I tried," I retorted.

"Well, shortly we'll know the truth. Then you can stop nagging me, and I'll have grounds to file for divorce."

Having revealed his plans, he didn't look very happy about them, and I was furious. Of all the cold-hearted, scheming . . . I forked up my last bite and ate it. Then I waved imperiously to the waiter. The sooner we made our visit to Lieutenant Boudreaux, the better. I didn't think I could stomach much more of Nils's company.

It was raining again as we set out for the Vieux Carre station, not a sheeting rain, but still, this obviously wasn't the most pleasant season in New Orleans unless you lived in the desert and craved the blessing of moisture. Nils complained about the weather every step of the way, but underneath the ill temper, I detected a certain unease. In his place, I would have felt uneasy. His wife had been missing since Saturday, and he had waited until Thursday to report it. If he was to be believed, his only reason for doing so today was to get me off his back and obtain grounds for divorce on the basis of desertion.

We were both scowling by the time we reached the station. There, to my dismay, we found that Lieutenant Boudreaux was away on official police business. The cynical sergeant took our information on Julienne — description, age, profession, social security number, home address and phone number, local address and phone number. He didn't seem much interested.

"Dr. Magnussen has been gone since Saturday," I finally interrupted with ill-concealed desperation, "and not seen since Sunday."

"Who saw her?" the sergeant asked.

Nils turned to look at me challengingly, and I hated to answer, knowing that any mention of Linus Torelli would set Nils off. "A waitperson —"

"A *what?*" The sergeant stopped writing and frowned at me.

"She's trying to be politically correct," said Nils sarcastically. "She means a waiter or waitress."

"— at Café du Monde Sunday morning, a bartender at the Absinthe House —"

"Don't sound to me like she's gone missin'," the sergeant interrupted. "Sounds like she's out on the town."

"— maybe someone at the voodoo museum, a street performer that evening —"

"Her lover, Linus Torelli." Nils added to the end of my list the name that my tongue just didn't want to voice. The sergeant stopped writing again and looked up with sharpened interest.

"Torelli isn't her lover," I snapped.

"When did *he* see her?" the sergeant asked with a smirk.

"After she left the dinner party," I replied unwillingly, hoping I wouldn't have to enlarge on that.

"And now Torelli's made an unexplained trip to Sweden, on which my wife undoubtedly accompanied him," said Nils bitterly. "Or maybe that's what he told his chair, and they've gone somewhere else together."

"His chairman is here in New Orleans. Torelli told someone else, who told the dean of science," I corrected. "And Julienne did not —"

The sergeant had closed his notebook. "We don't go lookin' for no folks who's run off with lovers an' such."

"She hasn't —" I started to protest.

"No problem checkin' that out," a voice from behind interrupted.

I turned, and there was Lieutenant Boudreaux. I fear that my relief at his appearance was only too obvious, for Nils inspected him closely as the lieutenant told the sergeant that he would take over the interview and ushered me solicitously into his office. Nils trailed behind. Only when we were seated was I able to introduce him to Alphonse Boudreaux.

"Well now," said the lieutenant. "The missin' husband."

"*I'm* not missing," snapped Nils defensively.

"Took you long enough to report your wife among the missin'," said Boudreaux dryly. "This lady's been frettin' all week 'bout Miz Magnussen. Don' seem you have."

"I'm not happy that my wife ran off with another man, but I don't know of any law that prevents her from doing so." Nils's tone was downright starchy.

"Easy to check out." The lieutenant took down Julienne's name and what passport information Nils could supply after he agreed that she did have a valid passport, the information on Linus Torelli, the probable city of departure, and the probable destination. Then he made a call. To Customs or Immigration or whoever checks passports. "Computers sure have eased our burden, us in law enforcement," he observed as he waited, phone to ear, smiling companionably at me. "How you doin', Miz Carolyn?"

"Very well, thank you, Lieutenant," I replied. Given the expression on Nils's face, I could only wish that I had been addressed as Miz Blue instead of Miz Carolyn. I didn't want any false impressions of my relationship with the lieutenant circulating in the academic community, although it occurred to me that Nils would love to tell Jason that I had an admirer in the New Orleans Police Department. Did I? Quickly, I put that thought aside.

"Been doin' any more sleuthin'?" the lieutenant asked amiably. "Hope you haven' run into any more local crime waves."

"Not today," I replied.

"Uh-huh. Uh-huh," said the lieutenant into the telephone. "Much obliged." He hung up and turned to Nils. "Dr. Linus Torelli's sure 'nuff left for Sweden, but yo' wife hasn't left the country, sir, so maybe we bettah be worryin' 'bout where-all she might be. When did *you* last see yo' lady, Professor?"

Nils sputtered and flushed. "Am I suspected of something?" he demanded angrily.

"Harm comes to a lady, husbands an' lovers are first on the list of suspects," the lieutenant replied. "So why don't you be cooperative an' answer mah question, sir."

Nils glared at me and replied, "The same time Carolyn saw her, when she stormed out of the dinner party Saturday night."

"An' why did she *storm out,* as you say?"

"We had words," Nils muttered.

"About what?"

"I don't know," Nils said, looking unhappy. "We're always having words about something lately."

"About the fella you say's her lover?"

"We didn't talk about that — not Saturday night, anyway," Nils replied in an almost inaudible voice.

"You did once she'd left," I added.

"But Miz Magnussen — she knows that's what you think?" the lieutenant pressed.

"Yes," Nils admitted.

"So what did you have words about?"

"Her dress," I replied since Nils either wouldn't say or really didn't remember. "He intimated that it was — improper. Actually, she looked lovely. And her decision to send their daughter to a private school. Nils said she was an indifferent mother, which is nonsense. Diane is a student at a very prestigious prep school in the East."

The lieutenant nodded. He was making notes. "We'll put out an APB on her an' send all the information to Missing Persons. Since she was last seen in mah district, Ah'll have mah men askin' questions on the streets."

"Thank you," I said, and believe me, my thanks were heartfelt. Maybe now, at last, Julienne would be found. A shiver went up my spine because I was so afraid that she wouldn't be found alive, that someone — some criminal, the missing Torelli, or even Nils — might have hurt or killed her. But I just couldn't let myself consider that terrible possibility. Julienne was the best, dearest friend I'd ever had, and I couldn't imagine life without our phone calls and E-mails and occasional meetings. I just couldn't.

"Bitch," Nils snarled at me as we exited the station. Having expressed his anger at a woman he must be holding responsible for the lieutenant's suspicions, Nils turned and strode away from me. I was stunned. I don't think anyone has ever called me that, certainly not anyone I've known for years. Of course, there was the purse snatcher. I recalled that he had called me a bitch. A stupid bitch, I believe, although one needn't be concerned with the opinions of criminals. And then there are motorists. Who knows what other motorists call one in the heat of that new bane of society, road rage? Sadly, I turned toward the hotel. I don't know where Nils was headed, but it wasn't there.

23

Chocolate Cake and Red Wine

As I stood in front of the police station contemplating Nils's unpleasant farewell, the memory of my dream came back. I was now glad that I hadn't mentioned it to the lieutenant. He was obviously a man who would put more faith in messages from the INS than those from the subconscious. In my dream Julienne had rescued me from a boat in the swamp. Did that mean she had gone there by herself? Or that someone had taken her there? And if so, who?

I went back into the station and asked to use their telephone. The desk officer refused and directed me to a public telephone, from which I called Philippe's room once more. He still wasn't answering. Could he and Julienne be in the swamp together? Philippe had been a fisherman once, morose but often successful. I personally hadn't wanted to share a boat with him because he never said anything and often didn't answer when spoken to. Depression, no doubt. So why didn't he take one of the many prescription drugs that relieved depression? His chairman had said, as an aside, something about Philippe's not being suited to the private practice of medicine. Small wonder. Who would want a doctor who neither spoke nor answered questions?

I tried to imagine being the patient of a silent doctor, one who conducted an examination, wrote a prescription, and walked out. That wouldn't be a successful approach to sick people. When you were telling Philippe your symptoms, you'd never be sure that he was listening. I can remember Julienne warning him that there was a black widow spider on his shirt collar. He never replied. Of course, there was no spider, but that was beside the point. Any normal person would have looked.

And how did he teach his classes if he didn't speak? Obviously, he now condescended to say something. Maybe depression allowed one to lecture but not to answer questions.

"You lost, ma'am?"

Good heavens! A helpful New Orleans

policeman, other than Lieutenant Boudreaux. How long had I been standing by the telephone neither using it nor leaving? "Where can I find a car rental agency, officer?" I asked, pleased to have been approached by someone who might know.

He gave me a lecture on hogging public telephones, then directions to a Hertz office, where I rented a car with no trouble. All one needed was a valid license and a credit card. I fear that having completed my transaction, I took up more than my fair share of time with the personnel, for I also needed maps, directions, and photocopies of the yellow pages that listed boat rental facilities.

A short, stocky man waiting in the office became impatient and left, much to the dismay of the clerk who had been helping me, albeit somewhat impatiently, when I showed no aptitude for map reading and little confidence in my ability to drive their car to any given destination. Perhaps the clerk's attitude indicated a gloomy presentiment that I would wreck their red Ford Escort rather than irritation over the loss of a potential customer. Have you ever wondered why so many rental cars are red? Is it to warn locals that tourists are wandering the roads, lost and befuddled?

At any rate, I set off in my rental car and promptly became lost, not an unusual occurrence for me. I had to make inquiries of several policemen. Some were in cars that pulled up beside me and asked why I was looking at a map instead of crossing on green. Some were on foot. One was on a motorcycle and every bit as sarcastic as the police cyclist I had asked for a ride to the convention center. And the last was directing traffic at an intersection jammed with drivers attempting to visit the drive-in daiquiri establishment.

That incident gave me pause. I did not find it reassuring to think that I was sharing the streets with motorists imbibing daiquiris; the policeman did not find it reassuring that I had got into the daiquiri line by mistake.

Ah, well. Finally, I reached the first boat rental facility. And the second. And the third. I lost count. No one had rented a boat for night fishing or photography to a woman matching Julienne's description, not on Sunday night or any recent night. Or to a man accompanied by a woman. I was driving along a barely paved road in a light rain, heading for the last place on my list, when I saw, in my rearview mirror, a dusty pickup truck roaring toward my rear bumper. Alarmed, I edged my rental car over a bit toward the shoulder, but not too far because I could see, in my peripheral vision, black water among the weeds.

The truck, revving its engine, pulled out to pass, and on a narrow, two-lane road! The driver must have been some mad-yokel type. Or perhaps he was drunk. I glanced nervously to the left and noticed, to my horror, that his truck was only inches from my front bumper and closing in. My heart accelerated madly as I cut the wheel sharply to the right and — the gods must have been with me that day — onto a rutted dirt road. As my car slewed in mud, I caught just a glimpse of a long-billed cap obscuring the head of the madman at the wheel of the pickup.

Then he was gone, and I was occupied with trying to keep my vehicle from flying off first one side of the miserable road, then the other. Because my wheels were sliding in the mud, I dared not brake, so I took my foot off the gas and steered, ulti-mately bumping to a stop in front of — I could hardly believe it! — the very boating establishment I had been seeking. Were it not for the drunk in the pickup truck, I would surely have missed the turnoff to the only place where I got so much as a nibble.

Shaking like an aspen leaf in a fall wind, I killed the engine and leaned my head on the steering wheel for a moment. Never have I experienced so frightening a near accident. When I looked up, somewhat recovered, I saw the unshaven owner of a rickety pier that had no boats tied to it. He was leaning against the frame of his door as he smoked a very odoriferous brown cigarette. I had to breathe through my mouth when I approached him. Then, before I could say a word, he asked what I thought I was doing, speeding my fancy red car on his private road. If he thought an Escort was fancy, what did he drive?

"I was almost run off the highway —" I waved vaguely in the direction from which I had come. "— by a madman in a pickup."

"Comin' which way?" he asked.

"I turned right into your road."

"Lucky for you, lady, you wasn' run off into dat dere slough along da highway. It's deep, dat one. You'd been breathin' mud by now, you drove into dere."

"Then I was fortunate indeed," I answered in a weak voice. "Doubly fortunate because I believe your establishment is the very place I am looking for."

"Won't do you no good. Catfish is bitin', an' Ah ain' got a single boat left for hire."

I speculated that savvy locals must think fish are put off their guard by rain. Had I been a catfish, I would have assumed that no sensible fisherman would be tooling around the swamp in an open boat on a rainy day. *I* certainly wasn't happy about being rained on. I had to go back to the car for my umbrella since the man in the doorway did not step aside to let me in. There wasn't even an overhang on his porch to protect visitor or inhabitant. His undershirt and the raggedy plaid shirt over it, not to mention his stained canvas pants, were getting wet. He didn't have to worry about his shoes because he was barefooted.

I returned with my new umbrella to inquire about recent rentals. (I had given in to necessity and purchased a new one to replace the one damaged against the purse-snatching mugger's head.)

"You don' wanna rent a boat, you?" he asked, evidently disgusted.

"You don't have any to rent," I retorted. "You just told me that."

Accepting the truth of my observation, he simmered down and answered my questions, ending every sentence with a pronoun. What an interesting speech pattern.

Had it evolved from the French spoken by the original Arcadian immigrants to the swamps? I didn't recall any such sentence structure from high school French classes or from the bit of conversational French I had picked up from Julienne and her family. Of course, they weren't Cajuns; they were Creoles.

What I found out from the soggy boat owner was that he had indeed rented a boat to a man who wanted to do some night fishing. This was on Sunday.

"Was he accompanied by a lady?" I asked eagerly.

The owner rolled a second cigarette, lit it from the first, which had dangled from his mouth during the rolling, licking, pinching process — quite a feat, I thought — and then he shrugged. "Coulda been."

In other words, he hadn't seen Julienne.

"What was your customer's name?"

The owner didn't remember. He didn't take credit cards, so he had no record, and he didn't worry about customers stealing his boats, because why would anyone want one and where would they go with it that some friend or cousin of his wouldn't see the boat, know it was missing, and reclaim it for him.

"Did your customer return the boat?" I asked.

He hadn't seen the return, that having occurred sometime between ten and dawn, but he'd rented that same boat out this morning to a man hungry for a mess of catfish.

"What did the man look like?" I asked patiently.

"Ray Ralph? Ray Ralph got him a glass eye an' —"

"So you do know the name of the man who rented your boat Sunday night?" I doubted that Julienne would have been with glass-eyed Ray Ralph.

"Ray Ralph Otis dun rented mah boat dis morning."

I sighed. "What did the man who rented it Sunday night look like?"

He stared at me suspiciously. "You a cop, you?" Then he took the cigarette out of his mouth. "Naw, you ain't no cop. Why you care —"

"I'm looking for a friend of mine."

"What yo' friend look like?"

Patiently, I described Julienne. He pointed out that the Sunday renter had been a man, not a woman, and he didn't remember what the man looked like, just that he had cash money and wanted to rent fishing equipment as well. I showed him the pictures. He didn't recognize anyone.

Then the roll-his-own entrepreneur closed the door in my face because, as he pointed out, "wrastlin' " was coming on TV, and he had a mess of gumbo in the pot calling him to lunch.

I could smell the gumbo and, being very hungry myself, decided that it would make an interesting chapter for my book if I survived the experience. Cajun boatman gumbo. Did he use catfish in it? However, that plan was not to materialize. He didn't answer when I knocked on his door again. Maybe it was just as well. He really had looked to be a disreputable character. Jason would have been horrified to think I'd invited myself to lunch with such a man.

As I drove back to town, the rain abated, and I let my imagination linger over the little information I had collected. A man had rented a boat, using cash, before midnight Sunday and returned it before dawn Monday. It could have been Linus Torelli, the chemist who had reputedly disappeared into the cold wastes of Sweden (actually, he was probably in Stockholm, but I didn't *know* that). Torelli had claimed that Julienne left his room in a huff because he wouldn't take her into the swamp, but he could have lied, either because something had happened to her there or because she had him drop her off somewhere and swear not to tell where she was. He might even still be in New Orleans, registered at some other hotel under an assumed name, although why he would — oh well, that was a useless avenue of speculation, and Lieutenant Boudreaux's sources said that Torelli had gone to Sweden.

It could have been Nils under the same circumstances, but I couldn't imagine why he wouldn't then admit that he knew where she was. After all, he'd finally reported her missing just this morning. And I suppose it could have been her brother. Maybe he was still in town because he had promised to rent another boat and pick her up from wherever she was hiding out. It might even have been Julienne, disguised as a man, who rented the boat, but then who had returned it? And if she had, where was she now? Not in Sweden. That's all I knew.

I imagined her meeting her brother, perhaps in a rented car, their going somewhere to talk about their mother's will, Philippe agreeing that he'd been out of line to think that everything should be his. "The silver? The china? Do you want those, too, Philippe?" she'd ask teasingly, and he'd have to laugh. Did Philippe ever laugh? How could he help it, at least occasionally, when he had a sister like Julienne, who could coax laughter from a statue?

They'd stop somewhere and have gumbo, which they had both loved since childhood, recall events from their early life in New Orleans, perhaps reminisce about trips to the lake cabin in Michigan. Did Philippe remember those summers with fondness? Then Julienne would say, "Philippe, let's go fishing again the way we used to. Remember going to the swamp with Papa? I'll take pictures, and you catch us some catfish. We'll find a place to cook them up in the morning," and Philippe would smile and agree. And off they'd go, out of the city, stomachs full of gumbo, minds filled with happy memories, traveling bumpy roads they'd taken in childhood until they came to that shack and rickety pier that belonged to the roll-your-own man. I should have asked Mr. Red (his sign said Red's Boats/Cash Only) whether he knew the late Mr. Delacroix. He might have been a fishing buddy or guide of their father's when he was a younger, less scruffy-looking version of himself.

And when they were sitting in the

motionless boat, listening to the eerie night sounds of the swamp, watching the permutations of moonlight on the brown water, Julienne would tell her brother about her problems with Nils and how angry and discouraged the situation made her. And maybe Philippe would suggest that she just take time out, the way the psychologists are wont to say; Philippe had probably visited his share of psychologists and psychiatrists. He'd remember an old rental shack on solid ground out in the swamp where she could kick back, think things over, and take pictures. He probably even knew a place to stop for supplies and knew where to pull in to ask the owner's permission to use the shack. In fact, since he wasn't answering his phone at the hotel, he might be there with Julienne.

No, he'd returned the boat, but he could have rented another, at a weekly rate, picked up the supplies in the morning, and returned. I was feeling almost cheerful when I returned my red Escort to the rental agency. My imagined scenario made sense. I could picture Julienne and her brother sitting lazily on a pier somewhere in the swamp, fishing, taking pictures of the strange trees and the alligators and snakes and other denizens of the mud flats and the water, getting reacquainted after so many years of following their separate career paths.

By the time I reached Jackson Square, I decided I deserved a treat, so I stopped again at La Madeleine's and bought a glass of red wine and a piece of chocolate cake with deep, rich frosting. My snack wasn't for the book; it wasn't particular to New Orleans. It was happy food, and I enjoyed every sip and bite as I sat at the window and watched the passing scene. Red wine and chocolate: food for the gods. Jason thinks it's a crazy combination, but what does he know?

24

News of an Untenured Adulterer

I returned to the hotel after my dose of comfort food on Jackson Square to find a voicemail message from Jason: "Caro, I talked to one of Julienne's colleagues this morning. The latest gossip from her university is that the dean of her college received an E-mail from Linus Torelli announcing that he'd just accepted a job in Sweden and wouldn't be back. Seems Torelli told the dean he was leaving because he's being blamed for Julienne's disappearance by, and I quote, 'some nosy friend of hers.'" Jason's delighted chuckle sounded in my ear as he asked, "Think you're the 'nosy friend'? Torelli also says he was not having an affair with Professor Magnussen and he resented all the vicious gossip about them, most of which he attributed to her husband.

"Maybe it was a mistake, but I called Nils with the news, and he seemed pretty upset," Jason added. "I don't know how it went this morning with the police, but I think you ought to check on him. OK? See you around five-thirty."

Torelli had resigned? That seemed a bit overboard to me if he wasn't guilty of anything, and I resented being characterized as the "nosy friend," even if the dean, whom I'd never met, didn't know my name. It's rather off-putting to think that one is being unpleasantly characterized on the Internet, which is not, as I understand it, a particularly private means of communication. And what an odd way to resign! Bad enough to disappear and resign in the middle of a semester without notice, but to do it by E-mail! That is hardly proper academic etiquette.

Feeling tired and put upon, I combed my hair and applied a bit of lipstick as I wondered what Nils was upset about. One would think he'd be glad to know that Torelli was gone for good, declaring Julienne's innocence in the process. But of course, that meant — if Torelli was to be believed, and I believed him even if I hadn't liked him — that Nils had been wrong about Julienne. He'd be upset because he was feeling guilty at having misjudged her.

As I put down my lipstick case, it also occurred to me that if Torelli had not been involved with Julienne, he'd have had no reason to do her harm, although he might have agreed to hide her out from her husband before he left. He might have been the renter of the boat. In fact, he might not be in Sweden at all. One can't tell where an E-mail originates. I had to remind myself once more that Lieutenant Boudreaux said Torelli had flown to Sweden. Could that be faked? In truth, I didn't know what to think. My speculations were unaccompanied by proof.

I picked up my handbag and headed for the Magnussen room. At least I didn't have to go out in the rain again, for it was pouring down from low-hanging, gray clouds. Even I, starved for the sight and feel of rain, was getting a bit tired of it. El Paso's perpetual sunshine might look good by the time we got home. I knocked on Nils's door, waited, knocked again harder, called his name, and finally got a response, although not a very welcoming one. Nils opened the door looking rumpled and unhappy, more so when he saw me.

"Did you come to say, 'I told you so'?" he asked bitterly.

"I came because Jason said that you

seemed upset after he called about Torelli's resignation."

"Why should I be upset?" Nils retorted sarcastically. "The man's gone to Sweden. He's not coming back. My wife didn't go with him. I'm delighted."

He didn't look at all delighted. His thinning blond hair stood up in ragged tufts, his face seemed bloated, his eyes puffy, and I could smell scotch on his breath. "Do you want to discuss this out in the hall?" I asked calmly. Getting impatient with a man so edgy didn't seem like a good idea.

He shrugged and waved me in. He had one of the rooms that overlooked the courtyard, while ours overlooked the street. I stood for a moment eyeing the greenery below, thinking it must be more peaceful at night than the front of the building where Jason and I could hear the voices and laughter of people on the street. On the other hand, the melancholy sounds of horns wailing in the night were romantic. People our age, parents of grown-up children, can always use a bit of romance in their lives.

Nils had dropped down on one of the twin beds, so I sat down on the other, facing him. He looked the picture of dejection, hands dangling between his knees, head hanging. "We'll find her," I said encouragingly. "Do you want to help me look? Maybe she's rented a place in the swamp."

His head came up abruptly. "Why would you think that?" he demanded.

I felt a stab of panic. After all, the only clue I had about the swamp was the fact that a man had rented a boat to go night fishing. No woman had been seen with him. What if the man had been Nils, and he felt that I was closing in on him, and he —

"You think she's so furious with me that she'd hide out in some moldy swamp so I can't find her and try to patch things up?"

"I . . . I don't know where she is," I stammered. "I'm just guessing." Patch things up? If he wanted to patch things up, didn't that mean he hadn't done anything to her that would prevent them from reconciling?

"I did some investigating myself," Nils continued, low-voiced. "After Jason called me about Torelli's resignation, I called this fellow in her department."

I nodded and guessed, "Mark somebody or other."

"How did you know that?" He looked alarmed, as if I had psychic powers and might be reading his thoughts.

"I remember Julienne saying this Mark

313

always knows everything that goes on. In her department, at any rate."

"Oh. Well, he does."

"What did he say?" I found that I was almost afraid of the answer.

"That she wasn't having an affair with Torelli. The son of a bitch has been dropping those hints in the department to cover up the fact that he was fucking the chairman's wife."

You can imagine my horror. No one that I know uses the "f" word, at least in my presence. Well, maybe some of the younger faculty. And the students. My son Chris used it once, and when I reprimanded him, he said, "Oh, Mom, everyone uses it." I was not happy to hear that. I suppose if I'd been part of the counterculture of the sixties and seventies, I might not have been so disgusted with Nils's language, but frankly I avoid R-rated movies because so many seem to employ a one-word vocabulary, which shows a woeful lack of inventiveness on the part of the scriptwriters, in my opinion.

"Well, aren't you going to say anything?" Nils snapped.

I managed to get my mind off the wording and onto the content of his revelation. In this case, the word in question wasn't just an expletive; it was used to describe an activity: Linus Torelli having sexual relations with his chairman's wife. Good heavens! I never cease to be amazed at the clandestine sexual activities that go on in the academic community. In this case, not just adultery, but adultery of the stupidest kind. Not that liaisons between students and professors aren't madness in these days of proliferating sexual harassment charges, but to become involved with one's chairman's wife was surely a suicidal impulse, professionally speaking. "Did he have tenure?" I asked.

"Tenure? That's your only comment? Did he have tenure?" Nils stopped looking woebegone and looked, instead, irritated.

It *was* a stupid question. Even insensitive, given Nils's obvious misery. Although I'm sure it would come to the mind of any person who has spent many years involved with college faculties. Even if the chairman's wife was the aggressor, the chairman wasn't likely to take that into account if he became cognizant of the affair. Would a chairman's wife seducing an untenured professor be considered sexual harassment? I wondered.

"He didn't," said Nils.

"He didn't what?" I had been lost in my

speculations, which only proved that I needed a nap.

"He didn't have tenure," said Nils impatiently. "My God, he was ten years younger than Julienne. He wasn't even coming up for consideration until the end of next year."

"Then why did you think Julienne would be interested in him?" I retorted.

Nils gave me a strange look. "You mean why would she go after someone without tenure when she was married to someone who had it?"

"No!" What a silly interpretation of my question! "I meant why would she be interested in someone ten years her junior? Or, why would you believe it of her?"

Nils sighed. "Because I'm a fool." He dropped his head into his hands. "I've been so stupid."

I had to agree with that, although I didn't say so aloud. "So why did he take off for Sweden in the middle of the semester if he was in love with the chairman's wife? Did the chair find out about it?"

Nils shook his head and mumbled, "Martha found out about the supposed affair between Julienne and Torelli. In fact, her husband called her from here to tell her about Julienne disappearing and Torelli being suspect and so forth, and the wife called Torelli and tore a strip off him, said she was going to tell her husband that Torelli had seduced her."

"Good grief! How do you know all this?"

"Torelli told Mark. So Torelli hopped a plane to go home and pacify the chair's wife and try to talk her out of screwing up his bid for tenure, and she decided that he'd just been after her because he wanted her to support him with her husband."

"Is that likely?" I asked, amazed. What a bizarre story!

"I don't know. Maybe. She's older than Julienne and doesn't look half as good. What the hell would he want with her if he weren't hoping to get something out of it? Anyway, he panicked and went to Mark for advice."

"Which is like telling your troubles to Barbara Walters on national TV. I remember Julienne saying this Mark is a terrible gossip," I mused. "He not only knows all but tells all. If Torelli's that indiscreet, maybe he did need someone to support his bid for tenure."

"Julienne always said he was a good scientist." Nils scowled. "If she hadn't kept saying that —"

"Oh, nonsense, Nils. Don't put your jealousy off on Julienne. Especially now that you know you were wrong about her. And *especially* since your jealousy drove her away, and we don't even know where she is."

Nils looked so guilt-stricken that I almost wished I hadn't reminded him of his culpability in all this. "So what advice did Mark give Torelli?" I asked to get his mind off his troubles.

"He said that Torelli was done for with Martha on his case, and he'd better take the job in Sweden if they offered it. They did, and he did. End of story."

"Surely Martha wouldn't have told her husband that he should fire Torelli because she had been having an affair with him."

"No," Nils agreed. "She'd have said both Julienne and Torelli should be fired because *they* were having an affair, which he'd have believed because he'd already heard the rumors. That way she'd have gotten even with them both."

"Julienne has tenure," I pointed out.

"She'd never have been given another raise. She'd have found herself teaching all the scut classes and lots of them. She'd have gotten all the bad committee assignments. You don't have to fire someone to get rid of them. Julienne wouldn't have put up with that kind of treatment, and Martha wouldn't have stopped nagging her husband until he forced Julienne to leave."

"And Torelli just went off and left Julienne to that fate? How despicable! And this Martha doesn't sound like a very nice person, either."

"Martha's a bitch," said Nils.

I was reminded that he had called me a bitch just this morning. While I was remembering that, Nils was rising from the bed and grabbing a raincoat that had been thrown across the desk chair. "Where are you going?" I called after him as he headed for the door.

"To get drunk," he replied and slammed out.

Well, that wasn't a very fruitful approach to the problem of his missing wife! I sat a minute longer on what must have been Julienne's bed before she disappeared. Without any new ideas about where to find her, I used Nils's telephone to try Philippe's hotel room again. Might as well let Nils pay for the call. Goodness knows, I had spent an insane amount of money on calls before I discovered what they were costing. I punched in the numbers. By now I had them memorized. Without much surprise I listened to the ringing of the telephone. Philippe still wasn't in.

I hoped that meant he was with Julienne. Maybe his failure to answer meant that they had left town together, and he had kept his hotel registration to foil attempts to find them. Was Philippe a loving enough brother that he would risk his own position at the medical school where he taught in order to comfort his sister? Perhaps, if not to the swamp, they'd gone to the family cabin on the lake.

But the weather there would be dreadful, worse than New Orleans.

Then suddenly Nils's words came back to me, or to be more exact, his verb tenses. "She'd never have been given another raise . . . . She'd have gotten all the bad committee assignments. . . ." As if nothing the chair's wife or the chair meant to do to Julienne made any difference. Because she wouldn't be around to take the heat for the alleged affair. What was Nils thinking? And why?

25

The Roux Morgue

It was after three-thirty when I returned to my room and sank down on the red bedspread, toeing my shoes onto the floor and stretching out. Although I was determined to have a nap, my mind refused to turn off. Nils didn't expect Julienne to return. Why? It didn't bear thinking on. And Martha, the chairman's wife. A spiteful woman. Would she seek revenge if Julienne did return? Surely, Martha could be persuaded that there had been no affair. Well, none but her own.

Still, that would be a difficult subject to introduce tactfully. What was Julienne supposed to say in her own defense? "I wasn't having an affair with Linus Torelli. You were." Actually, that approach, put more subtly, had merit. This Mrs. Chairman Martha might think twice about accusing Julienne if she knew that Julienne was aware of the jealousy that lay behind Martha's campaign to get rid of someone she perceived as a rival for the affections of a lover.

But there *was* no campaign to force Julienne out. Not yet. And Martha — I was calling some woman by her first name when I had never set eyes on her. This whole wild story about affairs and vengeance might be a figment in the imagination of another person I'd never met, Mark the Gossip. Still, Torelli *had* left the country. And Julienne *was* missing. Oh God, how I hoped that she was with her brother!

But where could she and Phillipe have gone? When did she plan to return? Why hadn't she called me? What kind of job had the amoral Professor Torelli been forced to take in Sweden? Where should Jason and I go for dinner? Preferably someplace with food interesting enough to write about in my book. I should look at the *Louisiana New Garde*, but I was so sleepy. My thoughts drifted and broke up as my eyes began to close.

The ringing jerked me awake. Time to get up, I thought groggily as I reached for the telephone. "Thank you for calling," I mumbled and swung my legs over the side of the bed. The telephone receiver was on its way back to the cradle when I saw the time. Four o'clock? They'd given me a wake-up call at four o'clock? Light shining through the windows told me that it wasn't morning, and I replaced the receiver against my ear in time to hear a male voice saying, "Miz Blue? Miz Blue?"

"Lieutenant?" Why was *he* calling?

"Miz Blue, Ah'm tryin' to get ahold a Professor Magnussen."

"Why?" I asked.

"Well." There was a long pause.

"Is something wrong?" Suddenly, I was no longer sleepy, but rather short-winded and anxious. "What's wrong?"

"Likely nothin', ma'am. But if you know where the professor is —"

"He's gone out to get drunk."

"Damn!" Another pause. "Sorry 'bout the language, ma'am."

"Why did you want to speak to him?"

"Well." The next pause made me even more nervous than the first. "Well, Miz Blue, fact is, we got this body in the morgue. Jus' came in."

"Oh, my God. It isn't —"

"Probably not, ma'am. We jus' thought, your friend bein' missin' an' all, maybe the professor should take a look."

"Where did you find the body?" He told me in great detail, little of which meant much to me as a nonresident of the area. However, I did gather that the body had been fished from the swamp by a tour boat, much to the dismay of the tourists. "Is it . . . is it . . ."

"Like Ah said, Miz Blue, we don' know who it is. That's why we need identification. Probably someone who lives out in the bayous fell off a fishin' boat or a pier. Somethin' like that. Been in the water a while."

"I'll come."

"Oh, now, Miz Blue, Ah don' think you wanna —"

"Where?"

"Well, the morgue, but —"

"I'll take a taxi. Will a taxi driver know where the morgue is?"

"Yes, ma'am. Likely he will, but Ah don' think —"

"Thank you for calling, Lieutenant." I hung up. *Oh lord, not Julienne,* I prayed as I stuffed my feet into my shoes and grabbed my handbag. *Not Julienne.*

With a sick dread, I sat on a bench outside in the corridor, waiting for Lieutenant Boudreaux to appear and usher me into the morgue. A policeman and a man in white medical scrubs were smoking cigarettes ten feet down the hall and chatting.

"I don't get it," said the officer. "Why are they callin' it the roo morgue?"

"R-O-U-X. Like you start with for gumbo," said the pathologist or tech or whatever he was. "We've had one sous chef, one maître d', and one waiter brought in in the same week."

"Yeah?" The cop frowned, puzzled.

"You never read *Murders in the Rue Morgue?*"

"I don' read much," said the cop. "It's a book about gumbo?"

"No, man, R-U-E in French means *street.*"

"So?" responded the policeman. He blew a smoke ring and watched it drift away.

"It's a pun," I said sharply, wishing they'd stop talking. Instead, they both turned and stared at me.

"She's right," said the tech. "It's a kind of joke, you dummy."

"Who're you callin' a dummy?"

I turned my back on them as the argument escalated. Then the lieutenant arrived to rescue me from tasteless puns and try to talk me out of viewing the body, which he evidently hadn't seen himself. However, I insisted. I had to know one way or the other, so he escorted me, reluctantly, through the door and into a cold room where an incongruously merry-looking man, his round stomach ballooning in a pregnant mound under a white lab coat, awaited us by a steel table. Shivering, marginally comforted by the support of the lieutenant's warm hand at my elbow, I nodded to the morgue tech, or was he the coroner?

As he began to draw the sheet back, the lieutenant swore. I retched. Because the face was gone, shredded by monster teeth, while the victim's arm had been devoured entirely.

"Ah knew this wasn't a good idea," said Boudreaux, his hand tightening on my arm. "Slater, why don't you —"

But I couldn't wait. Tearing my arm away from the lieutenant's supportive grip, I dashed into the now-empty hall and turned left toward a rest room I had noticed as I came in. Unfortunately, it proved to be the men's room, but I had no time to observe the niceties of gender separation. I catapulted through the swinging door and vomited into the first available receptacle.

"Hey, lady!" cried the policeman who

hadn't read *Murders in the Rue Morgue.* Before he protested, turned his back, and zipped up with frantic haste, he had been standing at the urinal next to me

I retched again. And again, impervious to his demands that I leave the "little boy's room," as he put it. "Lady, Ah'm gonna arrest you. It ain't right for ladies to come in here. Jus' 'cause you're hungover, don' mean you kin —"

Hungover? I gave him an indignant look, staggered to the sink, and cupped my hands under the faucet, then lifted the water to rinse my mouth. By the time I had splashed water on my burning face, the second occupant of the men's room had thought better of arresting me and gone.

Could that have been Julienne on the table? I wondered, appalled, and leaned weakly against the grungy wall tiles. Possibly. The hair — it might have been Julienne's. I scrubbed the tears away from my eyes and walked slowly back to the morgue, where Boudreaux intercepted me at the door.

"Miz Blue, if you'd given me the chance, I'da told you what they told me; there's just not enough left to identify unless you know the lady real . . . real intimately. Maybe we can get a print from the right hand. Ah should never a let you corral me into —"

"I doubt that Julienne was ever finger-printed," I replied. "And I *can* identify her." In my mind I replayed voices — Julienne's and mine — twelve years old, on a sleepover at her house, giggling and trying on each other's clothes.

"Look at that!" said Julienne, turning away for me and pointing unhappily at a light tan splotch just where her bottom rounded on the left side.

"It's so light you can hardly see it," I had protested. "Besides, nobody's ever going to see it except me . . . and your mom, I guess."

"What about my husband when I get married?" Julienne wailed.

The idea of anyone, especially a male someone, ever seeing one's naked bottom was too much for my twelve-year-old mind; I had suggested we listen to records. But I *could* identify Julienne — by that birthmark she had so detested. I wondered, sadly, what Nils had thought of it.

Slipping past Lieutenant Boudreaux, I walked back to the steel table on which, I prayed, no light tan birthmark would be in evidence on the poor, mangled body that lay there. "Could you turn her over, please?" I asked the potbellied man in his spotless lab coat. How would I have felt, I wondered, had that coat been splashed with blood? It didn't bear thinking on. The body was horrifying enough.

"Ma'am, Ah don't think a nice lady like yourself oughta to be lookin' at the backside a this here —"

"Please," I said, voice wobbly but determined, "if we're going to find out who she is, or isn't —" which is what I devoutly hoped to ascertain, who she wasn't "— you're going to have to turn her over."

Looking resigned, Lieutenant Boudreaux gestured to the man, who then stripped back the sheet. I had to close my eyes. Could that be Julienne? I was unable to tell because the body had been unbearably savaged. Mr. Slater lifted and turned the body. Very gently. I liked him for that. It was touching that, in such a grisly profession, he had maintained his humanity. And then I gasped, because the left buttock, on which I had based my confident prediction of identification, was virtually gone, gnawed away. I turned, weeping, and the lieutenant led me from the cold room.

"We're runnin' a fingerprint check right now on AFIS," he said consolingly. "Probably find out it's some woman been in

329

prison for years an' drowned herself because she couldn't make it on the outside. Not much chance it's your friend."

"I suppose not," I said.

He handed me a clean linen handkerchief. It must be a Southern thing, I thought. Julienne had carried linen handkerchiefs, too, while most of us philistines just use Kleenex. At the thought of Julienne and her lace-edged handkerchiefs, I started to cry again and used the lieutenant's. Of course, it had no lace, but I did notice a B embroidered in the corner. And now, having shown so little self-control, I'd have to get it washed and ironed before Jason and I left New Orleans.

26

The Intrepid Gourmet

Lieutenant Boudreaux sent me back in a police car. Still sniffling into his handkerchief, I climbed out in front of the Hotel de la Poste, only to be confronted by Carlene, Broder, and my husband.

"You poor girl," Carlene cried and pulled me into a motherly embrace. "What happened? Were you arrested?"

The policeman jumped out of his front seat and said, "Here. What are you doing?" to Carlene. "This woman's under my protection."

Evidently he thought I was being attacked. How ironic that the New Orleans Police couldn't wait to protect me from a friend's hug but were never in sight when one of the many crazies in the city really was attacking me. I could certainly have used his help yesterday when that madman in the pickup truck tried to run me off a country road.

"Caro," Jason cried, "what are you doing in a police car, and why are you crying?"

"Get your hands off her," the officer said to Jason.

"He's my husband," I protested, fearing Jason's imminent arrest.

"Oh." The officer climbed into his patrol car immediately, saying, "I purely hate domestic disputes."

"What dispute?" Jason asked, but the officer was already pulling away. My protection, needed or not, had been very short-lived.

"I've been to the morgue," I said, sopping up tears with Lieutenant Boudreaux's soggy handkerchief.

Jason and the McAvees looked stunned. I don't suppose any of them has ever been to a morgue. I certainly hadn't until today. "It was horrible."

"Julienne," said Broder. "Was it Julienne?"

"I don't know. I looked at the body, but I couldn't tell."

"How could you not tell?" Carlene asked reasonably. Although Broder seemed to be giving in to fear for our friend, Carlene remained calm. "Either it was Julienne, or it wasn't."

"The woman had been . . . been . . .

killed by an alligator." More tears. I couldn't seem to stem the flow.

"Oh, sweetheart." Jason put his arms around me, although this conversation was playing out on the street in front of the hotel, and Jason usually saved demonstrations of affection for private moments, as you'd expect of a long-married scientist with two more or less grown children. I cried some more, and he handed me a Kleenex, having failed to notice that I had a real handkerchief from Lieutenant Boudreaux.

"She was . . . was chewed up," I sobbed. "The woman in the morgue. But she had black hair. I think. It was muddy . . . just like . . . just like mine when I fell into the bayou." Before I could get any further with my description of the body I had gone to view, thunder rolled, drowning out conversation, and rain poured down as if dumped on us from buckets in the hands of angry rain gods. We all sprinted inside and dripped on the antiques in the lobby.

Carlene made me sit down, handed me another Kleenex, and said, "It wasn't Julienne," in a voice of absolute certainty. "Why would Julienne let herself be eaten by an alligator? She was a native of Louisiana. If anyone knows the danger of getting near an alligator, it's Julienne. She would never put herself in a position where an alligator could get anywhere near her."

"But —"

"You can take my word for it, Carolyn. She came to visit us one time and scared my children half to death with alligator tales. You never heard so much squealing and shrieking and giggling in your life. Children do love gore. Don't you agree, Broder?"

"Well, they've grown out of that phase," he replied defensively.

"True, but the point of this story is that Julienne knows all about alligators and how to keep out of their way, so the woman you saw was not Julienne. Now . . .." Carlene, who had been sitting beside me, got up, pulling me with her. "Now we're all going to dinner and have a wonderful meal. You can write about every bite we put in our mouths."

"Why did *you* have to go to the morgue, Caro?" my husband asked. "Shouldn't Nils have been asked?"

"He was, but he's out getting drunk," I replied, beginning to feel angry. There's nothing like a good gush of indignation to dry up one's tears.

"Drunk!" Broder frowned disapprovingly.

"Nils's conduct throughout this whole episode has been reprehensible. When a search for Julienne needed to be made through the dangerous streets of New Orleans, you and I had to take on that responsibility because Nils wouldn't. I think —"

"I think you're getting grouchy, love," said Carlene. "Is it the prospect of an expensive dinner? Or are you just hungry?"

"I'm getting tired of rich food," Broder admitted. "I'd like to eat some ordinary —" He paused, trying to think of what might be ordinary enough for a Midwesterner who had been subjected to years of oddball California cuisine and health food by his wife and who had now suffered through a week of French sauces and Cajun spices. "— some plain old steak and potatoes," he decided. "But I don't suppose steak and potatoes would do anything for Carolyn's book," he finished wistfully.

"On the contrary, I seem to remember . . . let me think . . . there was a delicious-looking recipe for filets and mashed potatoes." Broder looked hopeful. "Let's go up to our room to dry off while I look it up." I knew Broder and Carlene were staying at a B & B on the edge of the Quarter, so it wouldn't be very convenient for them to return there before dinner.

"I like mashed potatoes," said Broder, as he and Carlene trailed us up to the room.

I found the recipe under an entry for the Pelican Club, filets mignons with shiitake mushrooms and Cabernet sauce and garlic mashed potatoes with roasted onions. It sounded perfect for a cold, rainy night. I didn't mention the mushrooms and Cabernet sauce or the garlic in the potatoes to Broder, who was busy peering at a map with Jason, looking for the address on Exchange Alley. Carlene was in the bathroom toweling off her longish gray-white hair, and I was calling to secure a reservation for four.

"Oh, I'm sorry, madam, but I'm afraid a reservation for this evening would be impossible," said the person who answered the telephone.

"What a shame," I replied. "I had wanted to include the Pelican Club in my book on eating in New Orleans, but I suppose I'll have to substitute some more accommodating restaurant."

There was a brief pause. "Is this a guide book?" asked the man.

"No, it's a — how should I describe it? — a book about food, New Orleans food. The manuscript is due at the publisher's in six months, and I am due home on Saturday, so I'll just have to skip the Pelican Club, although I did want to sample your filet with shiitake mushrooms."

"An excellent choice, madam. If you'll give me just a minute, I'll see if a table can't be found for your party."

"Oh, good!" I said breezily. "I think I'd prefer the front room, which I'm told is quite elegant, and I do want to look at the paintings. Do you have any of particular interest? That would make a nice addition to my description of the ambiance."

"We have some very fine pieces," I was assured. "Consigned from excellent galleries."

"I'm delighted to hear it." While the reservation person was getting me a reservation, I had to suppress an undignified impulse to giggle at my own temerity. A certain rather crude member of Jason's department would have said that I had "balls." In this case having balls proved to be an excellent thing. We got our reservation, passed around towels to sop up the results of the cloudburst that had caught us in the middle of my personal cloudburst, combed hair, refreshed lipstick, used the facilities, borrowed extra umbrellas from the hotel, and ventured outside again, maps in hand.

Jason and Broder argued amiably over whether we should turn right or left (Exchange Alley runs parallel between Chartres, our street, and Royal, the police station street). Jason won, and we turned left, finding the restaurant at the corner of Bienville and Exchange Alley. Having lost the route debate, Broder argued with his wife about whether they should order courses in addition to the filets and mashed potatoes. Broder was worried about the extra cost of desserts and appetizers.

"We'll skip the appetizers and share a dessert," I suggested. "They're supposed to make a marvelous profiterole. The pastries are served three to a plate, but maybe I can talk them into four," I said cheerfully. I had been thinking about Carlene's statement that Julienne would never have put herself in the path of a hungry alligator. That seemed a reasonable assumption to me.

"They're not going to make the dessert bigger just to accommodate us," Broder complained. "They'll want to sell us four desserts."

"If I talked them into giving us a reservation on short notice, I can talk them into providing one more little profiterole and four forks," I assured him. After all, I told myself, I was a food critic with "balls."

27

Filets Mignons with Shiitake Mushrooms and Cabernet Sauce, and Garlic Mashed Potatoes with Roasted Onions

Somewhat the worse for rain, Jason, Broder, Carlene, and I arrived at the nineteenth-century townhouse in which the Pelican Club was housed. There we were greeted with deference and seated at an excellent table in the front room, which was as elegant as my guidebook had indicated. I felt a bit guilty at the thought of the party for whom the table had originally been designated, but goodness, academics aren't often treated like visiting royalty, so I decided to enjoy the windfall dropped in our laps by my new profession. Accordingly, I whipped out my new camera, purchased to replace the one that fell into the bayou. What an expensive trip this was turning out to be! Perhaps the new camera was tax deductible. While I took pictures, Carlene prowled the room looking at the paintings that were for sale. Other diners were staring at us, which was a bit embarrassing.

Then Carlene cried, "This one. I want to buy this one." It was a very pleasant, fuzzy picture with golden splashes slanting across the foreground. Broder, having leaned forward to see the price, gasped. "Now, love," Carlene chided exuberantly, "I have to have it. It looks just like a compound we're working on in the lab."

"Can't you just frame a picture from your electron microscope?" asked Broder, looking more and more alarmed.

"Broder McAvee, I make enough money that, for once in my life, I can afford to buy an oil painting that I like."

"Acrylic," murmured the female diner behind whose chair Carlene was standing.

"Especially one that looks just like the bioactive compound my team developed," Carlene continued. "Look, Jason. Doesn't that look like . . ." She came out with some long string of chemical designations that I couldn't have deciphered or remembered if I were to be quizzed on them the next minute.

Jason obligingly leaned forward to look at the yellow pools of light in a shadowy field of sometimes-translucent blue and black. "Could be," he agreed. "Certainly there's carbon there."

His vague answer, the twinkle in his eye, and the hint of a grin behind his beard told me that he probably wasn't even familiar with her compound, much less in agreement on the biochemical significance of the painting, and even I knew that there was carbon everywhere.

"Ah hate to rain on your parade, ma'am," said the companion to the female diner who could tell acrylic from oil, "but that's an impressionist renderin' of a New Orleans street at night."

"Nonsense," said Carlene.

"Ah know the artist," said the man, offended at having his expertise ignored.

I couldn't resist the impulse to participate in the fun. "There's a Lyonel Feininger quality to the layering of paint, don't you think?" I suggested thoughtfully.

"It doesn't look like Feininger at all," protested the acrylic lady with knowledgeable indignation.

"I'd call it a postmodern Renoir," Jason chimed in. He was now definitely on the verge of laughter.

"I can't detect a redheaded girl anywhere in that painting," I objected enthusiastically. There's nothing more exhilarating than talking absolute nonsense, something grown-ups so seldom get to do.

"Oh, stop it, you two." Carlene grinned at us, then turned to the maître d'. "I want to buy it."

Poor Broder groaned as if he thought the college educations of his remaining offspring would come to an abrupt halt because of his wife's spendthrift impulses. However, I knew what a broomstick skirt cost. Carlene was wearing another of her collection. She must have saved a fortune on clothes over the years with that posthippie wardrobe. Enough so that she deserved to buy a painting if she wanted to, even if it didn't look like a chemical to me.

Carlene went off to complete her purchase, calling over her shoulder, "Just order that filet for me." The rest of us retreated to our table and perused the menu. Broder was horrified at the price of the steak, so much so he didn't notice that it came with sauce, mushrooms of an oriental variety, and garlic in the mashed potatoes. Claiming to have my book in mind, Jason ordered an entirely different entrée, an assortment of seafood cooked in a clay pot with vegetables. The broth, according to the waiter, was flavored with, among other things, cilantro, which is very popular in El Paso.

"I read in the paper the other day that the Mexican drug cartels have been smuggling cocaine into the United States in shipments of cilantro," I said conversationally.

Broder looked horrified. "You mean there might be cocaine in our steak and potatoes?"

"Not at all," I assured him. "If there's a problem, it will be with Jason's seafood stew. Perhaps we should watch him closely to see if he shows signs of drug overdose."

The waiter looked bewildered.

"Thanks a lot," Jason said dryly. "Maybe we should call one of your acquaintances on the police force to bring in a drug dog to sniff my seafood."

"I assure you, sir —" the waiter stammered.

"You poor man," said Carlene, who had taken her seat during the cocaine remarks. "Pay no attention to these people. They're mad scientists, except for my husband, who is a thrifty Calvinist, and this lady, who is a mad food critic."

Then we ordered three filets in cabernet sauce, plus Jason's seafood flavored with possibly dangerous cilantro, and fell to discussing Julienne's disappearance. Carlene again assured me that the body I viewed could not have been our friend. She insisted on the logic of her contention. But Broder, surprisingly, made the argument that really resonated with me. He said that had the alligator-savaged woman been Julienne, my heart would have confirmed it.

"I have always felt that there is a continuing bond between the living and the dead when they have been close in life," he told me. "Do you really feel convinced that Julienne is dead?"

Did I?

"What did you feel when you viewed the body?"

"I threw up," I admitted. "In the men's room."

"Caro!" Jason exclaimed. "What were you doing in the men's room?"

"Really, Jason," Carlene chided. "Surely, you've noticed that there are always lines outside ladies' rooms while the men's rooms are always empty. What was she supposed to do? Throw up on the woman in front of her in line rather than use the men's facilities?"

"Insensitive of me not to have anticipated that situation," Jason admitted. "Sorry, Caro."

"I should think," said Carlene, a bit smug at having made her point. "I hope you're supporting the movement for equitable public toilet facilities for women." She was looking at my husband.

"I didn't know there was one," Jason replied.

At this point, I was feeling a bit conscience-stricken. Carlene was berating poor Jason when I had used the men's room because I hadn't seen a ladies' room. And in fact, the men's room hadn't been empty as Carlene assumed. There had been the unfortunate policeman urinating when I reeled in. I had to stifle an unseemly chuckle at the thought of his horror and indignation when he found himself sharing the trough with a retching female.

"At any rate," Carlene continued, "vomiting was simply a result of physical repulsion at a terrible sight. I think Broder has a point. Aside from the horror you felt, did you think you had lost your childhood friend? Do you have the feeling that Julienne is dead? I know I don't. I keep expecting to see her walk around the corner, grinning and apologizing for having missed my plenary address."

Actually, I didn't know how I felt. Having been consumed with worry for five days, buoyed one minute by optimism, then plunged the next into dread, my strongest emotion was confusion, which isn't so much an emotion as a mental state. Carlene and Broder might be right. Surely, I would have recognized my friend, no matter what the condition of her body. Surely, I would have experienced overwhelming grief. "Maybe she *is* alive," I said, feeling my spirits lift.

"Let's hope so," said Jason. He covered my hand with his own.

"We might as well expect the best as long as there's no reason to grieve," said Broder.

"Imagine. Optimism from a man who believes we're all destined from birth for heaven or hell," said Carlene.

"I've never really understood the idea of predestination," I chimed in, glad to change the subject. "Does that mean you can sin indiscriminately, and if you're pre-destined for heaven, you'll still get there?"

Before Broder could answer me, the waiter began to serve our entrées. Conversation pretty much ceased after that as we concentrated on our dinners, which were marvelous. Jason's crustaceans in a clay pot, the broth flavored with lime, chili, and cilantro, had the intriguing tang of a ceviche I've eaten in

Juarez on one of those rare occasions when the drug wars abated enough for dinner excursions across the border. If any cocaine had fallen off the cilantro into the broth, I couldn't tell. I believe cocaine is supposed to induce a feeling of exhilaration, but I must say I had found our foolish conversation about Carlene's painting more exhilarating than Jason's entrée.

As for the filets — ah, heaven! I had asked for mine medium rare, and medium rare it was. Between us, Carlene and I had managed to convince Broder not to order his filet mignon well done, although medium was the pinkest he would agree to, but Broder loved his dish as well. I even noticed him surreptitiously wiping up the last of the rich, flavorful wine sauce with a piece of bread and eating every mushroom. When he first spotted them on top of his beef, he claimed to be completely unfamiliar with shiitake mushrooms and to be suspicious of mushrooms in general, having heard from colleagues of Carlene's about a group of biologists in the Northwest who had been poisoned by eating gathered mushrooms.

We assured him that the event in question had been years ago and that efficient Japanese harvesters, who wouldn't dream of poisoning a customer, had undoubtedly gathered his shiitakes. I had to signal Jason to silence when he launched into a discussion of Japanese culinary toxins. The subject, which would not calm Broder's fears, was puffer fish or *fugu,* a favorite Japanese sushi, known not only for its nerve toxin, but served to special customers with enough poison left in the fish to give them tingling lips without killing them. At least that is the expectation.

I include the recipe for Chef Richard Hughes's filets with shiitake mushrooms for those who are overcome with a desire to spend several days in the kitchen. Otherwise, fly to New Orleans and visit the Pelican Club.

Filets Mignons with Shiitake Mushrooms and Cabernet Sauce, and Garlic Mashed Potatoes with Roasted Onions

To Make Filets for 4:
Preheat oven to 350° F.

Brown *four 8-oz. filets mignons* on all sides in *2 tbs. of butter* in a heavy, ovenproof skillet.

Bake in oven for 8 to 10 minutes or

until medium rare.

Set filets aside and keep warm.

Transfer filet pan to burner on stove top, add *1 tbs. chopped shallots* and *1 cup stemmed and sliced Shiitake mushrooms,* and sauté until shallots are translucent.

Add *2 tbs. bourbon,* protect face, ignite bourbon with long match, and shake pan until flames subside.

Add *¹/₂ cup demi-glace* (recipe follows), *¹/₂ cup Cabernet Sauvignon,* and *¹/₄ cup Madeira or dry sherry,* and cook over medium heat to reduce until thickened, 5 to 8 minutes.

Stir in *2 tbs. of butter, salt and pepper* to taste.

To Make 1 to 1¹/₂ Qts. Demi-Glace Sauce:
Place *5 lbs. cut veal marrow bones* in large baking pan and roast in a 400° F oven until brown, 30 to 40 minutes.

Add *2 cups peeled, diced carrots, 2*

cups diced onions, 2 cups diced celery, and roast 20 minutes more.

Add *2 tbs. tomato paste,* stir, and continue roasting 10 minutes.

Place on stove top, pour in *2 bottles Cabernet Sauvignon* and *1 bottle Madeira wine or dry sherry,* and cook over medium heat, stirring to scrape up brown bits from pan bottom.

Place in heavy stockpot, add *1 gallon water, 8 garlic cloves, 1 fresh thyme sprig, 3 bay leaves,* and simmer 24 hours.

Strain through fine-meshed sieve and cook over medium heat to reduce to consistency of heavy cream. Unused sauce may be frozen for later use.

To Make Mashed Potatoes:
Preheat oven to 375° F.

Rub *olive oil* on *1 unpeeled onion* and *2 garlic heads with outer papery husk removed,* and roast 30 minutes or until slightly browned and softened.

In large saucepan, boil *3 large white, peeled and cubed baking potatoes* in salted water to cover until tender, 20 minutes.

Peel onion and puree in blender or food processor.

Slice garlic heads in half crosswise and squeeze out garlic cloves; combine with onion puree.

Mash potatoes with onion-garlic mixture until soft. Add *6 tbs. butter, $^1/_2$ cup hot milk,* and *salt and pepper* to taste.

To Serve:
Pour sauce over filets and serve the warm mashed potatoes alongside.

While Broder was devouring his last bit of Cabernet sauce–soaked bread and wearing the expression of a man who would have patted his tummy in satisfaction had he thought his wife would let him get away with it, I managed to talk the waiter into a four-profiterole dessert plate. It arrived promptly, a lovely sight. Each profiterole was filled with homemade ice cream and topped with chopped pecans and a creamy chocolate sauce, the whole garnished with sliced, fresh berries. I do love the combination of raspberries or strawberries with chocolate. Combined with the last few sips of my red wine, the dessert was delicious.

"In answer to your question about predestination," Broder said to me over dessert, "I like to think that a soul predestined for heaven shows itself in the admirable behavior of its owner."

"So we can tell that a man like Linus Torelli is destined for hell because he was slandering Julienne while having an affair with his chairman's wife?" I asked.

Three pairs of eyes turned in my direction.

"Where did you hear that?" Jason asked.

"Nils told me. Someone in their department named Mark says that Torelli wasn't having an affair with Julienne; he just acted like it to cover up the fact that he was — ah — intimate with his chairman's wife."

"You can't be serious!" Carlene exclaimed and started to laugh. "That must be some exciting department to work in. So why did he take off for Sweden so suddenly?"

"Because the chairman's wife heard he was having an affair with Julienne and threatened to have him fired by her husband."

Carlene nodded. "Hoist on his own petard, as it were. What does that mean anyway? What's a petard?"

"It's from *Hamlet*," I said absently. "A petard is a thing for blowing holes in castle walls."

"I was asking a rhetorical question, not expecting an answer. How in the world would you know something like that, Carolyn?"

"Because I wasn't a science major," I retorted, laughing. "Anyway, this Mark told Torelli he'd never get tenure with the chairman's wife on the warpath, so Torelli took the job in Sweden. Now Nils is feeling terrible because he accused Julienne of being unfaithful when she wasn't."

"I never cease to be shocked at the sexual scandals in universities, where one would least expect to find them," said Broder, shaking his head over the sins of academe. "Happily, we don't have those problems at smaller colleges of religious origin."

"Oh, come off it, Broder," said his wife. "Have you forgotten the dean who used to pinch bottoms at faculty parties?"

"He was very old and somewhat senile," said Broder, "and he was gently nudged into retirement."

"Gently nudged, my eye," his wife retorted. "I saw that he got the boot after he pinched me."

"He pinched *you?*" Broder looked very unhappy to hear it. "Well, I'm sorry you had to put up with that sort of thing, Carlene, but I doubt that you were responsible for his resignation. Our president at that time, a man of great rectitude, got wind of the dean's problem and —"

"The president was moved to action at the insistence of his wife. The last time the dean pinched me, I walked her over to his circle, and of course he pinched her. Voila! That was it for the Dean of Bottoms, as we wives used to call him."

"I see." Broder looked stunned. Evidently, a lot went on at his college of which he was unaware. Hastily, he turned to me and remarked that, having heard about Linus Torelli's lamentable lapses of morality, he now wondered whether the young chemist might not have had something to do with Julienne's disappearance. "A man of loose morals might do anything," said Broder ominously. "And sinners do like to blame their own falls from grace on innocent bystanders. No doubt, he blamed Julienne for the very problem he created himself by slandering her."

I did not find that conjecture very reassuring, having, at that point, managed to convince myself that Julienne was probably safe and avoiding, with the help of her brother, undeserved recriminations from her drunken husband. Therefore, I made my last notes on the dinner with a heavy heart.

"Didn't you enjoy your food, Mrs. Blue?" asked the maître d', looking somewhat alarmed. He must have been alerted by my glum expression.

"If the rest of my visit to New Orleans had been as delightful as this dinner," I assured him, "I would be a happy woman."

The poor man didn't seem to know what to make of that accolade from a food critic who claimed to like his cuisine but looked anything but pleased.

28

The Faux Priest

I sat dispiritedly in the Café du Monde drinking a latte, munching on hot beignets, and wondering what to do. Of course, Julienne didn't appear at the café. I'd given up expecting her to. Philippe didn't answer his telephone. No surprise there. And the truth is, I had run out of ideas. I didn't know where to look next. Once again I brushed powdered sugar from my black raincoat, which, for a change, I didn't need. There was actually a stray sunbeam escaping from the usual umbrella of rain clouds that hung over the city. For lack of inspiration, I took my trusty *Frommer's New Orleans* from my pocket and thumbed through, scanning for likely investigation sites.

The French Market! Julienne had mentioned it. Although I didn't think I'd find her there, it would at least provide a destination. I followed Decatur Street from Jackson Square, entered the French

Market, and wandered in and out of stores, looking but not buying, then moving on to the farmer's market portion as I imagined how it had been in the 1700s when it was an Indian trading post at which Creoles could barter for sassafras from the Choctaws. The Spanish had put a roof over it, German farmers had supplied the produce as it evolved, and Italian immigrants sold food in its stalls, structures now swathed in garlic strings and offering, twenty-four hours a day, the most delicious in seafood, fruits, vegetables, and spices. The chef that cooked our meal last night must shop here, as well as many a New Orleans housewife who wanted to buy the freshest of food for her family.

I looked to my heart's content, then purchased some crab boil in cellophane packets. Jason would like that. The text on the label informed me that I could also use it for shrimp, lobster, and crayfish, whatever crustaceans I could find. Good! El Paso had shellfish but not always just what one wanted to buy at the time one wanted to buy them.

Then I spotted fresh pralines and purchased two. Something sweet to nibble on will often raise my spirits. Beyond the farmer's market was the flea market. My enthusiasm began to pick up, sparked by the pralines and the offerings. Table after table covered with merchandise that might or might not please friends and relatives beckoned to me. I'd buy a few mementos to take back home. I browsed. I picked things up and put them down, discovering that putting an item down lowered the price. Interesting. If I wanted to buy something, I'd be expected to bargain, not a talent at which I have any practice. Still, I was game.

On the edge of the pavilion a little Asian lady, wizened and in need of orthodontics, presided over a table of cloisonné pillboxes. Excellent presents for one's aging friends and even those not so old. I picked up a box decorated with a multicolored dragon and pressed the button that released the lid. The proprietor scowled at me. Evidently one wasn't supposed to open the box. I soon found out why. Once opened, it popped open again when I tried to close it. I put the dragon box down. She plucked up a prettier model with butterflies on it and handed it to me. Wiser as a result of my first experience, I persisted in testing the release and locking mechanism. This one worked. "How much?" I asked with a smile.

"Five dollar," she replied.

I put it down.

"Four dollar."

I shook my head.

"Tree dollar."

At two-fifty I bought five boxes in varying patterns, but I had to test eight to find five that worked, and every time I popped a lid open, she scowled at me. Still, they were pretty, and perhaps the pillbox lady had had a very sad life and had forgotten how to smile. Or maybe the state of her teeth made her self-conscious. Or her feet hurt. Mine certainly would if I had to stand behind a table of pillboxes all day. I planned to keep the blue and green one for myself. Maybe I'd keep two. One for Tylenol, a second for antacids. If any more friends disappeared on me, I'd be needing something for an upset tummy.

My next serious stop was at the mask table. Now, very few people actually need a mask, but these were so exotic. Of course, I realized that they weren't as gorgeous as some I'd seen in a Mardi Gras shop during my French Quarter tour with Broder, but those had been very expensive. These, after a haggling session, cost me three dollars each. How could I resist? Especially the ones with feathers. I purchased an orange yellow model with fuzzy feathers surrounding sad, downturned eye slits; a round, red felt mouth decorated with tiny black feathers; and black and yellow feathers trailing down below the mouth. Then I chose a model with red sequins around the eyes and a veritable plume of black feathers shooting up above the head, and last, my favorite, the gorgeous green mask with blue-eyed peacock feathers in an elaborate crown.

I wasn't convinced that I could get them home on the plane in mint condition, and I didn't know what I'd do with them once I got home. It's not as if I attend any masked balls or would feel comfortable with feathers tickling my face and neck all evening. Nonetheless, I was inordinately pleased with my under-ten-dollar collection of masks, so pleased that I wondered if El Paso had flea markets. I'd never patronized one before.

Of course, an El Paso flea market probably sold piñatas and Mexican pottery, and I had no need for a piñata and was afraid of Mexican pottery, having once read about a California family who contracted lead poisoning from a glazed juice set that they purchased in Tijuana. Because of Jason's research interests, I'm always on the lookout for unusual news stories about toxins.

With my pillboxes in my purse and my masks in a plastic bag, I set off toward Jackson Square thinking of lunch. But where? I sat down on a bench and studied my Frommer's. Should I try The Gumbo Shop on Saint Peter Street? Or Saint Ann's Café and Deli on Dauphine, an establishment reputed to have saved the sanity of a person just moving into town? I could use some psychic comfort, I decided, if I could find the place. I thumbed through to a map, pink and white with black lines, and looked for Dauphine. Ah, there it was. Decatur (where I was), Chartres, Royal, Bourbon, then Dauphine. Now where did Saint Ann cross Dauphine?

"Are you lost, my chile?"

I looked up to see a priest with a tanned, somewhat weathered face and reddish gray hair ringing a bald head. He was smiling at me and wearing a black . . . frock? What does one call a skirted priest's garment? Maybe he was a monk. But the gown had a high clerical collar. "I'm looking for the Saint Ann's Café, Father," I replied. If he was a monk, I supposed he'd tell me.

"It's right on da way to mah parish," he said, "if you like to walk along wit me."

How kind! And how charming! A Cajun priest! I recognized the accent. "Thank you, Father." I stood up and accompanied him along Decatur. Soon we were zigzagging through streets and alleys, and I was completely lost. Still, once I got to my destination, I could study the map during lunch and would, no doubt, find my way back to the hotel without too much trouble. It wasn't as if I'd thought of a more useful way to spend the afternoon. If the police didn't turn up news of Julienne, I was stymied.

As we entered yet another alley, this one quite messy, Father Claude was telling me an amusing story about a parishioner who had taken out a restraining order against the church because she was allergic to the flowers that customarily decorated the altar. "Downright disgustin' da way folks dump dere trash in dese alleys," said Father Claude, interrupting his own story. "Makes a mighty poor impression on our visitors."

"Indeed," I concurred, for I had narrowly avoided tripping over a wooden box from which spilled a few remaining salad leaves — arugulla, I believe. He had to take my arm to keep me from falling.

"Bettah we stop right heah," said Father Claude.

"Oh, I'm fine," I replied. "I'll be more careful about —"

"Right heah's a good place." He grasped my arm, quite hard actually, and then I felt something poking my chest, for he had swung me around and wore a very unpriestly look, a really sinister look.

I gulped and glanced about desperately. The alley was deserted. I peeked down at the object jammed against my breastbone. A gun! I was caught between astonishment and terror. "You're not a priest!" I exclaimed.

"Got dat right, missy," he replied.

It was then I noticed that the gun was, of all things, plastic. This faux priest was threatening me with a toy gun. That was really the last straw. I'd had quite enough of the criminal element in New Orleans. Without a second thought, I snarled, "Idiot!" and swept my free hand — free except for the plastic bag of masks — up against his hand, the hand clutching the plastic gun. I was planning to tell him I had no intention of giving up my purse to a man wielding a toy, but the gun went off.

Imagine my surprise and fright! Imagine his! He staggered back, blood streaming from his ear, an expression of astonishment and rage on his face. Then he ran away, leaving me in possession of the gun.

I leaned over to pick it up and examine it. Could a plastic gun shoot real bullets? Close to tears and shaking like the off-balance ceiling fan in my family room, I tottered down toward the end of the alley where my would-be assailant had disappeared, Several tourists who saw me emerge with the gun in my hand ran away. I can't blame them. Then a policeman approached me, drawing his own weapon.

"Oh, thank goodness!" I cried and fell, weeping, into his arms. It's a wonder we weren't both killed by mistake.

29

Father Claude's Ear

Officer O'Brien disentangled himself, gingerly removed the plastic gun from my fist, and called for assistance. To me he said, "Ma'am, this may be the Big Easy, but it don't make us cops easy to see ladies runnin' out of alleys wavin' guns."

"I was mugged," I sniffled and pulled out Lieutenant Boudreaux's handkerchief since Officer O'Brien didn't think to offer me one. Having had it laundered by the hotel at considerable expense, I hated to use it, but the lieutenant's clean handkerchief was the first thing that came to hand, and I was in desperate case.

"Well, likely that's one sorry mugger," said the patrolman dryly. "You got a permit for this here weapon, ma'am?"

"Of course not. It's not *my* gun." I gave my tear-filled eyes one last swipe, blew my nose, and stuffed the handkerchief into my raincoat pocket. "Shouldn't you put it into a baggie or something? Since it belonged to the mugger, it may still have his fingerprints on it."

Officer O'Brien evidently didn't have an evidence bag on him. Instead, he appropriated my mask bag and stuck the plastic gun in that. Of course, I protested because I didn't think having a weapon, even a plastic one, dropped in among the feathers would do them any good.

At that moment, a patrol car pulled up beside us, and Officer O'Brien murmured to the two men who climbed out, "Female wavin' a handgun on the street. Claims she was mugged an' disarmed the mugger."

"I didn't exactly disarm him," I tried to explain as they helped me into the backseat of the car, putting a hand on top of my head just as I'd seen it done to suspects on television. Officer O'Brien got in back with me while the other two took their places in the front seat. Because they had my mask bag, I leaned forward and knocked on the screen to get their attention. "Could you please place that gun in an official police evidence container before it damages the souvenirs I bought at the flea market?" I requested, feeling considerably calmer and much safer now that I was under the protection of the police.

After leaning back, taking a deep breath, and trying to get comfortable on the rather lumpy seat, I turned to Officer O'Brien. "Are we going to the Vieux Carre substation?" I asked.

"You been there before?"

"Several times"

"I'll bet," said the officer who was holding my mask bag and searching the glove compartment, presumably for an evidence container. These policemen did not seem to be very well equipped. It occurred to me that we needed an evidence *team* to take care of the mugger's gun, but I'd never seen a crime-scene van on the streets of New Orleans, although one can hardly watch ten minutes of a television police drama without observing one. In this case, it would seem that life did not imitate fiction.

We arrived under the familiar portico in no time and all climbed out, Officer O'Brien assisting me, as if I couldn't get out of a car on my own. Perhaps it was the Southern-gentleman training. Lieutenant Boudreaux had always been very gallant. I nodded to the sarcastic desk sergeant as we passed through the reception area and made our way to a small room where I was left after Officer O'Brien excused himself. I couldn't help noticing that he locked the door behind him, almost as if I was a prisoner. And they had not returned my masks.

I must have waited five minutes or more, staring at the peeling walls of the little room and trying not to notice that some very unacceptable phrases had been scratched on the table at which I sat. Then a black man in civilian clothes unlocked the door and took a seat across the table from me. He was accompanied by Officer O'Brien, who introduced him as Detective Rosie Mannifill. Rosie? What a strange name for a man. Perhaps his mother had named him after a very large football player named Rosie.

Jason, over the years, has watched some professional football on television, so I pick up a few names as I pass through the family room. Rosie Greer was one of those names, although I couldn't say what position he played, or plays, or for what team. The teams seem to proliferate like rabbits. Who but an ardent fan can keep track of their names? In fact, I may have heard the name *Rosie* when I was living at home. Mr. Delacroix watched football. Of course, my father didn't. I introduced myself to the detective and offered to shake his hand. He wrote down my name.

"O'Brien here says you told him you was mugged."

"Well, I suppose that would be the word for it," I agreed. "The man grabbed my arm and shoved his gun against my chest."

"An' you disarmed him?"

I thought about Detective Mannifill's phrasing. "I wouldn't put it quite that way, Detective. You see, when I realized that the gun was plastic, I thought that he was trying to steal my handbag by threatening me with a toy. After all, who ever heard of a plastic gun?"

"Anyone who knows anything about guns," said Detective Mannifill. "I got one myself."

"You do? Don't you consider it dangerous?"

"Dangerous as any gun, ma'am."

"I mean especially dangerous. When I tried to knock it out of his hand in a fit of pique, the mugger's weapon went off. It probably exploded. Western history, when untrammeled by the romantic myths about gunfighters, tells us that weapons misfired or exploded as often as not. And cannon explosions in earlier centuries . . ." I could see the detective's eyes glaze over and had to presume that his interest in history, even the history of firearms, about which I am not really an expert, was minimal. "At any rate," I resumed, "whatever happened, I certainly heard the explosion, and his ear bled copiously."

"You *shot* the mugger?" Detective Mannifill now looked as if he didn't believe me.

"Not in the sense that I pulled the trigger. I just gave his hand a sharp upward blow. However, he may well have been shot. Perhaps you should call local hospitals to check for someone missing an ear, or part of one." I thought for a moment. "And you'll want to check for fingerprints. Mine will only be on the barrel. If the mugger is a career criminal, no doubt his fingerprints will be on file."

Mannifill turned to O'Brien. "She was running out of the alley carrying the gun by the barrel?"

"Well . . . yeah," O'Brien admitted.

The detective rose and started to leave the room, presumably to call hospitals and ask for fingerprint experts. I called after him, "I would like to have my plastic bag with the masks back." He didn't reply, so I turned to Officer O'Brien and remarked, "I bought some charming feathered masks at the flea market."

"Yeah, my wife likes them. She got my

little girls some for Halloween."

"Oh, they must have looked adorable. How old are they?"

Officer O'Brien and I were discussing Halloween costumes favored by little girls when the detective returned and sat down. "So maybe you could describe this mugger, Miz Blue," he suggested.

"He looked like a priest."

Both men stared at me.

"Well, I'm not saying he was one," I amended defensively. "But he was wearing one of those ankle-length black gowns with the traditional clerical collar and —" I stopped to picture him. "— and he had reddish gray hair sprouting out around a bald head."

"Anything else?" asked the detective. He was taking more notes.

"He offered to show me the way to Saint Ann's Café and Deli on Dauphine Street. Naturally, I didn't hesitate to accept help from a priest. I mean, one doesn't really expect to be mugged by a priest, does one?"

"Where did the mugging occur?"

"In the alley. I have no idea which one, but Officer O'Brien should be able to tell you that. In fact —" I turned to the patrolman "— you may have seen him

371

running out of the alley. He was ahead of me."

O'Brien shook his head. "Didn't see no priests with bloody ears." He told the detective where he had first seen me, gun in hand.

"Anything else?" asked Detective Mannifill.

"He was about my height, five-six, and had olive skin, rather leathery, as if he'd spent a lot of time in the sun without using sunscreen." The detective raised his eyebrows. "I hope you don't think that you're safe from skin cancer because you're black," I cautioned him.

He scowled at me. "Anything else?" he prodded.

"He told me that one of his parishioners had asked for a restraining order against the altar flowers in his church. That was just before he grabbed me."

"Courts don't issue restraining orders against flowers," said the detective. "Anything else?"

What an impatient man! I searched my mind. "Only that he introduced himself as Father Claude."

"Well, shit," said Detective Mannifill. I gave him a disapproving look, but he didn't apologize for his language. "Since when is Father Claude mugging tourists?" He said this to Officer O'Brien, not to me.

At this point in what I could now see was an interrogation, Lieutenant Boudreaux entered the tiny room, completely filling up the last bit of space.

"Good afternoon, Lieutenant," I said. "I had your handkerchief laundered, but unfortunately, I've just had a very trying experience and had to use it again. However, I promise to get it rewashed and ironed, and this time I won't cry on it."

"Don't give it a thought, Miz Blue," he replied graciously. "My mama provides 'em by the dozen. Hear tell, you got mugged."

"By Father Claude," said Mannifill.

"Doesn't sound like his usual MO, muggin' tourists."

"Had him a Glock, one a them fancy plastic models," O'Brien chimed in.

Lieutenant Boudreaux looked worried. "Seems to me you're jus' gettin' more than your fair share of criminal attention, Miz Blue. You got any enemies out there? Anyone might have followed you from home with evil intent?"

"Heavens no, Lieutenant. I'm a faculty wife. And a food writer."

"Maybe she give some chef a bad review,

an' he put a hit out on her," said O'Brien facetiously. In response, he got a frown from the lieutenant.

"When were you plannin' on goin' back home, ma'am?" the lieutenant asked.

"Tomorrow, I suppose. Have you heard anything about Julienne?" He shook his head. "Or identified that poor woman in the morgue?" Again he shook his head.

How could I go home tomorrow when I didn't know what had happened to my dearest friend? "I just don't know what to do."

"Well, one thing you can't do, ma'am, is leave New Orleans until we get this matter cleared up," cautioned Detective Mannifill.

"Are you saying I'm a suspect of some kind?" I asked indignantly. "I believe that I am the victim in this incident."

"Sure looks that way, Miz Blue," the lieutenant agreed, "but until we catch up with Father Claude —"

"Like that's gonna happen," muttered O'Brien.

"An' we're sure the man with the ear injury's not gonna file charges against you," Mannifill added.

"But that would be outrageous, Detective. I didn't pull the trigger of his gun. I simply —"

"You never read about any a these burglars who wanna file charges when the homeowner catches 'em in the house an' shoots 'em?" asked O'Brien.

"I believe these two incidents would not be at all comparable," I said stiffly.

"An' you'd be right, Miz Blue," said the lieutenant soothingly. "So we'll let you know as soon as we catch the mugger or the evidence exonerates you."

"Oh well, that's all right then." The evidence could hardly fail to exonerate me. One can't shoot another person by holding the barrel of the gun. So unless Officer O'Brien's careless handling of the weapon in question had destroyed fingerprints, or contact with feathers had brushed away those little whorls —

Detective Mannifill cleared his throat to get my attention. "If you'll just write down your local address and phone number, we —"

"We got it, Rosie," said the lieutenant. "Miz Blue is by way of becomin' a daily visitor here." He turned to me. "Miz Blue, Ah'm gonna send you home in a patrol car, an' Ah hope this time you'll jus' stay in your hotel room with the door locked until it's time to go catch your plane. Ah'd be mighty relieved to hear you promise me that's jus' what you plan to do."

I smiled at him and replied that my plans included a nice nap in my room and dinner at some excellent New Orleans restaurant with my husband and at least four friends. He seemed to find that acceptable. They fingerprinted me for elimination purposes with respect to the plastic gun, gave back my plastic bag with the three masks, and drove me to the hotel. En route, I was pleased to discover that the yellow, orange and black mask, my least favorite of the three, was the only one crushed by Father Claude's weapon.

30

The Helpful Sibling

How in the world would I explain to Jason why I couldn't leave New Orleans tomorrow as planned? He had to get back to the university. Should I need to do any further research, we had planned to return here during the next vacation. Now I'd have to tell him about Father Claude with his gun pressed against my breastbone and my mistaken conviction that it was a toy weapon. Instead of Father Claude losing his ear, I could just as well have been killed myself. And now I might be charged with — what? Assault with a deadly weapon? Counterassault with the assailant's deadly weapon? That certainly didn't seem fair.

And why exactly had Father Claude, or whoever he was, pointed his gun at me? One of the officers had said robbing tourists wasn't his usual MO, which means, I believe, *modus operandi*. Surely he hadn't meant to shoot me! Why would anyone want to? Especially a stranger! Perhaps he had mistaken me for someone else. Officer O'Brien had jokingly said that some chef might have ordered my assassination. Was this Father Claude an assassin? If so, they should have told me. And they certainly hadn't seemed sanguine about catching him. "Fat chance of that," O'Brien had said. The situation was confusing and frightening and — yes — surreal. Especially, surreal. Things like this do not happen to faculty wives.

And there was Julienne. I still hadn't located her. Nor had the police. Earlier I had been worried about leaving New Orleans while she was still missing. Now I couldn't leave whether or not she was found. She probably wasn't in the city herself. Very likely her brother had helped her leave. With Philippe in mind, I called his hotel again. No answer. Then it occurred to me that I had been direct dialing his room. He could have left town, and I wouldn't know the difference. I could have been dialing an empty room or some other person now occupying Philippe's old room. I called the hotel desk to explain my problem.

"Oh, he's still here," said the clerk, after leaving me a short time on hold. "But I haven't seen him. Can't imagine why he never answers his phone. Hang on a minute." More time passed while I relaxed comfortably on my bed and thought about a nap. "He's been using room service every day," she said, "so he must be in there. In fact, he's got one whopping big bill, but it says here that he's a doctor, so he can afford it. Reckon he's one of our orthodontists, though why you'd come to a convention and never leave your room is beyond me. They're out there this afternoon at the pool having a high old time."

"Dr. Delacroix is not an orthodontist, but thank you for your help."

Philippe was there, staying in his room, ordering from room service, not answering his telephone? Depression! That explained it all. He'd fallen into one of his customary depressions. Perhaps about Julienne's situation. Perhaps because his chairman was threatening to fire him. Or just some chemical imbalance. But depressed or not, he could still give me news of Julienne. I rose, combed my hair, and grabbed my raincoat, although it wasn't raining, thank goodness. However, that didn't mean it wouldn't start.

Mindful of the money I'd spent on telephone calls and taxis, I prudently walked to the corner where the Superior Inn's free shuttle let guests off in the French Quarter and caught it back to Philippe's hotel. Without asking the desk clerk to announce me, I boarded the elevator to the second floor and was knocking at his door within minutes. Then I watched the peephole until I saw it go dark. Success! He was in there. If he didn't open the door, I'd just keep knocking. Even the most depressed person would get tired of someone pounding on his door.

However, the door flew open, and Philippe said, quite unpleasantly, "What are you doing here, Carolyn?" while he tugged me into his room and slammed the door. He didn't look depressed to me. He looked angry. In fact, he swore under his breath and said something like, "If you want something done right, you have to do it yourself," whatever that meant.

His attitude made me a little nervous, but I had a perfectly good reason for being here, even if he did consider my visit inconvenient. "Philippe, I'm looking for your sister, and you're my last hope of locating her. Why haven't you been answering your telephone?"

Philippe began to laugh, which I took amiss, and with good reason, given all the unpleasant things that had happened to me during my search. "Well, you may think this is funny, Philippe, but you wouldn't believe all the dangerous situations in which I've found myself this week while searching for Julienne."

Philippe laughed harder, obviously in a better humor than when I first arrived, for all that I found his amusement disconcerting. "I know all about your problems, Carolyn," he said with a final chortle.

"You do?"

"Of course. I know everything."

"Philippe, have you taken too much medication or something?" I knew immediately that I'd said the wrong thing, because his face twisted with rage.

"You're a stupid, interfering woman, Carolyn," he snarled and pushed me into a wing chair that stood in front of gently stirring draperies, which no doubt led to his balcony. *"Party Central,"* the Yellow Pages ad for the Superior Inn had said. *"Every room with a balcony overlooking our interior courtyard and pool."* I remember thinking that it didn't sound like Philippe's sort of place.

"You should have left well enough alone." He loomed over me in what I took to be a threatening fashion, although why Philippe would want to frighten me I couldn't imagine.

Well, I wasn't about to be intimidated. "Do you know where Julienne is?" I demanded.

"More or less," he replied, suddenly casual as he backed away and sat down at the foot of the bed. "Of course. And I know where you've been all week and what you've been doing."

Well, that was nonsense. He hadn't been out of his room, if the desk was to be believed. "Don't be silly, Philippe. Just tell me where Julienne is, and I'll be on my way."

"It was a mistake, Carolyn. You running around town getting people interested in things that weren't their business. Even you should have realized that by now. Couldn't you feel my power, my control? I'm the spider, spinning his web, pulling in the stupid little flies."

That wasn't depression. That was just plain craziness. Still, I had to approach him as if he hadn't become completely unbalanced. "I don't know what you're talking about, Philippe," I said, trying to sound calm and friendly. "You've been in your room all week as far as I know, but you must have helped Julienne to —"

"Oh, I did. I was very helpful to my sister, much more helpful than she ever was to me. And I've been trying to help you, too, little sister's friend. You were just too dumb to take the hint."

"Philippe, that's the second time you've called me stupid, which I'm not, and as for controlling me, that's silly. I haven't even seen you in years. If you didn't look so much like Julienne, I wouldn't have recognized you." He had Julienne's wild black hair but little else. In fact, he looked sick: terribly thin, his skin sallow instead of the rich olive that ran in the family, and he had great black circles under his eyes, as if he hadn't slept in weeks. "Are you ill?" I asked. "You don't look at all well, Philippe."

"How foolishly maternal of you to ask," he responded in a nasty tone. "But actually, I've never been in better health. If you didn't recognize me, it would be because you've only seen me when they were forcing me to subvert my real persona with medication, but that's over. I'm drug free and at the height of my powers now. I'm winning it all."

"Winning what? And what drugs? Antidepressants? Admittedly, you don't seem depressed."

"But that's what you'd like, isn't it? To see me whining and miserable?"

"No, of course not."

"So I couldn't control you."

"Why do you think you control me, Philippe?" Again I was trying to be the calm, reasonable faculty wife I usually am instead of scared stiff and confused.

"Were you afraid when the voodoo woman told you to leave town?" he asked.

"How do you know about her?"

"I sent her."

"You —"

"I'm watching you, Carolyn. My agent knows everything you do. Every ridiculous, futile move you make. The man with the knife who grabbed your purse. Remember him?"

I was speechless for a moment, then rallied to say, "He didn't get it."

"He didn't?" Philippe frowned. "You're lying. You're probably still trying to get your credit cards canceled and reinstated."

"I hit him with my umbrella."

"And falling into the bayou? Remember that? Too bad you didn't drown."

"If he got my purse, where did the money come from for the bus ticket to the bayou?" I asked sharply. I hadn't seen whoever pushed me into the water, but I *had* been pushed. And the purse snatcher, whom I hit with my umbrella, could he have been the same man? And the voodoo woman — well, she was a woman. Or not. She'd certainly been ugly enough to be a man.

"If you hadn't got here first, you'd be dead on the street, Carolyn, another tragic victim of random violence."

A shiver went up my spine. Father Claude. Philippe had meant to have me shot?

"Now we'll just have to wait."

"Wait for what?' My voice was quavering. I could only hope he didn't notice.

"He'll be back when he can't locate you, and since he obviously failed today, he'll have to do it here and find some way to dispose of the body."

Was that *my* body Philippe was talking about? He obviously didn't know that I had shot Father Claude's ear off, in a manner of speaking, and I certainly wasn't going to tell him. On the other hand, I had to get out of here before Claude plastered a bandage on his ear and reported in to "the spider." I glanced surreptitiously at Philippe. Now was the opportune time to say my good-byes, since it seemed that Philippe wasn't prone to doing his own dirty work.

"Nothing to say, Carolyn?" he goaded.

"I have to be getting back." I stood up. "Jason will be expecting me."

Philippe leapt up and pushed me into the chair. "You're not going anywhere, and Jason won't be expecting you for at least several hours."

"It's the last day of the meeting. Sessions end at three."

"No, they don't, not till five, and then he'll have a drink with his colleagues and doodle little chemical structures on cocktail napkins and trade academic gossip. Why, he probably won't be home until at least seven, by which time you'll be long gone. So don't try to lie to me, Carolyn. It won't work."

I gulped and settled into the chair, not even a particularly comfortable chair. What to do? It is very hard to make plans while in fear of one's life. Talk. I had to keep him talking. And hope Father Claude had become tired of failing in his missions, hope he wouldn't want to tell Philippe that he had been shot with his own gun by a forty-something wife, mother, and food critic.

Since he was known to the police, Father Claude must be a career criminal. In which case, this whole debacle would be professionally embarrassing. It would probably ruin his reputation if it got out. The police were looking for him. Maybe they'd find him. So I just had to — what? Get away from Philippe before he decided that he was crazy enough to do his own killing. Perhaps I should remind him of his Hippocratic Oath: *Do no harm.* But oh God, what had he done to Julienne? Or paid Claude to do to her?

"You're uncharacteristically silent."

Philippe was grinning at me with a curve of lip that seemed particularly malicious. That might have been my imagination. His smile had always been humorless, on the few occasions when I saw it, but not malicious. "Well, Philippe, since you don't want me to leave, I was just wondering what might be a good subject of conversation."

"So well brought up, Carolyn. I always admired that about you. Maybe if your mother had lived longer, she could have taught you to mind your own business as well as to function adequately as a good little hostess type."

How dare he bring up my mother? She had been the sweetest, kindest, gentlest, most rational person who ever lived, while he was a crazy would-be murderer. "What did you do to Julienne?" I demanded.

31

An Alligator's Dinner

"What did I do to Julienne?" Philippe rose from his seat on the foot of the bed and dragged the second wing chair over in front of mine. When he sat down, we were almost knee to knee, and his proximity sent a shudder through me. Then he leaned forward, arms on knees, hands hanging loosely, and thrust his face into mine. I could smell the faint odor of his breath, toothpaste overlaid with alcohol.

"I gave her another chance," he replied, seeming to take pleasure in the ambiguity of his answer.

"I don't understand." Did alcohol explain his strange behavior? He might be drunk instead of crazy, although I didn't find that a reassuring possibility, either.

"Of course you don't, Carolyn, because you know next to nothing about Julienne and me, especially about me."

"That's true," I agreed. "What kind of

chance did you give her?"

"That sounds like an accusation."

"No, Philippe, I was just asking for clarification of what you said, that you gave her another chance."

He nodded. "I did." Much to my relief, he settled back in his chair. "I made some requests of my sister, and she refused, so I gave her a chance to reconsider. I think that was quite generous of me. Considering."

"Considering what?"

Anger swept across his face, blazing in his eyes and tightening his thin lips, but just for a second. Then he became calm again. "Considering how much Julienne has taken away from me over the years."

Was he talking about his mother's estate? Diane had said he wanted it all because it was his right. "Primogeniture, you mean?" I asked hesitantly. "The estate?"

"That's part of it. I *am* the eldest son, the *only* son. Julienne got a dowry so she had no right to the estate."

A dowry? He *was* crazy. "Julienne had a dowry?"

"Of course. Mother gave her half the household stuff, not to mention all those bonds, when she married. I wasn't given any bonds when I married, no sheets, no dishes, no —"

"I didn't know you had been married," I stuttered. Had he? Julienne never mentioned it.

"That's because you don't know anything, even your own field. How could you have majored in medieval history and not know the rules of inheritance? Don't you know about primogeniture? And dowries?" His tone was hectoring, and he leaned forward again as if to intimidate me. With some success, I might add.

"Yes, of course I do, but . . . but Philippe, that was centuries ago."

"Oh, really?" Now his tone was scathing. "My mother didn't seem to think so; she's the one who talked about her daughter's *dowry*."

Now that he mentioned it, I did remember Fannie and Julienne joking about a dowry, but that's what it had been: a joke.

"Or maybe you want to talk about modern law? Or moral law? Or ordinary fair play, about which I'm sure you know nothing either? Well, Mother always favored Julienne unfairly over me, and Julienne exerted undue influence on her in the years after my father died. Any court would find in my favor."

"But Philippe, your mother wasn't of . . . of unsound mind."

"And I am? Is that what you're saying?"

"No," I whispered, because he really was frightening me. And how sound was his mind? This wasn't simple depression. Or clinical depression. It wasn't depression at all. It was something else entirely, something for which he refused to take medication, as he'd said himself.

"And the estate was the least of my sister's sins."

Keep him talking, I told myself, even though his mood seemed to bounce frantically from calmness to rage with each change of subject, each new thought that came to him. "What did she do?" I whispered.

"When my wife died . . ." His face became grim. "When my wife died . . ."

He couldn't seem to get beyond that phrase. "I'm sorry. What happened?" I prompted.

"She committed suicide."

How terrible! She'd committed suicide? And Philippe had always been prone to depression, at least in his youth.

"Oh, don't look so tragic. It was a whim."

"A whim?" I stammered.

"Yes, a whim. Postpartum depression, they said. She could have waited it out if she'd had any sense. I told her that."

391

Postpartum depression meant there had been a baby.

"And I protected her from their medications."

Good lord. His wife had been seriously depressed, and he hadn't allowed her doctors to relieve that depression? Perhaps repressed guilt over his wife's suicide had unbalanced his mind.

"But she was just as dead as if she'd had a good reason to kill herself. And then my sister — my *sister* —" His voice dripped venom. "Julienne, ever the helpful, greedy sibling, had me committed and took my child. With my mother's connivance. They said I was bipolar, a danger to myself and others, but that was just an excuse to dope me up and deprive me of the good times. My father . . ."

Bipolar. Manic-depressive, in other words. The new terminology was probably the result of some politically correct desire to mask the real nature of the disease. And he was in the manic phase right now, unmedicated. Because he *liked* the manic phase. He considered mania the *good times*. That explained all the talk of power, of being the spider who controlled the flies that ventured into his web. I was a fly. Had Julienne been a fly?

Now he was talking about his father. I concentrated on this new subject.

". . . just because he had periods of brilliance. Do you remember when he made all that money on the market? I'm doing the same thing right now, but I, fortunately, don't have my mother following me around, terrified that I'll lose the family savings." He laughed exuberantly. "I'm going to make more than my father ever did with no one to nag me to death the way she did. 'Promise me you'll nevah do that again, Maurice.' " His voice had assumed a feminine quality in a scathing imitation of Fannie Delacroix. " 'If you don't promise me, Maurice, Ah'll have to have you committed.' "

Oh my God! Was he saying that his father had been bipolar as well?

"She drove him to his death with all her nagging, but she never managed to control him, did she? No pills for my father. No loony bins."

Was Philippe saying that his father had committed suicide rather than submit to treatment?

"You're speechless, Carolyn. You didn't know all these things about your favorite surrogate mother, did you? The charming Fannie. My mother hated men. She'd rather have had you for blood kin than me."

"You're wrong, Philippe," I cried, hoping to head off the rage into which he was working himself. "She was very kind to me, but you were her son. She *loved* you."

"Shut up!" He was shouting in my face. Then his voice dropped abruptly back into the normal range. "But let's talk about Julienne. Your dear friend. How much did you ever know about the estimable Julienne? Nothing! Did you know that she couldn't be bothered to have a child of her own? And why should she bother when she could appropriate mine? And keep her."

"Diane?" I whispered.

"Diane. *My* daughter. Julienne wouldn't even let me tell her that I was her father."

I wouldn't have, either.

"Wouldn't let me have any say in her upbringing. When I wanted her back, Julienne shipped her off to that girls' school. So I gave my sister a choice — about the money, about Diane — and she refused."

"When was this?" I asked with dread.

"When *she* wanted something from *me,* I always agreed. Even the last time I saw her."

"What did you agree to, Philippe?"

"To take her out in the boat, of course.

You knew that. You were driving hither and yon asking about boat rentals, weren't you?"

"She agreed to go out in a boat with you?" Why would Julienne have done that? He was obviously dangerous.

"Of course she agreed. I was on my best behavior; she thought I was taking my medication. She thought boating would be good for my nerves, remind me of those happy times when we were children, sailing around the swamp with crazy old Dad, fishing poles in our hot little hands and all that crap. So I took her there."

I didn't want to hear what happened next, but I couldn't get away from him, and I couldn't —

"Don't you have other questions, Carolyn? I'm sure you do." He was leaning forward again. Crowding me.

"What happened that . . . that night? In the swamp?"

"Why, she fell off the boat. Always taking chances in order to get the perfect picture. Don't you think that's just like your friend Julienne?"

That malicious smile spread across his lips, and I felt as if a permanent chill had entered my bones. "She fell out of the boat?" I repeated.

"Do you doubt me? You think I gave her a push when she flatly refused to do the right thing? I did her a favor. I gave her the chance to reconsider."

"You mean you'd have helped her back into the boat if she —"

"No, little sister's friend, I mean if she made it to shore, she'd have time to think over my offer while she was slogging her way back. All she had to do was come here and tell me. I've been waiting. But she hasn't come back, has she? Always resisting me. That's my sister."

"Philippe, you know that those waters are full of . . . of . . . ." I saw in my mind that poor savaged body on the morgue slab. An alligator's dinner. And I knew it must have been Julienne. Tears began to trickle down my cheeks because I finally had to admit that she was dead. That Philippe had killed her.

"Tears, Carolyn? What for? Julienne was always a strong swimmer. Better than you. Better than me. Girls' champion all those summers at that wretched lake with our parents fawning over her. She could very well be alive. Probably is."

"Philippe, she's dead! I saw her body at the morgue," I cried.

His eyes narrowed. Had he really

thought she was waiting in the swamp, planning to come back and expose him? Or agree to his terms? Or perhaps he was afraid that I had been able to identify her. I hadn't.

"Well, that's all right. If she's dead, I can claim my daughter and my daughter's inheritance, which should have been mine, anyway." He looked quite pleased with the outcome but then frowned. "Did you identify her?" he asked sharply.

"No, but —"

"Well!" Philippe stood up. "I know about your trip to the morgue. Claude told me. And if she's dead and you think you know it, that's the end of our conversation, isn't it?"

"What do you mean?"

"Claude's obviously not coming back, so I guess it's up to me to end this." Before I could panic or try to push him away, just a second after I lurched to my feet, Philippe swept me up in his arms. As if I were Scarlett O'Hara and he Rhett Butler about to carry the heroine up the broad staircase.

"What are you doing?" I tried to struggle free, but he was surprisingly strong for such a thin person. Surely, he didn't mean to rape me, I thought in a panic. But no. He swung around my chair and brushed right through the drapes. They were dusty and, in sweeping over my face, filled my nose and throat with fine, dry grit. Once past the drapes, he lifted me high and tossed me away, as if he were launching a kite into the air.

Then I was falling, terrified, with the sun in my face.

32

Mardi Gras King Cake

I was spread-eagled in the sky while my clothing fanned out in a vain attempt to buoy me up in the unresisting air. Turning my eyes desperately to the balcony, I saw Philippe's back as he disappeared without a backward glance through the door and the drapes, whose dust mixed in my throat with the acid of terror. I thought of Jason and the children. I didn't want to die! And I was so afraid of the terrible pain I'd feel, even if only momentarily, when my body slammed into the courtyard below.

And then I did hit, but I bounced. It was like playing on the trampoline in the backyard when the children were little. I could almost hear their screams of delight and my own laughter as we bounded on our feet and our bottoms. However, the second time I bounced, I heard the harsh sound of tearing canvas. Then I was falling again, my second of relief and remembrance gone as I plummeted once more and jarred into stillness.

Oh, I hurt! But worse than the pain and fear, I couldn't breathe. There was no air in my lungs, nor could I draw more in. This must be death, even though I had fallen into something that offered little initial resistance. I opened my eyes to look one last time at the sun. Instead, I saw men surrounding me, grotesque faces peering down from odd angles while some drew back and turned to one another in an uproar of unintelligible babble. Glasses and goblets in hand, laughing, talking, frowning, the men began to look less surreal as I blinked my eyes; then the babble separated into understandable speech, understandable in its separate words, if not in its meaning.

"Hell, Alistair, how come she didn't pop *out* of the cake?"

"Couldn't you a found us someone younger?"

"Better yet, someone *nekked.*"

"She squashed da hell out of da cake, her."

"Ole Alistair always did have a flair for the dramatic."

"That li'l lady put out the Tooth Fairy Candle with her butt." Uproarious laughter followed most of the remarks from these men. I now saw that they were wearing sport coats, tieless shirts, and casual trousers. Then I was able to drag in my first breath and knew that I wasn't dead and that this wasn't some all-male hell peopled by a swarm of aliens with abominable taste in clothes — checked jackets, yellow pants, even a pink sport coat — all drinking and obviously the worse for liquor.

One staggered forward to peer at me and spilled beer on my face. When I tried to push myself away from him, my hands sank into the surface upon which I had landed. When I tried to wipe the beer from my face, I saw that my fingers were covered with green, gold, and purple grit. I was dazed, still unable to breathe deeply enough to satisfy oxygen-starved lungs, and evidently very messy.

"Did you fall from heaven pretty, overaged, lady?" asked a leering fellow in a lime green sport jacket and dreadful green-striped pants. All he needed was a straw boater and cane to be dressed for vaudeville.

"I was thrown . . . off a balcony . . . by a madman," I croaked.

Some of the men laughed. I saw one pounding another's back and shouting,

"That's a good one, Alistair." Alistair, for all he was wearing a frightful golf shirt with an emblem of an alligator eating a golfer, looked sober and confused. Again I reassured myself that I wasn't dead, just surrounded by ill-dressed, drunken ghouls. But Julienne was dead. Tears of grief and shock began to roll down my cheeks, and the men stopped laughing. One even tried to comfort me on the failure of my appearance in their conference cake.

"I need to call nine-one-one," I replied, reluctantly employing what little breath I had to speak.

Alistair offered me a cell phone. Others, realizing with surprise that my abrupt descent through the canvas of the tent and into their cake wasn't a bizarre convention act, fished out their phones as well. Within seconds, I had my choice of at least twelve cell phones. I took the nearest. Men on either side of me seized my elbows and sat me up, causing clouds of Mardi Gras–colored powder to swirl around me. Cake and icing squished out from beneath me and oozed onto the tablecloth which, much to my horror, was decorated with teeth of many colors. The act of sitting elicited a groan.

"Don't move her, Mort," cried Alistair.

"You want to get sued?"

"She's covered with frosting and sugar," Mort protested. "That's not gonna be good for mah cell phone."

Alistair tried to push me back into the cake. "The police wanna see the body jus' wheah it landed."

"Yo' not supposed to disturb a crime scene, fella," said another person.

"I'm not dead," I protested. "Not moving the body is for dead people." My breathing had evened out. Obviously the breath, not the life, had been knocked out of me.

"How about a nice margarita, lady?" The man in the pink jacket tried to thrust a salt-edged cocktail glass into my hand, but I resisted both the margarita and the attempt to lay me out once more on top of the cake.

"You got real nice teeth, ma'am," said the man in the lime green outfit. "Musta had a good orthodontist." He bent over to study my teeth at closer range. "Real good bite there."

Of course, I thought. I had landed in the midst of the Southern Orthodontist Society conventioneers. Which reminded me vividly of Philippe, although he was not one of them. Still, he'd be getting away while I was being ogled and cosseted by dentists. I ignored Mort's fears for his cell phone, which I still clutched in one sticky, multicolored hand, and dialed 911.

Then, taking a deep breath and steeling myself to make a brief, cogent statement of the facts, I said, "My name is Carolyn Blue. I am at the orthodontists' convention at the Superior Inn, and I have just been thrown out a second-story window by the man who killed Dr. Julienne Magnussen. Her body, I believe, is in your morgue. The killer's name is Dr. Philippe Delacroix."

"Damn conventioneers!" said the 911 operator, which I thought very unprofessional of her. The orthodontists were all protesting loudly that no orthodontist would throw a lady out of a window. They were making the same mistake made by the desk clerk who had assumed that any doctor at the Superior Inn was an orthodontist.

"Could you please send the police?" I requested.

"You need an ambulance?" asked the operator, her voice sounding doubtful and suspicious.

"I don't know," I replied. My arms and legs moved, although I had a number of aches and pains. "I haven't tried to stand up."

"Well, don't move. Help is on the way. This isn't some kind of drunken joke, is it?"

"I assure you that I am neither drunk nor amused by being thrown off a balcony. And the . . . the perpetrator is dangerous."

"He armed?"

"I don't know, but he is certainly unbalanced." And probably already gone during the time wasted with questions from the orthodontists and the operator. "Couldn't you just send the police before he gets to the airport and flies away?'

"They're already comin', ma'am. How far did you say you fell?"

"Two stories."

"What did you light on?"

I eyed the remains of the cake, a huge artifact made of twisted brioche dough, formed in a circle, frosted, and covered with the aforementioned purple, green, and gold sugars. "My research would lead me to believe that I landed on a traditional, if giant-sized, king cake." Absently, I stuck a frosting-and-sugar-covered finger in my mouth. Interesting. The frosting contained a touch of anise flavoring and bits of candied orange peel. A very nice combination. Was that traditional? I thought not. But how ridiculous that I should be assessing the flavor of frosting when I had nearly lost my life and my dearest friend had suffered a terrible death. Tears began to seep out of my eyes while the operator said, "Well, honey, if you got the baby Jesus, you have to give the next party."

"I think not," I replied severely. I had no intention of giving a party for the Southern orthodontists, no matter what New Orleans king cake traditions might apply.

A man in a sensible, dark business suit was standing beside me saying to Alistair, "We do want our guests to enjoy their stay with us, but we deplore damage to our facilities. Not only do I fail to see why the Superior Inn should pay for the destruction of your cake, but somehow or other, your members have ripped a hole in the tent we provided, and we will expect to be reimbursed for the repairs."

"Damn Yankee," said Mort to the manager, who sounded like a fellow Midwesterner. Then to me, Mort said, "You think this fella will be comin' after you? The one threw you off the balcony?"

"I doubt it. Sir, do I take it that you are a representative of the hotel?"

The dark-suited man turned to me, and his face lighted with a smile. "Let me guess," he exclaimed. "You're from Wisconsin."

"Michigan."

"I'm from northern Illinois."

"Carolyn Blue," I said, extending my hand. The two of us looked at it, he obviously reluctant to make contact with the multicolored icing, even for the sake of a fellow Midwesterner. I withdrew the hand and fought off the temptation to sample the interesting anise and orange flavor again. "If you have a security person or persons, could you send them to room two fourteen to detain Dr. Philippe Delacroix? He's the man who threw me off the balcony."

"Close personal friend?" asked the manager. "Significant other?"

"Madman," I replied, aggrieved that he would think my predicament the result of a lover's quarrel. "And if he's not there, my raincoat and handbag are. I'd appreciate their return." Then the siren wailed in the distance, moving ever closer. I hated to greet my rescuers while sprawled in a cake, but I was really afraid to move in case I did myself some further injury than to my pride.

The king cake is a Mardi Gras tradition, a sweet briochelike confection, iced and dusted with sugars in Mardi Gras colors: purple, green, and gold. It is first served on Twelfth Night in honor of the Three Kings and continues to be served at parties and even at coffee breaks during the Carnival weeks that lead up to Mardi Gras or Fat Tuesday, the day preceding Lent. A prize, either a plastic baby figure representing the Christ child, a ring, or a gold bean, is baked into each cake.

In Europe, the person who is served a slice of king cake containing the prize must play one of the three kings. In South America, the partygoer who gets the Christ child figure also wins a year of good luck. But in New Orleans, the receiver is considered "king for a day" and may be expected to give the next party. One wonders how many New Orleans prizewinners conceal their good fortune in order to avoid the expense of hosting a Mardi Gras party.

Entering the words "king cake" into a search window on the Internet will provide you with a recipe. Even better you can put your order in to Mam Papaul's for cake mix, plastic baby, filling, glaze, and colored sugar in one handy package.

Carolyn Blue,
Eating Out in the Big Easy

33

She Jumped?

The paramedics arrived, tested me, and helped me off the cake table after declaring me free of broken bones and spinal cord injuries. When I was upright, frosting and festive sugar from my shoulders to the back of my knees, the orthodontists gave me a standing ovation, and Mort again offered me a margarita. I took it, but a paramedic snatched it away from me. "You might have a concussion, ma'am," he pointed out.

"I didn't hit my head," I replied and retrieved my drink. However, it was an inferior version of the margarita I had first tasted at Martino's in Juarez during a lull in the drug wars. Jason and I took a German scientist to dinner there, at his insistence, and ordered a pitcher. The New Orleans margarita was too sweet and was undoubtedly made with those large, pulpy, flavorless limes instead of the tiny, flavorful, nut-hard Mexican variety. Or perhaps — I sipped again — this one had been made with — horror of horrors — a mix.

While I was assessing the margarita on a scale of one to ten — I gave it a five because at least it had alcohol in it, and I was in need of calming — Mort discovered the good luck plastic baby Jesus stuck to my posterior and presented it to me. I assured him that I did not intend to host the Southern Orthodontists at their next party.

Alistair assured me that they wouldn't expect it and ordered a table knife from a passing waitperson in order to scrape frosting from the back of my clothes. Ordinarily, I wouldn't have welcomed such familiarity from a male stranger, but being plastered with frosting tends to skew one's perceptions of propriety. Also, if the hotel security people returned with my raincoat, I didn't want to ruin the lining with king cake remains. When the scraping of my back wasn't particularly successful, Alistair — I never did learn his last name — prevailed upon the hotel manager to provide me with replacement clothes. I changed in the pool house, since the orthodontic festivities were being held in the patio that contained the swimming pool.

You'd think the manager would want to

placate a woman who had been tossed off one of his balconies, if not for humanitarian considerations, then to avert a lawsuit. Not so. Either he had no suitable female clothing available, or he was being deliberately offensive, for he provided me with a dun-colored skirt and jacket sized for a woman who weighed several hundred pounds. I emerged from the pool house looking like a bag lady.

Fortunately, the security people arrived with my raincoat, umbrella, and handbag shortly thereafter, and I put on the raincoat. "What about Philippe Delacroix?" I asked anxiously. "Did he escape?"

"Who's that?" asked the house detective.

"The guest registered to the room where you found my raincoat," I replied impatiently. "Tall, unruly black hair, gaunt face, black circles under the eyes, very strong, dressed in black, arrogant. He'd have been acting like a megalomaniac."

"Guess they didn't get him," said the detective. "All I saw was some cops trying to talk to a guy who was sitting on the floor in the clothes closet. He was crying."

Crying? That didn't sound like the Philippe I had encountered upstairs. Having heard the answer to my question, the orthodontists were staring at me suspiciously, and the manager looked smug. What were they thinking? That I had *jumped* off that balcony and then blamed Philippe when I survived? I myself interpreted the security man's news to mean that Philippe had locked some terrified hotel employee in the closet and then escaped, which meant that he was still at large and could come after me. The thought of being thrown off another balcony or possibly fed to alligators, as he had done to his sister, turned me cold with fear.

"I don't think Dr. Delacroix seemed the type to throw anyone off a balcony," the manager murmured to Mort. "A very respectable person, that's how he struck me. However, if he did, I shall hold the Southern Orthodontists responsible for the damage to the tent."

"He's not one of ours," Alistair protested. "You seem to have forgotten that our cake was ruined when she tore through your tent."

Before I could argue with such a self-serving apportionment of blame, plainclothes detectives arrived, spotted and identified me, and asked for a statement. Having donned my raincoat to cover up the clothes provided by the hotel, I retired

412

with the detectives to the manager's office for the interview.

"You made the nine-eleven call, ma'am?" asked Detective Dennis McCrow after inviting me to take off my raincoat. Naturally, I refused, given the abominable suit I was wearing. Detective McCrow was a redheaded youth in his midtwenties with a face scarred, in all probability, by a serious case of teenage acne. Why don't more parents avail themselves of the many treatments now available to prevent such disfigurement? Chris had been so plagued in his teens, and we promptly took him to a dermatologist. Although Chris persisted in referring to the specialist as Dr. Zit, he did cooperate in the rigorous skin-care and medication routine prescribed. Now twenty-one and acne-free, Chris has hardly a mark on his face. But poor Detective McCrow! Of course, one can't commiserate with a scarred person. One can only ignore the problem. I smiled and started to reply.

"We need to establish her identity first," said Detective Virgie Rae Boutaire, a short, anorexic black woman with hair clipped to within an inch of her skull. She looked as if a passing breeze would blow her away, but I surmised that she was all wiry muscle, enabling her to deal with violent malefactors. At least, I hoped so. As for the haircut, it was rather startling, but I could see the advantages: coolness in hot weather, time saved in hair styling, and so forth.

"You got a problem with mah hair?" she demanded.

"I was thinking how pleasant it must be during hot and muggy weather."

"You got that right," she agreed suspiciously. "Name?"

"Carolyn Blue."

"ID."

Surprised, I fumbled through my handbag and produced my wallet with my Texas driver's license. Detective Boutaire took the whole wallet and called in the information on the license as well as my social security number. She had a cunning little microphone pinned to the shoulder of her jacket.

"What are you doing?" I asked with interest. Up until this week I'd had very little to do with the police and found myself intrigued by their work habits.

"Checkin' your record."

"Oh, I imagine you'll find me listed a good deal in your files," I said. "I was in several times to report a friend missing and once to try to identify a body at your morgue." I had to blink back tears when I said that, because I was now reasonably sure that the body *had* been Julienne. "Also, I was accosted by a female practioner of voodoo; I was the intended victim of a purse snatcher; I was pushed off a pier in the swamp boat tour area, almost run off a country road; and finally, a man attempted to shoot me."

"An' today you claim someone threw you off a balcony," Detective Boutaire finished for me. "You been havin' a real bad week." As she talked, her shoulder mike squawked at her, and she checked off the various attacks I had mentioned. "Anyone actually see any of these incidents?"

I must admit that I was quite taken aback by her question, which seemed to imply that she thought I was making all my troubles up, including the plunge into the tent and the cake below. "They were all orchestrated by Dr. Philippe Delacroix," I replied. "With the help of someone named Claude. Philippe told me so before he threw me off his balcony."

"An' why would he do that?" asked the detective.

"Because I wouldn't stop looking for his sister, and he had pushed her off a boat in the swamp Sunday night, after which she was . . . was eaten by an alligator." The thought of Julienne's fate sent a wave of nausea over me, and the two detectives, foreseeing an unpleasant event, teamed up to push my head down and advise me to breathe deeply. However, that was as far as their concern went.

"An' why would he dump his sister in a swamp?" Detective Boutaire asked once I was upright again.

"Because she wouldn't turn over her half of their mother's estate and give him back his daughter, whom she had adopted while he was in a mental institution."

The two detectives exchanged glances of such skepticism that I was forced to review what I had just said. It did sound peculiar. "I believe that Philippe is manic-depressive, that is to say, bipolar. He was certainly manic this afternoon. He talked as if he controlled the world from his hotel room, and . . . well . . . he threw me off the balcony because Father Claude hadn't succeeded in killing me. That's hardly the action of a sane person."

"You say this Father Claude tried to kill you?"

"Yes, he had a gun, but since it was plastic, I assumed, incorrectly as it hap-

416

pened, that his weapon was a toy. I hit his gun hand and, during the altercation, he lost his ear. Or so I assume. It was bleeding profusely when he ran away."

"You shot a priest in the ear?" Detective McCrow asked disapprovingly.

"I doubt that he was a priest, and, no, I didn't shoot him. The gun —"

"The *gun* shot him? So you're one a them gun-control people? Guns shoot people, not people? You probably don't think citizens got a right to carry arms or hunters to —"

"Oh, shut up, Dennis," snapped Detective Boutaire.

"I guess you're one of those NRA people," I said angrily to Detective McCrow. "Well, for your information, I am quite unfamiliar with guns. If I belonged to the NRA, I'd have known that Father Claude was carrying a real gun. Then I wouldn't have tried to knock it out of his hand, and I'd be dead. And in answer to your first question, I *am* the person who called nine-eleven. The orthodontists were too busy making facetious remarks about ladies jumping in and out of cakes and trying to give me a margarita."

"What orthodontists?" asked McCrow.

"Can we get back to the interrogation?"

Boutaire interrupted.

"If that's what this is," I exclaimed indignantly, "maybe I need a lawyer."

"Get one if you want," said Boutaire, "but we don't usually bother to prosecute suicides. We might try to have you committed."

"Me? You want to commit *me?* I assume you mean to a mental institution. You should be looking for Philippe. He's the one who needs help."

"Far as we know, we found him," said McCrow. "All curled up in a corner of his closet and didn't hear a word we said to him, jus' kept sobbin' like a big baby an' sayin', 'she jumped.' Didn't seem too dangerous to me."

"Shut up, McCrow," said his partner. "Now, ma'am, were there any witnesses to these alleged attacks on you?"

"An' how come you're out shootin' priests?"

"Shut up, McCrow."

"I don' know why you keep tellin' me to shut up. Jus' because Ah'm new on the squad don' mean I don' git to ask no questions."

I took a deep, calming breath. It was hard to believe that somehow I had become the suspect after all my close calls with Philippe's minions. Or minion. For all I knew everyone who attacked me was Father Claude. "May I suggest the following," I said, trying to sound as calm possible. "One. Check mental health records on Dr. Delacroix. He's unstable and has been for years. Two. Compare DNA between the body in your morgue and Philippe. You'll find that they are brother and sister. Three. Check the will of their mother, Mrs. Fannie Delacroix. That will provide you with Philippe's motive, other than insanity, for pushing his sister off the boat. He wanted all the money."

I didn't mention Julienne's daughter having told me that and wouldn't unless I had to. The poor child didn't need to know that her uncle — no, her natural father — had killed her mother — well, adopted mother. Oh lord! It then occurred to me that Diane was the natural daughter of a man suffering from bipolarity, and that her father was fathered by a man who had probably suffered the same mental condition. The periods of silence, the wild plunge on the stock market, the car accident that might have been suicide — Maurice Delacroix had probably been bipolar just like his son Philippe. What did that say about Diane's chances of escaping the family curse? The situation seemed more tragic every time I thought further on it.

With difficulty, I pulled myself together and went on. "Four. Show a picture of Philippe to Mr. Red at Red's Boat Rentals, or have Mr. Red pick Philippe out of a lineup. He rented Philippe the boat. Five. Check the fingerprints on the gun I turned over to the officers at the Vieux Carre substation to see if the prints match those of a criminal named Father Claude. Six. Check Philippe's sleeves for fibers from my clothes, which are in the pool house downstairs because, Detectives, I did *not* jump! I changed clothes in the pool house because I was covered with cake frosting and had to — *why are you laughing?*"

Both detectives were convulsed with mirth. I couldn't imagine why. I thought all my suggestions not only practical but impressively technological, perfectly in line with criminal investigation methodology I had seen on TV.

"Lady, do you know what it costs to do DNA tests?" asked Detective Boutaire. "You think the department's gonna spring for that? It's not like we got a murder here. An' even —"

"Julienne's been murdered," I said and

began to cry again. At that moment, and much to my relief, Lieutenant Boudreaux walked in, checked us all out, and handed me a handkerchief. I was so embarrassed. I hadn't yet returned the last one.

Then the interview started all over again. While I was getting myself together with the help of the lieutenant's handkerchief, he interviewed the two detectives, who treated him with much more deference than they had me. They didn't have that much to tell him. Philippe was in custody, but he wasn't talking now, not even to say, "she jumped." As far as anyone could tell, he wasn't even hearing. Did that indicate deep depression, catatonia, or deception? I wondered.

Then the lieutenant interviewed me, showing every indication of sympathy for my ordeal and great interest in what Philippe had told me about Julienne's death. "If we can't get him to talk, we'll have to do a DNA match on the two of them," he mused. His fellow officers looked shocked. I tried not to look smug. "Better yet, we can probably identify her by dental records."

"Am I under suspicion?" I asked my police friend and champion.

"No, ma'am, Ah wouldn't think so," said

the lieutenant, patting my shoulder.

"Say, she could be making the whole thing up," said McCrow. "If it turns out the body is this Julienne, maybe Miz Blue pushed her off the boat an' then blamed it on that poor nut upstairs. Maybe she made up all those attacks. No one saw nothin'. We only got her word."

"Except that the fingerprints on the Glock are Father Claude's," said the lieutenant. "Hers are only on the barrel. You can't shoot someone while you're holdin' the barrel of the gun. Anyway, the gun was stolen two years back in the robbery of a pawnshop, an' she's a professor's wife from El Paso, Texas. Not likely she was here two years ago holdin' up pawn shops, but that bastard — 'scuse the language, ma'am — we got his fingerprints at crime scenes all over the Quarter. Nevah got him, not even a mug shot, but we're lookin', an' now we got a bettah handle on what he looks like. All those disguises not gonna hide the fact that he's missin' an ear, not when we catch him."

Detective McCrow looked crestfallen that I was not guilty of killing my friend, manufacturing attacks on myself, and attempted suicide. I suppose he had believed Philippe and thought I'd been overcome by my guilty conscience and jumped. But then, even his partner, Detective Boutaire, didn't seem to value his intelligence highly. And what had Philippe meant when he said, "she jumped"? The antecedant of "she" could have been me, but it could also have been Julienne. Either way he was lying.

"So detectives," said the lieutenant heartily, "Ah think you all bettah take yo' nutcase downtown an' see if you can get a confession out of him, an' Ah'll take charge of Miz Blue here, who's lookin' mighty peaked. She's had her a real hard week."

Amen to that, I thought and left willingly with Lieutenant Boudreaux. When I thanked him for his kindness, he said, "Think nuthin' of it, ma'am. An' call me Al. You evah had crawfish boil an' hush puppies?"

"I don't believe so," I replied.

"Then Ah'm takin' you to the best place for crawfish an' hush puppies in the whole city, an' that's sayin' somethin'."

34

Crawfish Boil and Hush Puppies

The lieutenant's car was parked squarely in the middle of the taxi zone in front of the hotel and guarded from ticketing by a uniformed officer. "They seemed to think I might be guilty of something," I said, amazed. Lieutenant Boudreaux nodded, helped me into the car, then took the wheel himself, and pulled out into very heavy traffic.

"Most people we deal with are guilty of somethin'," he replied mildly. "They jus' din' know the background a the case."

"But I told them."

"Sure, but you're a civilian. Don' take offense, Miz Carolyn. Cops get lied to so much, they come to expect it, an' Ah'm not gonna let you be arrested. So you jus' try not to think about all that bad stuff. Think about hush puppies and crawdaddies."

But that was hard. As depression settled over me, my interest in food disappeared. I was sure the crawfish and hush puppies would be delicious, but I was about to ask that he take me back to my hotel when Lieutenant Boudreaux said, "Sorry fo' the loss of you friend, Miz Magnussen. Reckon we're gonna' find that's who our unidentified body is."

I nodded. How terrible that Julienne, so beautiful and vivacious in life, should be lying in a drawer in a cold room, unrecognizable even to me, her best friend. "They won't let Philippe go, will they? He might hurt someone else."

"Not from what Butaire and McCrow had to say. Man who won't move or talk, he's not likely to —"

"He could be faking. When I was up there, he was . . . he was like a . . . malicious spider. He called himself a spider, luring us into his web, using that . . . that Claude —"

"Claude was workin' for him? He said that?" The lieutenant glanced from the traffic on a narrow neighborhood street we had entered to my face and caught my nod. "Wonder what their connection is?"

"Goodness only knows. Philippe did live here until he was almost a teenager. Maybe they knew each other from childhood."

Boudreaux nodded. "Could be. We don' know hardly anythin' about Claude ourselves, jus' talk among criminals an' crimes we think he committed. Don' even know if that's his real name, but if Delacroix called him that, maybe we can trace them back."

"Is he a . . . a . . . killer?"

"He seems to do whatever comes to hand long as there's money in it."

"Then Philippe was paying him to stalk me?"

"Likely, unless Claude owes him favors, somethin' like that."

He swung the police car into a bus zone near a small neighborhood grocery store that had a hand-lettered sign offering Best Crawfish Boil in Town — Take Home a Pound or Four. While talking, I had forgotten to ask for a ride to the hotel instead of lunch. What did the lieutenant expect me to do, stand in the aisles of the store eating crawfish with my fingers? Maybe he planned to go back to the Moonwalk, sit on a bench as we had with the muffulettas, and eat the repast. If so, I hoped the crawfish were shelled. Otherwise, we'd make a spectacle of ourselves and ruin our clothes.

He came around and handed me out of the car and into the little store, where he was greeted with enthusiasm and jokes by the proprietors, two short, rounded people, an Asian female and a Cajun male.

"This here's Miz Carolyn. She's a woman had a real hard week. What she needs is some of your fine, spicy crawdads an' a bag of de-licious hush puppies, Pierre."

Pierre swept me a bow and told me that his "crawdaddies" were good for whatever ailed me. I doubted that, although the place smelled enticing. His wife, giggling girlishly behind her hand, began to scoop hush puppies from a deep pot of bubbling fat and drop them into a bag.

The lieutenant snatched one from the bag and held it out to me. "Blow on it first so you don't burn your mouth," he cautioned.

I felt very foolish and not a little self-conscious about blowing on a hush puppy held in the fingers of a police lieutenant while the lady, whose name was Yashi, beamed maternally at us. However, her hush puppy was amazingly good: hot and crunchy outside, light and oniony inside. The tears came to my eyes when I thought of how Julienne would have loved this experience.

"Why she cry, her?" asked Pierre, who

had been fishing spice-encrusted crawfish from the crab boil.

"She jus' lost a friend," said the lieutenant, who then peeled and fed me a crawfish. "Best crawdaddy you're ever likely to taste," he announced, smiling.

I nodded. It really was, and I wanted to ask Pierre for his recipe, but somehow I didn't have the heart because I'd never be able to pass it on to Julienne. I could imagine the conversation we'd have had. "You couldn't possibly have a better crawfish recipe than I have," Julienne would have said, and I'd have replied, "Winner has to do the rowing next summer?" The tears rolled down my cheeks at the thought that we'd never have that conversation, never go out together on the lake again on a fine summer day.

"She still cryin', her," said Pierre.

"Better you buy beer, too," Pierre's wife advised Lieutenant Boudreaux.

The lieutenant went to inspect the beer selection. "Well now, we got Turbo Dog, Voodoo. Here we go . . . How about a Dixie longneck?"

"I've never tried any of them," I replied, sniffling. However, I certainly should. German immigrants had been the primary brewers of beer in New Orleans, a city proud of its local brands. In fact, the word *Dixie* was of New Orleans derivation, having come from an American mispronunciation of the French word for ten displayed on one side of a ten-dollar bill printed in the 1800s for circulation in the city. "But I choose the Dixie longneck," I added, always interested in things of historical significance.

The lieutenant pulled a six-pack from the refrigerator and paid for the two sacks and the beer while I used a corner of his handkerchief to stem my tears. "Well," he said, once we were back in the car with the enticing odor of his purchases wafting through the grill from the backseat, "where shall we go to eat this?" He put the key in the ignition and turned to smile at me. "My place all right?"

Oh, dear, oh, dear. Somehow or other, the lieutenant had gotten a very wrong idea about our relationship. Kind as he had been, I had no intention of . . . no desire to . . . I glanced, panic-stricken, at my watch. Worse and worse. It wasn't lunchtime. It was five-thirty. Jason would be arriving at the hotel just about now, wondering where I was, and now this handsome policeman evidently expected me to accompany him to his place.

Unfortunately, I couldn't take that to mean the Vieux Carre substation. He expected me to join him for a private feast of crawfish, hush puppies, beer, and goodness knows what else. I closed my eyes and wished myself elsewhere. What an absolutely dreadful week this had been, and somehow or other, I had to write a book about it. How would I ever manage? How would I ever manage to explain to Lieutenant Boudreaux that I wasn't amenable to . . . to New Orleans cuisine followed by late-afternoon adultery?

"Ah can see you're jus' speechless at mah suggestion," he said, his tone somewhat wry.

Reluctantly, I opened my eyes. "Lieutenant, I'm a happily married woman. Very happily married. If I have somehow given you the impression that . . . well . . . well, I'm so sorry. And embarrassed. And —"

"Mah mistake," he said, sounding perfectly amiable.

Thank goodness for that. What if he'd made a scene? Which perhaps he had a right to make. But what had I done —

"Saw you look at yo' watch," he continued. "Reckon yo' husband might be comin' home to the hotel jus' about now? Not stayin' fo' any talk about teeth an' such?"

"He's with the American Chemical Society," I replied earnestly, glad to get away from the topic of afternoon trysts, "not the Southern Orthodontists Society." Hadn't I told the lieutenant that before? Yes, I thought I had, which only goes to show that men don't really listen to women. "I only know the orthodontists from falling into their dessert," I continued. "Well, actually, I don't know them at all, although they were reasonably gracious about the destruction of their king cake."

"And so they should be," said the lieutenant gallantly. "A pretty lady like you. Ah hate to think what bad memories you're gonna have of our city." He shifted and pulled out into traffic. "When you leavin'? I recollect you said somethin' about tomorrow."

Oh, he remembered that, did he? Just like a man, even a pleasant one. He had been looking forward to a one-night stand, with the lady in question, me, conveniently disappearing the next day on an airplane.

"Tomorrow afternoon," I replied.

"Well, you'll need to come on over to the station tomorrow mornin' to make a statement."

"Another one?"

"Formal statement. Signed statement.

You wanna tell her husband the news?"

"I don't even want to see him," I said bitterly. "If he hadn't berated her at the dinner, she wouldn't have left, and then —"

"No use, thinkin' that way, Miz Carolyn. If her brother was set on killin' her, likely he'da found another opportunity. Anyways, we'll take care of notifyin' the husband."

"Thank you." We were back in the Quarter. In fact, we were on Royal Street, and I wondered if he planned to make me walk home to the hotel from the substation.

However, that thought did him an injustice. He drove me right to the Hotel de la Poste and even insisted that I take the dinner he had purchased. Of course, I protested, and, of course, he insisted. "Jus' so you remember us kindly," he said, smiling. He didn't offer to escort me inside.

35

The Last Crème Brûlée

Le Bistro Crème Brûlée

Preheat oven to 325° F. In a medium saucepan, scald *1 qt. heavy whipping cream* and *2 vanilla beans, split lengthwise,* over medium heat.

In large bowl, whisk *6 egg yolks* and $^2/_3$ *cup granulated sugar* together until thick and lemon-colored. Remove vanilla beans from cream. Slowly whisk hot cream into yolk mixture until smooth. Strain through a fine-meshed sieve.

Fill ten 4-ounce soufflé dishes to $^1/_4$ inch from top. Place cups in baking pan and add 1 inch warm water to pan. Cover cups with aluminum foil or baking sheet. Bake 30 to 45 minutes or until set. Remove from oven and cover each cup with plastic wrap. Chill for at least 8 hours.

To serve: Preheat broiler. Evenly spread *5 tablespoons raw or brown sugar* on top of custards. Place under broiler about 4 inches from heat until sugar is caramelized. Let custard cool and tops harden before serving.

Serves 10.

When I opened the door to our room, Jason was lying on the bed with his shoes off, watching the national news on TV. He took one look at my face as I came in, my arms loaded with paper bags, and clicked the remote to turn off the program. "What's wrong, Caro?"

"She's dead." I set the bags down on the dresser in front of the ornate mirror. By the time I turned, Jason was there to put his arms around me. He didn't need to ask who had died.

"Does Nils know?" he asked after a minute.

"Not from me. The police will tell him. I couldn't bear to talk to him . . . I guess because I hold him partly to blame."

Jason led me over to the bed and sat down beside me, his arm around my shoulders. "What happened?" he asked quietly.

"She and Philippe went out together on a boat. He pushed her overboard, and an alligator got her." I swallowed a sob.

"My God." Jason sounded horrified. "I guess that means they found the body?"

"Yes."

He remained silent for a moment, then said firmly, "They'll need someone to identify her. I do *not* want you to volunteer, Caro. Let Nils do it."

"I've already seen the body. I just didn't know it was her."

He thought a moment. "When you went to the morgue? That was . . . well, of course it was. Still, Nils can damn well be the one to go over there a second time."

"He won't be able to tell, either."

"That bad?"

"Yes. They'll have to use dental records. Or a DNA comparison between her and Philippe." I was beginning to feel numb, as if the real me was standing back watching this Carolyn Blue as she answered questions with little apparent emotion.

"But why would Philippe —"

"Because he's sick . . . mentally ill. Bipolar, and paranoid too, I imagine. He thought their mother had unfairly favored Julienne over him in the division of the estate. And he claims Diane is his daughter and Julienne wouldn't give her back."

Jason looked astonished. "Could that be true?"

"About the money? Not really. About Diane? I just don't know, but, Jason, if she is Philippe's daughter, we'll have to think long and hard about telling Nils or her."

Jason nodded. "It's not news either one would be happy to hear, especially not after he killed Julienne. What an awful mess."

"I know." It made me even more miserable just talking about the situation, and I tried to change the subject. "I brought home dinner. A police lieutenant took me to this little grocery store."

"Good idea," said Jason absently. "You probably don't feel much like eating out again."

"No," I agreed.

"You realize that even if we say nothing about Diane and Philippe, he probably will."

"Right now, according to the police, he's practically catatonic. Maybe he'll never recover." I spread newspapers across the bedspread, unloaded the paper bags, and pried the tops off two Dixie longnecks. "In fact, I hope that's what happens. I hope they commit him to some archaic mental institution and never let him out."

Jason looked somewhat taken aback at my vehemence, but he said nothing and accepted a helping of crustaceans and hush puppies. Lieutenant Boudreaux might be given to hitting on married ladies, but he did know his "crawdaddies." They were delicious, although I had to page through one of the tourist magazines the hotel provided to find the directions for eating them.

"All right," I said to Jason. "First, twist the tail off." He did so. "Now, hold it by the bottom and peel off the top ring." Jason peeled. The juices dripped. I read further. "Now, pinch the bottom of the tail between your forefinger and thumb, and pull the meat out with your teeth."

Jason did that and smiled at me. "Terrific," he said.

I nodded and rose to take off my raincoat. I didn't want to get crawfish juice, no matter how delicious, on the garment that had been the most useful to me during this dreadful visit. My mind was on Diane, that sweet girl in boarding school who didn't know that her mother was dead and her biological father — I shook my head and devoured two crawfish in the prescribed manner. Nils obviously didn't know that his adopted daughter was also his niece-in-law. With any luck, neither of them would have to face that dilemma.

"Why are you wearing that awful suit?" Jason asked.

"My other clothes were ruined."

"How?" He looked puzzled.

"Philippe threw me into a cake." I didn't mention from what height, anticipating that Jason would be upset that I'd been thrown from a two-story balcony. Time enough for the whole story later, when neither one of us was in shock.

"A *cake?*"

"A big one. It belonged to a bunch of orthodontists."

"Maybe you could explain that?" We were both cracking open the crawfish and sucking the tender, spicy morsels into our mouths.

"Well, I told you Philippe was crazy. I wasn't exaggerating. He's not only crazy, he's violent." Did Nils know that his brother-in-law was bipolar and probably his father-in-law as well? Evidently it was a genetic disorder.

"Good lord! He attacked you, too?"

Jason exclaimed in response to my remark about Philippe. My husband shook his head and opened a second round of beer for each of us. We were drinking straight from the bottles. I suppose we could have used the glasses in the bathroom, but it didn't occur to us. My mind returned compulsively to Diane and Nils. Perhaps, after all, I was obligated to tell him that his daughter might be at risk? But then he'd watch her like a hawk, looking for signs of abnormality, perhaps seeing symptoms that weren't there. He could ruin her life. Everything about the situation made me want to weep, to hide my head in the sand, to pretend none of it had happened and I knew none of the tragic details.

"My paper got an excellent reception," Jason told me. By that time we were finishing off the last of the hush puppies.

"I'm glad."

"Now, you think of something good that happened on this trip."

It was an old game of ours. When everything was dreadful, we tried to think of good things. "Well," I said listlessly, "a handsome police officer asked me out."

Jason looked surprised but, on consideration, remarked, "Just goes to show the good taste of the New Orleans Police Department.

What's his name? I'll file a complaint."

"No need. I didn't accept the date."

"That's good news." He opened the last two bottles of beer and handed me one. "Want to drink a toast to Julienne?" he asked.

I set the bottle down. "No, I have a better idea. Do you remember Julienne saying that the three of us should go together to Le Bistro for the crème brûlée?"

"When did she say that?"

"At the alligator dinner." Oh God, I'd have to stop thinking of it by that awful name.

"I like crème brûlée," said Jason.

"Correction. You love crème brulee! So let's go there and have dessert. In her memory."

"But do you think they can fit us in? At this late hour, and just for dessert?"

"I'm a food critic! Of course, they can!" And they did.

In Memory of
Julienne Delacroix Magnussen
Brilliant Scientist
Best of Friends
We loved the crème brûlée, and you, Julienne.

Carolyn Blue,
Eating Out in the Big Easy, Dedication

Recipe Index

*Catfish Pecan with Meunière Sauce   270
Chef Dick Brennan, Jr., Palace
Café, New Orleans

*Filets Mignons with Shiitake Mushrooms and Cabernet Sauce, and Garlic Mashed Potatoes with Roasted Onions   348
Chef Richard Hughes, Pelican
Club, New Orleans

*Le Bistro Crème Brûlée   433
Chef Randy Windham, Le Bistro
at Maison de Ville, New Orleans

*Taken from *Great Chefs: The Louisiana New Garde* by Nancy Ross Ryan with Chan Patterson (New Orleans: Great Chefs Television & Publishing, G.S.I., Inc., 1994).

About the Author

NANCY FAIRBANKS is a pseudonym for Nancy Herndon, who is the author of the Elena Jarvis mystery series for Berkley. She has also written historical romances under the name Elizabeth Chadwick. She lives in El Paso, Texas, with her husband, a chemistry professor and chairman at the University of Texas at El Paso. She travels widely and frequently with her husband throughout America and Europe, enjoying new places, good food, opera and scientific conferences.

We hope you have enjoyed this Large Print book. Other Thorndike, Wheeler or Chivers Press Large Print books are available at your library or directly from the publishers.

For more information about current and upcoming titles, please call or write, without obligation, to:

Publisher
Thorndike Press
295 Kennedy Memorial Drive
Waterville, ME   04901
Tel. (800) 223-1244

Or visit our Web site at:
www.gale.com/thorndike
www.gale.com/wheeler

OR

Chivers Large Print
published by BBC Audiobooks Ltd
St James House, The Square
Lower Bristol Road
Bath BA2 3BH
England
Tel. +44(0) 800 136919
email: bbcaudiobooks@bbc.co.uk
www.bbcaudiobooks.co.uk

All our Large Print titles are designed for easy reading, and all our books are made to last.

TELL THE WORLD THIS BOOK WAS

GOOD	BAD	SO-SO